WHAT WE DID TO SURVIVE

ALSO BY MEGAN LALLY

That's Not My Name
No Place Left to Hide

PRAISE FOR *NEW YORK TIMES* BESTSELLING AUTHOR MEGAN LALLY

PRAISE FOR *THAT'S NOT MY NAME*

"Secrets. Lies. Betrayal. Get ready for a roller-coaster ride where nothing is what it seems. *That's Not My Name* begs to be read in a single adrenaline-fueled sitting."

—April Henry, *New York Times* bestselling author of *Girl, Stolen* and *Two Truths and a Lie*

"With her masterful use of carefully placed details to build suspense, Lally asks: Just because something is obvious, does that make it true?"

—Jessie Weaver, author of *Live Your Best Lie*

"A gripping, emotional page-turner with an undeniable tenderness at its center. This book will leave you breathless."

—Rachel Lynn Solomon, bestselling author of *Today Tonight Tomorrow*

"A thrilling delight right up to the unexpected and bittersweet conclusion."

—*Kirkus Reviews*

"A suspenseful thrill ride."

—*Publishers Weekly*

PRAISE FOR *NO PLACE LEFT TO HIDE*

"Lally's sophomore novel will keep you guessing all the way from its suspenseful beginning to its shocking end."
—Trish Lundy, author of *The One That Got Away with Murder*

"Lally masterfully drives you to a high-speed collision of an ending."
—Courtney Gould, award-winning author of *The Dead and the Dark*

"[A] propulsive tale of revenge."
—*Publishers Weekly*

"Unputdownable."
—*Booklist*

"Highly enjoyable and highly recommended… Lally continues to prove herself one to watch in the genre."
—*School Library Journal*

WHAT WE DID TO SURVIVE

MEGAN LALLY

sourcebooks fire

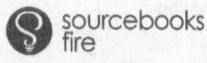

Copyright © 2026 by Megan Lally
Cover and internal design © 2026 by Sourcebooks
Cover design by Sophia Chunn
Handlettering by Erin Fitzsimmons/Sourcebooks
Cover images © Victor Torres/Stocksy
Title page image © Olga Pankova/Getty Images
Internal design by Diane Cunningham/Sourcebooks

Sourcebooks and the colophon are registered trademarks of Sourcebooks.

All rights reserved. No part of this book may be reproduced in any form or by any electronic or mechanical means including information storage and retrieval systems—except in the case of brief quotations embodied in critical articles or reviews—without permission in writing from its publisher, Sourcebooks.

No part of this book may be used or reproduced in any manner for the purpose of training artificial intelligence technologies or systems.

The characters and events portrayed in this book are fictitious or are used fictitiously. Any similarity to real persons, living or dead, is purely coincidental and not intended by the author.

All brand names and product names used in this book are trademarks, registered trademarks, or trade names of their respective holders. Sourcebooks is not associated with any product or vendor in this book.

Published by Sourcebooks Fire, an imprint of Sourcebooks
1935 Brookdale RD, Naperville, IL 60563-2773
(630) 961-3900
sourcebooks.com

Cataloging-in-Publication Data is on file with the Library of Congress.

The authorized representative in the EEA is Dorling Kindersley Verlag GmbH. Arnulfstr. 124, 80636 Munich, Germany

Manufactured in the UK by Clays and distributed by
Dorling Kindersley Limited, London
01-356599-Mar/26
10 9 8 7 6 5 4 3 2 1

*For all my fellow anxious travelers.
This book probably won't help your
anxiety much, but your next vacation can't
possibly go as badly as this one…*

CHAPTER ONE

Unrequited love, thou art a bitch.

I lean against the smoothie stand's mosaic countertop and try not to look at him, but I fail. As always. I have no self-control when it comes to Jackson. My gaze slips across the pool in the middle of the U-shaped resort to the white lounge chairs where my best friend's older brother reclines shirtless, one hand flung above his head. The other holds open the Ted Bundy book that's had the full scope of his attention since we landed in Mexico.

Thank god my sunglasses are dark enough to hide where I'm looking.

He shifts in his seat, turning his head just enough that I spot the Bluetooth headphones in his ears. He's undoubtedly listening to a true crime podcast while he reads. I swear Jackson's one of those humans who uses one hundred percent of his brain capacity. There's no other explanation for how he's able to listen to one thing and read another, but I've seen him do it a thousand times.

He's impressive *and* gorgeous.

It's honestly rude.

I force myself to look away. Emmy's down on the beach, and the last thing I need is for her to pop up and catch me ogling her stupid brother. As far as she knows, my crush died years ago. As it *should* have.

This resort is quite possibly the most beautiful place I've ever been in my life.

Pristine white sand beaches, huge palm trees, and perfect weather every day. There're six restaurants, a taco bar, smoothie stand, and crepe cart poolside. The spa is also incredible. Emmy tried to convince her parents that we required at least one spa service a day in the name of "sacred best friend time," and when that argument flopped, "We need this before we go our separate ways after graduation!" did the trick.

It should be the perfect vacation.

And yet, all I can think about is the boy on the lounger who hasn't said more than three words to me since he threw my luggage onto the weight scale at the Portland airport. He's ruining everything and has absolutely no idea.

The combination of butterflies and annoyance starts to make me a little sick to my stomach. I turn my back on the pool.

When Emmy's parents invited me to Puerto Vallarta for spring break, I couldn't see a single downside. It's our last chance to decompress before senior year gets even more hectic with finals, grad party prep, prom, and graduation. One last hurrah before I leave for college and Emmy takes off to explore the world. It never occurred to me that he'd come with them. Jackson's barely been home since he left for college the year before last.

Except for Christmas.

A spasm of regret races down my spine, and I shake my head to clear the memories.

By the time I found out Jackson was coming to Mexico, there wasn't a graceful way to bow out. The Coles would have been sad and worried, Emmy would've been pissed, and my dad would have had to eat the cost of my nonrefundable flight. Jackson's the only person who'd know why I bailed, and I'd rather eat my own flip-flop than give him the satisfaction of knowing I canceled an entire vacation to avoid him.

I wish I knew how to let him go, but it's been ten years, and this stupid crush is as strong as the day it formed—even though he's given me every reason to abandon it. I'm starting to think I'll be seventy years old, gray from head to toe, and still what-if-ing about Jackson freaking Cole.

A woman in a bright blue resort polo holds up two smoothies. "I have a strawberry banana and a mixed berry for Hannah?"

"That's me." I thank the woman, sign for the room charge, and take the drinks. A waft of banana works up my nose from Emmy's cup. I curl my lip and hold it away from me. I hate bananas.

I make my way to the beach without glancing in Jackson's direction.

Emmy's sprawled across a lounge chair down on the sand. Her long strands of bleach blond hair dance in the breeze. She's got her phone screen pressed to her nose, ankles perfectly crossed, showcasing the hot pink pedicure she got on our last spa day, trying to get the perfect photo for her Insta story. I put the smoothies on the wooden table between her lounger and mine, and she twists in her seat to show me the screen.

"What do we think? Is this cute or not?"

I cup the screen to block the sun so I can see. The photo is a fantastic shot of her legs, with a perfect wave crashing against the sand as a backdrop. A palm frond from the tree above us dips into the upper left corner. I give her the thumbs-up. "A-plus Instagram material."

She lets out an excited little squeal and posts the photo. "God, I love this place. Everything is gorgeous. I've literally never been so relaxed. Though I don't know why anyone bothers to sit around that pool. We have those back home. This, however," she says, waving two open arms at the view in front of us, "is unique perfection. I'd never choose a pool over the ocean."

As per usual, Emmy's sentences blur together in her excitement. She doesn't need me to respond, so I settle into my lounger and sip my smoothie, nodding as she shifts to wondering what's responsible for the particular smell of sunscreen, how often it rains in Puerto Vallarta, and whether or not paddleboarding is hard, before she finally settles on what spa treatment we should try next. I just listen to her go, smiling wider and wider as her face turns pink between breaths.

I love her so damn much. The situation with her brother might be annoying, but I'm so grateful to have this time before we're separated by thousands of miles.

In the fall, I'll be at Linfield University, and Emmy will be on her world tour, starting in Italy. She has a thing for adventure, for new experiences. Emmy was never going to apply to college, move into a dorm, and put down roots. She's been tacking travel photos to her walls since the sixth grade. They've become a chaotic wallpaper behind her bed frame, everywhere from Cusco, to Marrakesh, to Beijing. She doesn't care about the order or have much of a plan for how she's going to get from one place to the next. She wants to, and I quote, *See where the wind takes me.*

Emmy is my opposite in many ways, but especially in this one.

She's all about the unexpected, and I prefer the familiar. Emmy's always looking to make new friends, meet new boys, have new experiences, while I like the few friends I have and have liked the same boy for a decade. Emmy wants to explore new places, and I get anxiety when I have to drive somewhere new and don't know the parking situation. Emmy's the captain of the volleyball team at Waldorf, while I'd rather eat glass than play a team sport.

But opposites must attract, because we've been friends since the day my dad bought the house beside hers.

"You're being quiet," Emmy says.

I startle out of my thoughts. Emmy's twisted in her lounge chair, staring at me with a mostly empty smoothie cup in her hands. How long have I been spacing out?

"Sorry," I say brightly. "Enjoying the view."

She eyes me. "No. You've been a grump for months, and now you're zombie-ing through our epic vacation. What's up with you?"

I set my smoothie on the table and gather my best "I'm fine" face. "Nothing's up. I'm a little tired from the sun, but I'm not complaining."

She flops back onto her lounger. "Fine. Lie to me. It's cool. I'll be here when you want to talk."

I hate and love how well she knows me.

"Was Jackson by the pool?" she asks.

"I think so."

It comes out so calm, so casual that I want to pat myself on the back. As if I haven't been clocking his exact location since the moment he emerged from the hotel.

Pa-the-tic.

"Has he looked up from his book yet?"

I roll my eyes. "Unlikely."

She plops the empty smoothie on the table and glares back in his general direction. "We're at a resort with miles of beautiful beaches at our fingertips, and he'd rather stick his nose in a book? A book he could easily read back home, or on the plane, or in his stupid dorm at his stupid college. He's wasting the sun."

I can't hold back a smile as I adjust the strap of my bathing suit. "He's enjoying vacation his way too, I guess."

She scoffs. "Don't defend him. He's dumb. You're proof of that."

My hand stills on the strap. "What do you mean?"

"He dropped the ball big time when he fumbled you," she says with a wink. "One day he's going to find out about your crush, and he's going to feel like the biggest idiot on the planet for missing out."

Flashes of winter break flood my mind, and another spasm of guilt hits me. I take a long drink of my smoothie so I don't say something stupid. Like, *He already knows. Didn't make a difference.*

I'm not a fan of keeping secrets from my best friend, but I don't know how to tell her about something I don't understand myself. Winter break was so monumentally embarrassing that it's best to pretend it never happened at all. Emmy's not good at pretending. Especially not where I'm concerned. The only way this stays quiet and firmly in the past is if she never finds out about it.

So I keep my mouth shut.

Emmy rips her aviators off her face and jumps to her feet. "Oh my god, I know what you need!"

"Um...what?"

"A vacation fling."

I put up my hand to stop her. "No, thank you. That's more your alley than mine. No judgment. Just facts."

"Come on! You haven't crushed on anyone since Jackson. You need a no-strings-attached palette cleanser. A rebound crush so you can jet off to Linfield with a fresh mind!"

"That sounds like the worst idea ever," I say, sipping the smoothie I no longer want. "I don't need to make out with a stranger to clear my mind. Consider it translucent."

"Come on. Best case scenario, you spend the rest of our trip hanging out with a hot guy. And worst case... I don't know, you get herpes."

"Emmy! Seriously? Why are you like this?"

She throws her head back and laughs. "Kidding. About the herpes part anyway. Not about the rebound."

I stare at my best friend, the hot-pink-bikini-wearing, mermaid-haired goddess that she is, and sigh.

"Come on," she says. "There are tons of cute guys here. I'm on vacay boyfriend number three. One for each day of the trip."

She doesn't have to tell me that. In between spa treatments and tacos, I've had to watch each of them drool over her while she sunbathes.

Emmy has two modes when it comes to boys: All Boys Are Disposable and My Boyfriend Can Do No Wrong. She's in the first mode ninety-nine percent of the time, going through boys like gum that loses its flavor too fast. And then, there's the other one—also known as my personal nightmare. Every once in a while, Emmy attaches to one boy in particular, and it's like she becomes another person entirely. One who makes excuses for bad behavior in the name of "love."

Thankfully the resort has been full of the "disposable" kind.

I stand and put my hands on her shoulders. "Thanks, but no thanks."

"Oh fine! You're a real stick in the mud, you know that?"

I smile. "And you're the human equivalent of a golden retriever, but I love you anyway. There's no one else I'd rather be here with."

Emmy grins and drags me away from the loungers. "Come on, let's go swimming. My soul craves the ocean, and I must heed the call!"

Like I said, mermaid.

We run down to the water, our feet sinking into the warm sand. There's only a handful of people on the beach. We have this whole section of the coast to ourselves. The water washes over my new sunset red pedicure, and it's gloriously warm. We jump over the incoming waves and wade out to boob depth before Emmy turns to me with the biggest smile on her face.

"Can we stay here forever?" she asks.

I laugh. "I don't think your mom and dad would be on board with that."

"They have no sense of adventure."

She swims on her back, riding up over waves, her hair turning white and fanning out in the brilliant blue water. A new emotion curls my stomach, and I look away as she swims out farther. I'm really happy for Emmy. She's been saving every penny for three years to fund this world tour of hers, but knowing she's leaving and her *actually* leaving are two very different things.

I'm not sure what my life will look like without her beside me.

Not that I'm unhappy with my chosen future. As long as Emmy's dreamed of Seoul and Nepal, I've imagined myself in scrubs. The Linfield University School of Nursing is one of the best nursing programs in the state, and it was my first-choice school.

We're both headed for what makes us happiest, but that won't make the goodbye easier.

I slip beneath the waves, and the water tugs and twists me around before I resurface. I don't open my eyes right away. Instead I imagine the water pouring off me into the sea, taking all my worries with it. No goodbyes. No Jackson. No new-school jitters. Just sunshine.

"You look extremely peaceful."

I yelp and shove myself away from the unexpected voice, only to find myself staring at a pair of legs standing on the water. My brain glitches out for a second before it makes sense of what I'm seeing. Not legs on the water, legs standing on a paddleboard. I shield my eyes and look up at the boy smirking down at me.

"Or you did, before I scared you. My bad," he says.

He's...good-looking. Like incredibly good-looking. He's practically the male version of Emmy. Golden skin, perfect blond hair, and a smile that could melt even a seasoned pessimist like myself.

I clear my throat to say something smart and interesting—because that's what you do when you run into hot boys on vacation—but a wave takes me out before I have the chance.

I come back up sputtering, salt water dripping out of my nose.

Hot Stuff crouches down and grabs my hand. I brace myself on the end of his board to keep my head above the water.

"You okay? That one snuck up on you."

I shake off my embarrassment and smile at him. "Yeah, rotten luck."

"Well, can't be beautiful and lucky. That would be too much for one person."

I laugh. "Nice line."

He sits and slips his feet into the water on either side of his board as he grins at me. "It may be a line, but it's also the truth. I'm Ben."

He holds out his hand, and I shake it. "Hannah."

"Very nice to meet you, Hannah. Do you need a ride back to shore?"

"No, I'm out here with a friend." I turn and search the water for Emmy. I spot her a few hundred feet away, leisurely floating on her back. "She's over there. I'll head back in when she does."

"Ah, fair enough."

I push away from his board and try to dip my hair back into the water to clear the awkward strands from my face. "Thanks for the assist though."

He winks at me. "No problem. Are you staying at the resort?"

"Yeah. We're here until the end of the week."

"Me too. I checked in last night. Maybe I'll run into you again."

He holds my gaze for a second too long, and Emmy's rebound crush suggestion comes to mind. This super cute boy would probably love to hang out. What would it feel like to spend time with someone who likes me back? Who—gasp—actually talks to me?

Even as the thought crosses my mind, I know I'd be watching Jackson for a reaction the entire time. No matter how flirty or cute or seemingly available Ben may be, he's not who I want.

I shrug and start to swim away from him. "Maybe. It's a big resort."

Ben throws his head back and laughs. "I see how it is. Don't worry I like a challenge."

A flash of blond appears beside me. I see the exact moment his focus falters and his pupils turn into little hearts. Just like that, Ben becomes vacation victim number four. Emmy's a siren, lulling the poor boy to drown himself. It's hysterically predictable.

"And who do we have here?" she asks, gliding effortlessly through the water to his paddleboard. She folds her arms across the top and rests her chin on them.

"I'm...Bennett Mulholland."

One, I don't know why he paused. Did he forget his name? And two, why did he give me the nickname and Emmy the long version? Still, I'm struck by how much he *looks* like a Bennett. "Ben" might casually attend a resort. "Bennett Mulholland" sounds like someone who might own it, and the fact that he presented himself like this to Emmy seems to indicate he wants to be perceived as such.

"Emelia Cole. But you can call me Emmy. Only my parents call me Emelia. Mostly when I piss them off."

Ben-Bennett throws his head back and laughs. "Want me to teach you how to paddleboard, Emmy? It's a blast."

"I'd love to! I've always wanted to learn."

I tell them to have a great time and that I'll meet Emmy back at the room later. There's an audiobook that's calling my name. She waves me off, never breaking eye contact with her newest flirtation, and I turn to swim ashore. I should probably feel a little put off that Ben was all about impressing me until Emmy came along, but I can't bring myself to care. Let Emmy have all the boys in Puerto Vallarta.

I only care about the one who doesn't want me.

God, I need therapy.

My feet finally touch sand, and I wring out my hair and shake water from the ends as I wade in. I'm about waist-deep when I look up and lock eyes with Jackson. He's standing on the shore, toes at the water's edge, his book tucked beneath his arm. Still shirtless. Still gorgeous.

Only now, he's staring right at me.

I freeze. The shallows stretch out in front of me, separating us by a good twenty feet, but the entirety of my attention is on him and the serious expression on his face. I blink as memories better left buried fill my mind. Falling Christmas lights. Hands wrapped around a warm mug. A bored face beneath a tree on a street corner. A familiar flash of anger settles like a rock in my gut.

His mouth forms the shape of my name, but the sound is carried off in the wind.

Why did he look up from his stupid book *now*?

Did he see me talking to Ben and suddenly grow a—

A wall of water slams into my back, and I'm thrown forward. The wave knocks me off my feet, sucks me under, and spins me around like a pillow in a washing machine. Water rushes up my nose and burns through my sinuses. The wave regurgitates me out of the ocean, and I land face down in the wet sand, coughing up salt water as froth collects around me.

I hear the ghost of Emmy's laughter somewhere behind me, and I will the beach to open up and swallow me alive. But no such luck. I push back on my knees and spit granules of sand from my teeth. My hair hangs in a salty mess down my face, and when I glance up, Jackson is crouched in front of me.

His mouth is pinched, but humor dances in his hazel eyes like he's desperately holding back a laugh. "You okay? Not gonna lie, you look like the lady from *The Grudge*."

I sigh. Of course.

He holds out a hand to help me up, and I stare at it for a full ten seconds before he lets it drop, the humor vanishing from his face. I climb to my feet, and he does too, pointing at the surf.

"You shouldn't turn your back on the ocean. It's as unpredictable as my sister."

And with that, he does something the opposite of unpredictable, and walks away.

Because that's what Jackson Cole does best.

CHAPTER TWO

People talk a lot of crap about being the third wheel, but when you're best friends with Emmy Cole, you either get used to it or you find yourself a fourth wheel. Finding a date is never high on my to-do list, so I roll with the perks like the third-wheeling gold medalist that I am. And oh, have there been perks to Ben tagging along with us for the last two days.

For instance, without him, I wouldn't have been treated to poolside massages with Emmy. I wouldn't have gone jet skiing yesterday—rentals paid in full by Mr. Moneybags—and I absolutely wouldn't have found myself wandering a gorgeous farmers market today.

Ben charmed Emmy's parents into letting us go with him. It didn't hurt that Ben's dad and Emmy's parents went to the same college, only a few years apart. They didn't know each other at the time but found they had some mutual friends, and after a mini college reunion at the bar last night, Mr. and Mrs. Cole declared the Mulhollands "good eggs" and were more than happy to send us off on a shopping adventure with their son this morning.

We've been so busy, I've almost blocked out the mortification of face-planting on the beach in front of Jackson the other day.

Almost.

I stop beneath a full street of colorful banners stretched overhead and sigh. I've eaten everything I could get my hands on today. The food here is incredible. And there's music playing on every street corner. Fresh fruit stands. Dresses and T-shirts in intensely colorful shops. Merchants showcasing wearable displays of sunglasses, turquoise earrings, seashell necklaces, and woven beach bags. Hand-painted art on pottery, canvases, wind chimes, and plates. Emmy and I found a vendor who makes woven friendship bracelets with gold beads, and we each got one that matches our respective pedicures—pink for her, red for me.

This place is alive with a thousand conversations happening all at once, and I can feel the energy buzzing beneath my skin. I turn around, looking for Emmy, and find her and Ben stopped at another merchant. Ben examines two lighters, one gold and one silver, both with a sea turtle etched into the side. Emmy picks up a vibrant turquoise pendant on a silver chain and smiles happily as it spins in the sunlight. Ben hands a wad of pesos to the merchant, holds up the gold lighter, and nods toward the necklace without Emmy even asking for it. He pockets the lighter and slips the necklace from her fingers, stepping behind her to fasten it around her neck. She beams up at him and turns to show me.

"Isn't this the prettiest thing you've ever seen?" she asks.

I nod.

"Not quite. *You* are the prettiest," Ben says, planting a kiss on the side of her neck.

I try not to make a face at how horrifically cheesy that was. Or point out that he just called her *a thing*, because I'm fairly certain that was unintentional. They wander off ahead of me, Ben carrying at least ten bags of stuff he's bought for her in the crooks of his arms. He offered to buy a number of things for me too, but I declined.

Ben may be a wonderful tour guide, but I'm beginning to suspect his money is his most prominent personality trait. Emmy doesn't seem to mind though, and I've seen her attach to worse in the past. At least Ben is charming and kind. Even now, as I watch them strolling down the street, hand in hand, he looks back to make sure they're not leaving me behind.

Emmy stops at a rack of stickers, and I slide up beside her. Almost all of them say "Puerto Vallarta" with some illustration of a sun or a sea turtle or a palm tree. Emmy grabs one and holds it out to me. "This has 'Hannah' written all over it. For your water bottle collection?"

It's a neon pink sticker with a black palm tree that says, "PUERTO VALLARTA EST 1851." I reach into the coral-colored mesh bag I bought here this morning and pluck my water bottle from the bottom. The surface is nearly all covered in stickers. A sloth wearing a beanie, a "Stay Positive" skeleton flashing a thumbs-up sign, Dutch Bros, a "Save Our Oceans" sticker with an orca, an anatomical heart with anatomy labels, a brain with eyeballs that says "let me overthink this," a symbol for the Red Cross, one from Powell's Books, and a blue holographic sticker from the Waldorf student store. There's one more open spot near the bottom I've been looking to fill for a while now.

I hold the Puerto Vallarta sticker against the empty space, and it fits almost perfectly.

"Sold," I say, with a grin. I pay for the sticker before Ben can offer.

He rolls his eyes at me, but he's smiling.

I put my water bottle back in the bag and pocket the sticker for later.

Ben looks down at his watch. "We should catch a taxi, or we're going to be late."

He nods toward the end of the street, where traffic is racing back and forth, and we head in that direction. We said we'd be back at the resort by four.

Emmy loops her other arm in mine and leans her head on my shoulder. "Can you believe we only have one more day here? I'm not ready to go home yet."

I stop to admire a skirt with the most eye-catching emerald stitching. "It's technically two days. We don't get on the plane until six on Sunday."

"The last day never feels like a true vacation day though. It's too stressful to do anything with all the packing and watching the time and double checking outlets for lost chargers. There's only one day of fun left, start to finish. I'm going to spiral into situational depression on the flight home."

"Dramatic much?" I poke her in the side, and she laughs. "We'll make the most of the time we have left; don't worry."

She meets my gaze, and her blazing blue eyes are so sad it makes my heart pinch in my chest. "I'm not ready for…the rest of the school year."

Translation: She's not ready to say goodbye.

I pinch the end of her nose and smile. "No sadness on vacation! Fun only. Isn't that your number one rule?"

Besides, if she starts crying about goodbyes and going our separate ways, I'll lose it too.

"Yeah, okay. You're right. I'm just not ready to go back to the routine yet." She sniffs and takes a deep breath as we step onto the wide sidewalk at the end of the street. She starts to speak, but something behind me catches her attention. Her face brightens. She points at one of the little tourism kiosks on the street corner. It's covered with posters advertising local attractions. The side facing us has a giant print of a grinning man, speeding through the treetops in a harness.

"You know what would be fun? Zip-lining! One of the people at the front desk told me they filmed *Predator* here, and they turned the filming location into a zip-line tour. They even have the crashed helicopter from the set and guides who dress up like the alien and everything."

I feel my features pull tight around a smile that does not belong on my face, but if Emmy wants to zip-line with some aliens, I love her enough to make that happen.

"Or... I have a better idea," Ben says, turning to face us as he backs closer to the road. "What if we charter a boat?" He stops at the curb, and a heavy flow of traffic whips past on the cobblestone street behind him.

"Like one of the group tours?" Emmy glances toward other posters on the kiosk. Sailboats, double-decker pontoon boats, sleek-looking mini-yachts—all ready and waiting to take us to dozens of locations around the bay.

"Yeah! Maybe a sailboat? The three of us can sail and swim, and make the most of your last full day in paradise. They typically go out in the morning and come back before dinner, and they usually provide lunch and snorkeling equipment and anything else we might need. Could be fun." He catches my eye. "Maybe more fun than zip-lining?"

Okay, so he is a bit cheesy, but he clearly clocked my aversion to flying through the jungle and produced another option. One he lumped me into without it being an afterthought. *The three of us can sail...*

He's been very nice to me, and he clearly doesn't have to do that to get Emmy's attention. It's actually cool as hell. Ben's not so bad.

"Oh. My. God. I'd love to go sailing!" Emmy squeals so loud that a group of locals walking past us turn to stare at her. She doesn't notice.

Ben stops to hail a cab, and one screeches to a halt beside him. He opens the door to let us in ahead of him. I take the outside, Emmy slips into the middle, and Ben piles in last, then smoothly tells the driver where we're going in seemingly perfect Spanish while rearranging the shopping bags in his lap. The cab lurches away from the curb, accelerating wildly, and I bite back a grin. I love how they drive here. It's chaos, and I'm obsessed with it.

"So it's settled," Ben says. "I can arrange everything, if you'd like?"

"I have to ask my parents, but if they were cool with us going to the market with you today, I don't know why they'd have a problem with a boat trip."

My enthusiasm dies a bit. I highly doubt Mr. and Mrs. Cole will be as "cool" with this excursion as she thinks. There's a big difference between spending a few hours shopping in town and voyaging out to sea. Our final vacation hurrah might be dead in the water.

"I can charter a private boat; that way there aren't a bunch of strangers with us. Would that help? I can also talk to your parents myself, before I go back to my room."

Emmy beams at him. "You're so considerate."

"Anything for you."

I imagine hurling out the window, but I wouldn't do that to the driver. He shouldn't have to clean my vomit off the outside of his cab because my best friend is being gross with a boy—who's conveniently forgetting he's a stranger too. A very generous stranger. But a stranger nonetheless.

A day on a sailboat does sound amazing though. I think of huge white sails and a gorgeous sparkling sea. Of diving into the warm water with a snorkel and a mask, and watching fish swim around me. I wish it didn't come with a heaping dose of Emmy sticking her tongue down Ben's throat, but so is the life of the third wheel. If they manage to sell this plan to Mr. and Mrs. Cole, I'm positive I'll find plenty of other things to look at on the water besides the two of them sucking face.

The taxi comes to a screeching halt outside the sweeping entrance to the resort, and we all pile out. Ben tips the driver, and the man drives off in a flash. We ride the elevator to the fifth floor (Ben's staying in another wing, in one of the penthouse condos), and Emmy swipes her key card.

Our modest little suite unfolds before us. A kitchenette with cherry cabinets sits directly inside the door, and a seating area with a Murphy bed that Jackson's been sleeping on is beyond that. Two double beds fill the room to the left—ours for the week—and the primary bedroom and the bathroom are through the door to the right. Everything is white and blue, from the linens to the mosaic tiles that match the ones on the smoothie stand.

I spot Jackson out on the balcony. Emmy's mom and dad are on the couch, watching a movie. They look up at us as we enter and smile.

"Just in time. We were about to start brainstorming dinner options. How was the market?" Mrs. Cole asks.

Emmy's a carbon copy of her mother; both have the same long blond mermaid hair, only Melissa Cole wears dark-rimmed glasses, and Emmy doesn't. Mr. Cole is tall, bald, and possibly the friendliest person I've ever met in my whole life.

Emmy takes her bags from Ben and holds them aloft. "They had the best stuff. Peak shopping experience. Look at my necklace."

She drops her things on the floor and bounds across the room to show her mom what Ben bought for her. Mrs. Cole touches the pendant like it might break and makes a sound like she's cooing at a baby. "It's beautiful, Emmy. What a find."

"I'm going to look for a dress this color to wear to prom."

"That's a fantastic idea."

Mr. Cole eyes Ben and then me. "How did you like the market, Hannah?"

I plop down in one of the chairs at the table and groan. "I. Ate. Everything."

He laughs with his full body. "Sounds like you all had a fantastic day."

"Actually Daddy," Emmy says, perching on the coffee table in front of them both, "it was so much fun that it got us talking about what we're going to do tomorrow."

Mr. Cole raises his eyebrow, probably clocking the combination of "Daddy" and the eyelashes she's batting a mile a minute. "And?"

"We were thinking a sailboat excursion." Ben places his hands on Emmy's shoulders. "I thought the girls might enjoy spending their last day on the ocean, and the tour companies offer sailboat charters. We can book through the resort. Would you be comfortable with that?"

I shake my head. God, he's such a pro at schmoozing.

The sliding glass door opens. Jackson pops into the living room with his Ted Bundy book, the bookmark resting between the cover and his thumb. He must have finished it. He goes straight for the kitchen, and nobody seems to notice him but me.

Mrs. Cole laces her fingers together and sets them in her lap. "I don't know. Going to the market is one thing, but out on the ocean? We can't go with you tomorrow. We have reservations at the spa and then a golf tour. We might be able to make it happen on Sunday, before our flight?"

Ben frowns. "The tours leave in the morning and last most of the day. They likely won't return to the marina in time for you all to get to the airport before your flight."

"Please, Mom?" Emmy begs. "Please? Let us go tomorrow. We want our last day here to be as epic as possible. Ben says he can book a private boat so it's just the three of us. No randos. It'll be totally safe, and I won't even go into the water without one of those ugly orange life vests. I promise."

Mrs. Cole winces and looks to her husband. Mr. Cole scratches his head with a sigh.

My shoulders slump. They're going to say no.

Jackson slams the refrigerator door and drinks straight from the OJ container.

"Jackson Cole, if I've told you once, I've told you a thousand times: Use. A. Glass!" Mrs. Cole shouts. "Nobody else needs your spit in their orange juice."

He freezes mid-gulp and wipes his mouth. "My bad."

Mr. Cole squints over at him. "What if Jackson goes with them? To keep an eye on things? That way they can go on their boat trip, and we can have a bit more peace of mind."

Emmy slaps her hands against the coffee table. "What? No!"

"That works for me," Mrs. Cole says.

Oh, sweet baby Jesus. Stuck on a boat with Jackson *all day*?

I'd rather drown.

Emmy leans toward her mom. Her eyes are huge and pleading. "Jackson doesn't even want to go on the boat. Don't make him babysit. We don't need that. Plus...look at him. He's ninety percent library. His skin is practically paper. He isn't equipped to deal with full sun all day. He burns so easily."

Everyone turns to Jackson and his perfectly sun-kissed skin. He blinks at us like he has no fucking idea what we're talking about. I don't think he's ever had a sunburn in his life.

"That's the deal, Em. Jackson goes, or you keep both feet on land. Those are the terms," Mr. Cole says, leaning back on the couch. "Take it or leave it."

I glance at Jackson and find him staring at me.

"What's this about?" he asks.

"Emmy wants to go sailing tomorrow, but we can't go without you." I shrug. "You don't have to. We can find something else to do."

He frowns at Ben, and then at Emmy, who's practically vibrating in her seat.

"Please, Jack? I really want to go sailing. I'll do some boring thing you like in return? Please?"

Jackson snorts and folds his arms. I can already see the *no* forming in his mind. He doesn't like the open water. No way is he going to spend the whole day sailing with his little sister, her annoying friend, and the random guy they met at the beach.

He looks at me again and drops his arms. "You all really want to do this?"

"More than anything," Emmy insists, at the same time I say, "*She* does."

He sighs. "I guess we're going sailing tomorrow."

Emmy screams. She straight up screams and twists around to dive into Ben's arms. I stare at Jackson, because I can't imagine why the hell he'd want to do this. But he smiles, watching his sister celebrate, and I wonder if he's feeling the weight of her impending goodbye too.

He sits across from me at the table.

"You really don't have to do this, you know. Water and books don't mix. And I'm sure your mom would eventually cave and let us go without you," I offer. "We don't want you to be miserable all day. This is your vacation too."

"It's not a big deal," he says, and for the first time in months, he looks at me. Really looks at me. "I don't want to take anything else from you."

With that, he stands, walks to his suitcase on the stand by the TV, grabs another book, and goes back to the balcony. Like he didn't just punch a hole in my chest.

Emmy bounds to my side with the biggest smile. "Isn't this the best!?"

I take a deep breath and force a smile onto my face. "Absolutely!"

She plants a kiss on my cheek, taps her friendship bracelet against mine, and dances toward the door to walk Ben out. I slip into our room and flop back on my bed to groan in peace.

Nothing about this vacation has gone to plan, but ignoring Jackson's disinterest has been a lot easier while jet skiing or at the spa or wandering the markets. It's going to be much harder when he's one of five people on a private boat with no escape.

I shake myself. It doesn't matter. Jackson doesn't matter. He's the chaperone. It's not like he's going to participate. He'll probably spend the entire time below deck reading his new book.

I sit up. We have one last full day of sunshine in one of the most beautiful places in the world. I need to chill the heck out and let some of Emmy's infectious joy sink into me. We're going to have the time of our lives on that boat, and there's no way I'm letting Jackson ruin it for me.

Besides, what's the worst that could happen?

CHAPTER THREE

This can't be good.

Emmy and I lean against the railing on the hotel balcony, staring wordlessly at the dark, angry clouds in the distance. Humidity rolls off the ocean in waves. It feels like standing in the bathroom with the shower temperature turned all the way up. Eight in the morning looks more like late evening. But the sky directly above us is still blue.

I glance at Emmy, and she frowns. "The boat leaves in an hour. He would have texted us if the trip was canceled, right?"

"You tell me. When did you last hear from him?"

"He sent me the time the boat leaves and the address for the marina. He said he'd meet us there. We'll need to pay a port fee and go through security to get to the docks. It's a single metal detector, so it doesn't take that long. And then we get on the boat."

"Did he send you all that this morning? As in, after he would have seen that sky?"

"No, last night. When he booked everything."

"You might want to text him."

Her phone dings, one message after another, and considering the way she smiles at the screen, I know it's him. She shows me the messages.

BENNY BEAR:

> Today is going to be a blast. 🐻
>
> You guys leaving soon? I'm already here.
>
> Don't forget water! I've got the snacks covered. 🍪

Gag me with a spoon. "Benny Bear? Are you serious, Emmy?"

She rolls her eyes. "Oh, shut up. That's not the point. I guess it's still on?"

"You should ask him to confirm before we take a thirty-minute cab ride for nothing."

She types out a quick response, and her phone dings within seconds of her pressing send. She holds it out to me again.

ME:

> Are you sure it's still on? The weather looks a little sketchy.

BENNY BEAR:

> Absolutely! Captain says we're good to go. ⛵🐟

I cast another wary look at the clouds rolling in. I guess the boat captain would know what counts as bad weather and what doesn't, but I don't love the look of that sky. I guess we could always come back early if it gets choppy? I don't want to spend the day getting tossed around and hurling over the side of the boat. The clouds *are* out on the horizon. Maybe they won't reach us until tonight?

The sliding glass door opens behind us, and Jackson sticks out his head. He's wearing navy swim shorts with tiny white anchors on them and the black "Game of Holmes" T-shirt Emmy got him for Christmas. The front is a graphic of Benedict Cumberbatch sitting on the Iron Throne. Jackson spins his sunglasses around by one of the earpieces. "Is this thing canceled or what?"

He sounds so hopeful that it instantly sparks Emmy's annoyance. "Sorry, you giant wet blanket. The boat trip is still on."

"Em, look at that sky. Nobody with half a brain is going to take a boat out in that. The waves are going to be insane."

"Ben says it's fine."

Jackson laughs so loud it echoes. "Yeah, because Ben Mulholland is an expert in sailing and ocean conditions."

"He knows how to sail!"

"He knows how to pay someone to sail for him."

"You're such a dick!"

Jackson slips on his sunglasses, and the blue mirror lenses throw our reflection back at us. "She says, to the person who can put a stop to this whole day by sitting my ass on the couch and refusing to leave… Smart move, airhead."

"You wouldn't—"

Jackson slams the door.

"I'm going to kick him into the ocean," she grumbles.

I gently nudge her back inside. "We have to get to the ocean first, and if we don't hustle, we're going to be late. Come on. Chop, chop."

Emmy grabs her white lace beach cover-up and throws it over her pink bikini. She takes a second to smooth the frills in the mirror, then grabs the woven straw bag Ben bought her at the market from the foot of the bed and fishes through it to make sure she's got everything she needs. Next to her, I look frumpy as hell in my navy blue two-piece and black jean shorts. She's all strings and bows and bright colors, and the shoulder straps on my sporty bathing suit are wider than the fabric on her hips. I'd bet mine is more comfortable though. And less likely to malfunction when we jump into the ocean.

I pull one of my beach cover-ups from my suitcase. This one is a dark teal, and I throw it over my head so my stomach isn't showing as we walk through the lobby. Stuffing my phone in the pocket of my shorts, I'm ready to go.

Emmy blows a kiss at her reflection, and I grab my bag off the bedroom door handle as we leave the room and throw the strap over my head. It's stuffed with a towel, sunscreen, my freshly PV sticker-ed water bottle, a waterproof lanyard pouch for my phone, and my sunglasses.

Jackson's waiting in the kitchenette with nothing but his phone and a scowl. "This century?"

Emmy sticks her tongue out at the back of his head, and I stifle a laugh.

We take the elevator down to the lobby, and they have us in a taxi almost immediately. We whip around traffic and down the highway until the outer edges of Puerto Vallarta come into view.

The road curves around the bay where the cruise ships are docked, and I have to duck to see the tops. I never gave much thought to how big a cruise ship is. It's like a floating skyscraper, and looking at them makes me a little sick to my stomach. Or maybe it's the way the roads wind back and forth. Either way, I'm queasy by the time we pull up to the circular drop-off in front of the marina and pile out of the car. That doesn't bode well for this sailing adventure of ours. Maybe I should have stopped at a pharmacy to get some Dramamine.

Jackson stops beside me on the sidewalk, staring off at the cruise ships. "Those things look like a waking nightmare. Cross that off my bucket list."

I nod. "You couldn't pay me to get on one."

Emmy puts her hands on her hips. "I would. Looks like a blast. Some of them have roller coasters on board."

"Nothing more exciting than flying off roller coaster tracks, straight into the ocean," Jackson mumbles.

I nod. "Yeah, that's a no from me."

"You guys are super boring. Where's Benny?"

Jackson pretends to puke into a bush by the entrance, and I snort laugh. He's in a surprisingly good mood for a hostage.

Emmy stalks toward the glass doors. Before she reaches them, one opens, and the man himself emerges with his arms flung wide. He's wearing expensive-looking khaki swim trunks and a short-sleeve white button-up.

"Welcome to today's adventure!" Ben says, waving us inside. "You all ready? We only have a half hour until the boat leaves."

It only takes about ten minutes to pay our port fees—Ben generously covers them for everyone—and then we wait in a small line of cruise ship employees and tourists to go through a metal detector. Once we're through, wide glass doors at the end of the hall open to docks upon docks full of boats.

The cruise ships sit down the way in their own docking, and wide concrete aisles take up most of the left side of the marina, jutting into the water between large boats with giant colorful tour company logos on the side. We pass empty double-decker pontoon boats, their awnings furled. Ben veers to the right, down the farthest concrete aisle, and we pass nearly a dozen boats with no passengers.

Jackson clears his throat as we make our way farther from the building. "Hey, ah, Ben. There're a lot of boats here. Like…a whole lot. Are you sure tours are still going out today?"

Ben spins and walks backward as the dock shifts from concrete to wood planks. He plays with that gold lighter he bought at the market yesterday, flicking the metal lid open and closed, open and closed. The metal-on-metal click is more than a little annoying.

"Of course! My stuff is already on the boat. It's only a few dark clouds. Nothing to worry about."

Click, click, click.

I frown. There really *are* a lot of docked boats. Maybe it's still early? We walk past a small fleet of yellow sailboats, quietly rocking in the little waves. A middle-aged guy pops his head up as he tugs on the ropes securing a sail cover before he leaps off the boat onto the dock and heads toward us. Away from the water.

This doesn't bode well for our adventure.

Click, click, click.

I'm going to chuck that damn lighter into the ocean.

The guy from the boat stops and nods toward the water. "You kids might want to check your reservation," he says, with a light Spanish accent. "Charters are canceled. A couple of storms are coming down the coast—the first should hit Banderas Bay midday. No tours are going out until they pass. For safety reasons."

He smiles apologetically, as if the storms are somehow his fault.

"What?" Emmy whisper-shrieks. "No!"

Ben smiles at the older man and, finally, blissfully, snaps the lighter shut and sticks it in his pocket. "We'll check with our boat. Thank you for the heads-up."

The man smiles. "No problem. Have a nice day. Stay dry!"

Emmy grabs Ben's arm. "Is it really going to be canceled?"

Ben gently tugs her forward, down the dock. "Nah. Keith has it covered. Don't worry."

Who. The fuck. Is Keith?

Jackson raises an eyebrow at me, but we follow them to the farthest dock.

Ben stops at what must be a fifty-foot sailboat. He gestures to it like a game show host. "Here we are!"

I look for the logo on the side, like the other charter company boats have, but it seems like a normal boat. I glance at the others docked around us. They're *all* normal boats, in varying size, some sailboats and some powerboats. None have logos. We're definitely in the personal vessel section of the marina. When Ben steps to the side, the boat's name pops into view, painted on the back in bold, navy letters.

The *Be-Yacht-Ch*.

I stop dead in my tracks and grab Emmy's arm. "Hold on. There's no way this is a tour charter."

All three of us look at Ben as he climbs from the dock onto the sailboat. "It's not."

"What do you mean?" Jackson asks.

"I tried to book at the resort, but none of the tours were taking reservations because of the storm. So I came down to the marina and found someone willing to take us."

"Someone as in...a random guy with a boat?" Jackson asks.

Ben rolls his eyes. "Not some random guy. Keith's a professional."

As if he's been summoned, a frat-boy-looking white guy with a bright orange Hawaiian-print shirt pops up from a hatch in the middle of the boat and drops a clear tote on the deck behind Ben. Ben throws an arm around the stranger's shoulders with a grin. "Keith's been living on this boat for the last twelve years. He does private trips like this at whatever port he's visiting that month. He's a total pro. He's sailed this thing back and forth from San Francisco, like, seven times all by himself."

Keith grabs onto one of the metal supports that run from the deck to the mast and smiles at us. He's probably in his mid-thirties, average build, with messy blond hair and a wide smile. His eyes are the same color as the ocean behind him, and he's got a handlebar mustache he's clearly gelled into submission—the curls don't even move in the wind.

"Hey! Nice to meet'cha. You can call me Captain Keith. It's a pleasure to take you out today."

Jackson folds his arms. "No. Nope. No way."

"What do you mean?" Ben asks.

"There's no way we're going on some random guy's boat when all the professionals are smart enough to stay home. If the tour companies aren't going out, we should go back to the resort."

"Don't be a baby," Ben says. "The tours are overly cautious, that's all. Keith told me all about it."

Captain Keith nods. "It's really not going to be a problem. There'll be no harm in tasting the sea for a few hours. Besides, we'll be back long before the bad weather hits the bay. The weather report has the first storm making landfall around five or six tonight."

"If that's true, why are none of the tour charters going out?" I ask.

He shrugs. "Incoming storms typically create bigger waves, bigger waves mean more seasick tourists, and the tour companies don't want to deal with vomit and whining and refund requests. Which reminds me, if you gotta yack, aim overboard. I don't want to clean up after you either."

"See?" Ben grins at his new BFF, who looks shockingly like a window into Ben's future self. Confident? Check. Obnoxious? Check. Charming? Check. Peaked in high school? Check. "Captain Keith has it handled. Now let's get going before we waste all our sailing time standing around on land."

He reaches out for Emmy's hand. Surprisingly, she looks to Jackson and doesn't move. None of us do. Jackson frowns, but he says nothing.

Looks like our adventure's ending before it began.

Captain Keith sighs and stares into the distance at the dark clouds. He takes a breath. "Okay, how about this: If you're worried about the weather, I'll have you back at the marina by three at the latest. That's a solid two hours before the storm is supposed to hit. And if the wind changes, the forecast shifts, or anyone on the boat gets worried, we turn around first thing."

"Good enough for me," Emmy says, and practically lunges for Ben's outstretched hand.

Jackson reaches for her. "Em, no w—"

But Ben's already hauling her on board. She plops onto a cushion in the cockpit before Jackson can finish.

She laughs. "Too slow, big brother."

"Emmy, get off the boat. I'm not kidding. We're not doing this."

"If you're not up to it, Emmy and I can go alone," Ben suggests. "I'll make sure she gets back to the resort in one piece."

Jackson glares at him. "My parents would lose their minds."

"So don't tell them."

Emmy stands and wraps her arms around Ben, smiling from ear to ear. "Do what you want, but I'm staying with Ben, and we're having a fun day on the water. If you want to wimp out, that's your choice. This is mine."

I pinch the bridge of my nose. *For the love of common sense, Emmy.*

Captain Keith nods at the tote. "Take off your shoes and stick 'em in there. I'll stash the bin below deck until we get back. Flip-flops and wet boat decking don't mix."

They drop their shoes into the tote and scramble around to the front of the boat, where they disappear behind half-unfurled sails, leaving me and Jackson standing on the dock alone. Captain Keith hops down beside us and starts working on the ropes tying the boat to the dock, unhooking them one by one.

"I don't like this," Jackson says, taking in the clouds on the horizon.

"Me neither. What do we do?"

Jackson takes a deep breath and blows it out again, pulling at his shirt. "You should go back to the resort. I'll make sure my adventure-happy sister gets back in one piece. We'll meet you there later."

Captain Keith climbs onto the landing at the back of the boat and holds out a hand. "It's now or never, kids. Charter's bought and paid for. Are you in or are you out?"

Jackson sighs and climbs on without taking Captain Keith's hand. "My sister's on board, and I doubt I'll get her off this boat without a screaming match, so I'm in by obligation."

I nervously spin my friendship bracelet around my wrist. Honestly, not having to spend the whole day with Jackson while Emmy and Ben suck face sounds great. But can I really go back to the resort alone? What would I do on our last day of vacation all by myself?

I glance at the marina building, then at the boat.

Captain Keith is still hanging off the back, hand extended. He catches my gaze and smiles. "No obligation, girlie. I'll take care of your friends if you want to stay ashore. It's totally up to you. Either way, everyone's coming back safe."

A loud giggle comes from the front of the boat, and I see a flash of leg on the other side of the mast. A second later Emmy's lace cover-up flutters to the deck and Ben laughs.

With a groan, I grab Captain Keith's hand and let him pull me safely on board. I can't leave Emmy, and as much as I hate it, I can't abandon Jackson to deal with the two irresponsible lovebirds on his own. Emmy never listens to anyone, least of all Jackson. And if I go back to the resort, I'll spend the whole day worrying about them anyway.

Jackson's throwing his sandals into the tote when I step on the boat. His eyebrows shoot up his forehead. "You sure?"

"Not even a little bit." I chuck my flip-flops in a little angrier than intended.

The captain takes the tote down to the cabin.

The boat looks...kinda old? Or old*er*, anyway. The teak decking is worn. Long bench seats with vinyl cushions frame the wheel in a U shape. A tall metal mast juts into the air three quarters of the way to the front of the boat. Big white sails are piled atop a horizontal bar that stretches out above the opening Captain Keith descended into. Another sail looks to be wrapped around a wire that runs from the very front of the boat up to the top of the mast.

Ropes. Are. Everywhere. Piled on the deck, strung up between the sails, lashed to hooks and spool-looking things. Wrapped against a reddish-orange donut-shaped life ring along the boat's back railing.

Wires cut through the sky above our heads. There are cranks and pulleys all over.

One glance, and I'm convinced sailing is out of my depth. Learning what all these things do feels more daunting than the SATs. It makes me think a little more of Captain Frat Boy. Marginally.

I run my hand along the shiny metal railing and frown.

"It'll probably be fine," Jackson says, staring up at the sails. "We'll go out for an hour or two, Emmy will probably get seasick, and then we'll be back in the resort hot tub before we know it."

I almost laugh. He says that as if we're in this together, as if he's spent any of this vacation in that hot tub or anywhere near me. I don't say that though; I just nod and smile and try to put some distance between us by heading toward the front of the boat to see where Emmy ended up.

I come to an abrupt halt when I find her and Ben furiously making out. I glimpse a flash of tongue, and I spin on my heel, stomping back toward the wheel to sit on one of the cushions. I drop my mesh bag beside me and sigh. And so it begins.

Jackson plops down unexpectedly beside me, and I look at him in surprise.

"What? I don't want to see them sucking each other's faces either."

Right, that makes sense.

Captain Keith emerges from the cabin. "Where are the other two?"

Jackson wordlessly points toward the front of the boat, and the captain laughs.

"Okay, we'll do this without them, and you two can fill in the lovebirds later." He waves a hand at the boat. "A few safety items before we take off. There are life vests below deck. Please let me know if you're not a strong swimmer, and I'll get one for you now. Otherwise, you're free to sit without one."

"Hannah's a lifeguard," Jackson offers. "You don't have to worry about her. I'm good too."

Captain Keith nods. "Lifeguard? Making my day easier and easier. What about the other two?"

"My sister can swim in a pool. I wouldn't trust her in a current though. No idea about *Mr. Moneybags*."

"I'll ask them when they come up for air." He walks over and taps a hand on the wire railing that circles the boat. "Watch the lifelines. They are low on a boat like this, and we don't want anyone leaning over too far and ending up in the ocean." He points at the long horizontal piece the big sail is attached to. "That there is the boom. It shifts back and forth when I turn the wheel. If you aren't paying attention, you could get knocked on your ass by the boom's swing. Keep an eye on that at all times while walking around. It's safest if you stay seated while we're underway to avoid that problem."

He points at the life preserver. "There's a life ring in case of an emergency—but please, no emergencies. I have snorkel equipment below deck for later. Please no sunscreen spray on your feet. Nobody likes a slippery deck, and it's terrible on the teak. The head is below, straight back through the galley. Door on the right. You can put your bags in the cabin or keep them up here with you; just don't put anything near the side or you're likely to lose it. Boats are bumpy on a good day, and we're likely to rock a bit more than normal because of the weather. Like I said, if you have to puke, aim for the ocean. Otherwise, sit back and enjoy the day."

Huh. Okay. Captain Keith sounds pretty legit. Maybe Ben's desperate last-minute selection isn't a total lost cause. Jackson adjusts the sunglasses on his face and leans back in his seat. I wonder if he feels any better about this.

The sailboat's motor whirls to life. Captain Keith releases the last rope keeping us in place, the boat jostles a bit, and we're free of the dock. We pick up speed once we clear the marina, slowly cruising into the bay.

Captain Keith messes with some settings behind the wheel and speakers kick on. A high-tempo David Guetta song blasts across the boat. I watch the marina get smaller and smaller behind us, and I don't realize my knuckles have turned white around my water bottle until Jackson pokes one of them.

"You okay?"

I nod, but I don't meet his gaze. "Yup. I love cruising straight into the eye of a storm with California Keith, captain of the bros. This is fine. I'm great," I say under my breath.

Jackson scoots forward until he's in my line of sight. His pretty hazel eyes bore into me. "If it gets rough out there, I'll make this guy take us back. Everything will be okay. Besides, he seems fairly competent."

We both turn to Captain Keith, who's donned a pair of aviators and shed his Hawaiian shirt. He stands at the wheel, grinning into the wind, bare chested. His smooth waxed skin is a little too shiny to be natural. A large tattoo stretches beneath his puka shell necklace that says, "NICKELBACK."

"I should have stayed behind when I had the chance." I grip the edge of the cushion for dear life. "Puka Shell Keith is the stuff of nightmares."

Jackson nudges my shoulder with his. "Don't worry. I'll keep you safe."

My teeth grind together. "I don't need you to protect me."

His laugh takes me by surprise, and when I glance at him, his expression is part annoyance, part humor. "Oh, believe me, I know that."

Snippets of unwelcome memories fly through my mind. Jackson standing with a sobbing Emmy in the middle of a dark, deserted road. A driveway illuminated by a single floodlight. Me towering over smashed pieces of plastic and wire.

He looked at me the same way that night. Like he was both shocked and amused by his sister's quiet best friend causing a—well-deserved—scene. At the time, I was thrilled to surprise him. That look on his face felt like a quiet victory in my near-constant quest for his attention.

But now? Now it pisses me off.

"I'm going to take some pictures."

Jackson starts to say something, but I get up and move to the opposite side of the boat before he can speak. At the helm, Captain Keith tugs a few ropes, and the sails raise, catching the wind as he aggressively sings along to "#SELFIE" by The Chainsmokers, which is quite possibly the most annoying song on the planet.

Captain Keith winks at me as we rocket out toward the open ocean.

I fold my arms. "How exactly did Ben find you?"

"He caught me as I was pulling into the marina—I'd just sailed up from Manzanillo. He was walking up and down the docks, knocking on boats, and helped me tie up. Offered me a thousand dollars for the day. Half up front, half when I get you all back in one piece." He laughs. "Just like that. A thousand bucks. Saved my ass, honestly. I was running low on supplies, and it can be tricky to find private charters these days. Everyone wants the affiliated tours with the fancy polos and the catering and the amenities. Nobody wants to appreciate the simple beauty of the sea anymore."

I realize my mouth is open and snap it shut. Sure, sure. Who wouldn't pass up a fleet of shiny new boats full of food and a professional crew when you can have…

Nickelback's biggest fan?

"Lucky us," I say.

"Watch the boom!" he shouts to nobody in particular. He turns the wheel while pulling on a rope. The horizontal arm swings to the left, and he scurries off to secure the rope in place. "With the cash I can make some much-needed repairs to my baby before our next adventure." He pats the fiberglass tenderly. "She's been a little neglected lately. When we get back to shore, she's getting a spa day, let me tell ya."

"Did you just say 'neglected'?" Jackson asks, his voice tight.

Keith shrugs, walking back to the wheel. "Usual wear and tear. Nothing to panic about."

I catch Jackson's eye across the boat.

What the hell have we gotten ourselves into?

CHAPTER FOUR

Banderas Bay is a *lot* bigger than it looks. We cruise through the water, picking up speed the farther we head into the bay, but after a half hour we're still working our way toward the middle.

Sailing is surprisingly relaxing. The water is smooth, and sunlight filters through the clouds in a pretty way—so long as we ignore the dark and grumpy clouds on the horizon. Birds fly beside the boat. Locals in water taxis wave at us and Captain Keith, and I'm relieved to see some other people on the water.

We reach the crowded main stretch of Puerto Vallarta. The beaches are packed with colorful lounge chairs, straw umbrellas, and beachfront restaurants.

"That's Los Muertos Beach and the pier," Keith shouts at us over the wind, turning down the volume on his dance pop playlist or whatever's been screaming through the speakers.

The pier juts out into the water with curved walkways around a sail-shaped sculpture of twisted metal. It looks pretty cool.

"At night the pier lights up and changes color, and the beach is really nice on the south side here. A little crowded though." He looks over at us with a glint in his eye. "Legend has it, the beach got its name from a brutal pirate attack. A group of gold miners were supposedly caught unaware while loading up their riches. Pirates killed them all and left their bodies on the beach. There are probably still bones beneath all those lounge chairs…"

I'm clearly more freaked out by the idea of a bunch of skeletons buried beneath families eating lunch than Jackson is. When I glance over at him on the bench seat across from me, he's got a familiar glint in his eye—one that only makes an appearance when he hears a particularly terrifying true crime story.

"I'll never understand your fascination with the dead," I tell him.

Jackson grins. "What can I say? I love a good murder mystery, and who doesn't appreciate a pirate twist? That makes everything more entertaining."

His eyes almost sparkle, and my stomach does somersaults.

I force myself to look past him at the water. "Sorry, matey," I tell him, "but the survival stories are better."

"This is why you're going into nursing, and I'm studying criminal science. You want to save the living, and I want to avenge the dead."

"Even dead miners who may or may not have existed?"

He splays a hand across his chest in mock offense. "Justice has no expiration date, Hannah Banana."

As much as I try not to, I laugh. That's the problem with Jackson: He's so damn consistent. He's charming, *and* kind, *and* funny. He's always showing up for Emmy—and for me. There's a reason I've been crushing on him for a decade, and it's not because he's hot as hell. Well, not *only* because he's hot.

He's also good. To his bones, he's good. It's hard to get over someone like that.

As we make our way south, Captain Keith points up the sheer cliffs at huge houses clustered at the top. "We're getting a glimpse at the rich and famous. This is Conchas Chinas, or as I like to call it, the Beverly Hills of Puerto Vallarta."

The boat cuts through the water, casting spray at my face. The breeze almost instantly dries it, only to be misted again a second later. The sail is gigantic, shifting slightly every time Captain Keith pulls another rope or adjusts our direction. Ben was right, Captain Keith really knows what he's doing. He commands the boat like it's an extension of himself, easily bounding around to tend to this, move that. Smiling the entire time.

I suppose the Nickelback tattoo can be forgiven.

Almost an hour down the coast, Captain Keith turns more inland to show us a cove with a smattering of buildings along the sand. Dozens of boats are anchored inside the cove.

"This is Yelapa," he shouts. "If Banderas Bay is a clock, the north end of the bay at twelve, then Puerto Vallarta is at three o'clock, Conchas Chinas is at four, and Yelapa is straight down at six o'clock. Seven o'clock through eleven o'clock is straight ocean, baby."

A blur of motion to my right makes me jump, and Emmy plops down beside me with a giant grin. Her lips are pink and puffy in that "just made out for over an hour" way.

"What did I miss?" she asks, brightly.

"Um, everything."

She smiles and turns to the captain. "Captain Keith! What did I miss?"

He laughs over the sound of the waves, but he obliges her. "I was telling your friends that this is Yelapa. It's a cove town, only accessible by boat."

"Seriously?" Emmy holds a hand above her eyes so she can see. Her sunshine hair blows toward me as she does.

"Seriously. A lot of these little coastal towns are only accessible by water taxi. The jungle is so thick and dangerous it makes roads impossible. Not to mention those mountains back there?" He points to the rolling hills of jungle beyond. "Those are the Sierra Madre mountains. Some would argue that's the most dangerous mountain range in Mexico."

Jackson slides over to our side of the bench as we move along that imaginary clock of the bay, leaving Yelapa behind. "Wouldn't want my boat to break down out here."

Captain Keith nods, pushing his sunglasses up his nose with a knuckle. "That happened to me once. Not here in the bay, but much farther north." He lets out a shrill whistle. "That was one shit afternoon. If my temperamental radio chose that day to crap out, I could have been out there for days. There was nothing but water and empty beach for miles and going ashore and hiking in is not an option. These mountains don't mess around. Getting stuck on a stretch of mainland between towns is a bit like washing up on a deserted island."

Emmy's eyes are the size of sand dollars. "That's...awesome."

Captain Keith grins at her. "Don't worry. We're not recreating *Cast Away* on my watch." He takes a deep drink from his water bottle by the wheel.

A gust of wind catches in the sails, blowing our hair over our shoulders, and the boat leans to the right. I grab the railing along the back of the bench seat as our side lifts into the air.

Ben wobbles up beside Emmy and wraps an arm around her. "Are you guys seriously talking about getting stranded? Where's your sense of joy? Bunch of downers over here." He pulls his other hand from behind his back and thrusts a full bottle of tequila at us. "Luckily I brought the cure for downers."

"Did you also bring the cure for your future hangover?" Jackson asks.

Ben lets go of Emmy and leans over to slap Jackson on the shoulder. "How's that stick up your ass, man? Any plans to remove it or what?"

Jackson scowls at him, and Ben throws his head back and laughs. "Come on, we're supposed to be making the most of your last full day in Mexico. Time to relax."

He grabs Emmy's hand and starts hauling her toward the front of the boat, and she reaches back to drag me with them. When we reach the front, Ben spreads out a blue-and-white-striped hotel towel and flops down. I sink cross-legged on the edge, careful not to sit on the flat square hatch beside me. I cup a hand against the dark acrylic window and peek in, looking down onto the lower corner of a mattress. Probably Captain Keith's bedroom. Emmy all but climbs into Ben's lap, and Jackson leans silently against the front of the boat. I'm shocked he followed us.

Ben produces a stack of plastic cups and grapefruit-flavored soda from his backpack. He pours a generous splash of tequila and soda into each cup and hands them out. When we each have one, he holds his aloft with another grin.

"The poor man's Paloma. When in Mexico, right?"

Ben and Emmy are the only ones who drink. I set mine politely at my feet, and Jackson dumps his over the side when he thinks nobody's looking. He's never been much of a drinker.

Ben slaps his hand against the deck. "So, Stick in the Mud. What's your life like when you're not babysitting your beautiful sister?"

Jackson mimes another gag.

"He's studying criminal justice," Emmy answers for him. "He's in his second year at Portland State."

"Ah, that explains the murder books you're always carrying around," Ben says. "And that shirt."

Jackson says nothing, but he frowns down at his shirt like he's offended on Sherlock Holmes's behalf.

"So you're going to be a cop or something?"

"Not exactly. I'm not sure what I want to do yet. I'd like to be a criminal profiler or work in forensic science or crime scene investigation. Lately I've been leaning more toward victim advocacy."

Ben frowns. "What the hell is victim advocacy?"

The boat rises and falls over a wave, and Jackson holds onto one of the wires attached to the mast until the boat levels out again. "Exactly what it sounds like. Victim advocates work with victims of a crime to help them navigate the justice system. Sometimes they accompany victims to court. They gather resources, help with legal aid, get financial assistance, develop safety plans—that kind of thing. They basically make sure that the cops and courts respect a victim's rights, so they don't get lost in the system."

"Hmmm." Ben blows out a breath. "Sounds boring to me, but okay. What about you, Hannah?"

Boring? Making life easier for survivors to get justice sounds boring to him? My fingers find the friendship bracelet, and I start spinning it around my wrist. "What *about* me?"

"Emmy said you're sticking close to home for school next year. Where did you get in?"

"I'm going to Linfield University in the fall. It's about a half an hour from home."

"Do you know what you're going to school for?"

"Nursing. I want to work in trauma."

I see Jackson smile from the corner of my eye, but Ben seems confused. "That's...a choice. I bet your parents are thrilled. Trauma nursing sounds impressive. Not as impressive as being a full doctor, but up there."

My hand freezes on my bracelet. Did he just insult me and the entire nursing profession at the same time? "Yeah, my dad is pretty happy about it."

"And your mom?"

I pause, but I'm not sure why. It's not like it's hard to talk about at this point, and it's far from a secret, but it is a bit of a downer. "It's just me and my dad. My mom left town when I was six, and I haven't seen her since."

Ben looks pleasantly uncomfortable, so I keep talking. "My dad is great. He's the reason I'm going into nursing. He's been a pediatric nurse practitioner my whole life—"

Ben laughs out loud. "A male nurse?"

"Nurse practitioner—"

"Does that make a difference?"

My teeth grind together. "Yeah. It makes a difference. But there's also nothing wrong with male nurses."

Jackson steps closer to me. "And what does your dad do again, Ben? Does he spend his days taking care of sick and injured little kids, or...?"

"Don't be a dick, Jackson," Emmy mumbles.

"No need when Ben's doing such a good job of that himself."

But Ben seems entirely unbothered. "Nah, he's right. My parents both sell corporate real estate in Miami. Nothing noble. I didn't mean to throw shade at your dad, Hannah. Putting casts on clumsy kids is admirable."

I trail my finger around the rim of my cup and shrug him off. Honestly, I shouldn't have said anything in the first place. Once we go home, we'll never see this guy again. It doesn't matter what our future plans are. He won't be around, so why give him the opportunity to voice his opinion?

Emmy takes a nervous drink and puts on a megawatt smile. "Nursing will be such a great job for Hannah. She even worked as a lifeguard the last two summers to amp up her applications. She's so damn smart. I could never."

I frown at her. She totally could. Emmy is way smarter than she gives herself credit for. "If you wanted to be a nurse, nothing would stop you. It's not your passion, and there's nothing wrong with that."

Emmy leans her head on my shoulder. "Yeah, maybe. School just isn't in my blood. I can't imagine willingly signing up for more of it after graduation. If I never see another quiz or narrative paper again, it'll be too soon."

Ben crosses his long legs at his ankles. "I'm not an academic person either. I'm passing all my classes, but they're boring as hell. I'd much rather be traveling. I probably will after I graduate, at least until I figure out what I want to do long term."

Emmy sits up. "Oh my god. Me too!"

Ben gets that shimmery, happy sparkle in his eye again. "Where do you want to visit the most? If you could go anywhere in the world?"

"Italy," she says. No hesitation. "I'm starting there when I take off on my grand adventure."

He finishes off his drink. "I love Italy. I'll text you all my favorite hidden gems. I spent six weeks in Venice a couple summers ago, and I almost didn't come back."

The sound Emmy makes is part squeal and part gasp. "That sounds like a dream. I can't wait to wander. Getting lost in new places is my most favorite thing."

Ben uncrosses his ankles and recrosses them, staring pensively at his bare feet. "Maybe I'll come with you."

I raise my eyebrows at Jackson as Emmy claps her hands in excitement.

"I'd love that!" She looks up at him with wide goo-goo eyeballs that make me want to puke in my cup. "We could go all over Europe too. I have a list of destinations in my phone. We could check them off one by one!"

Ben grins. "Whatever it takes to keep that smile on your face, gorgeous."

Red flags wave frantically inside my head. I try and catch her eye, but it's like Jackson and I have ceased to exist in the wake of Ben's offer.

It's very Emmy. Her first priority is always whatever boy has her attention, however fleeting that may be. But she's never once considered inviting any of them on her big adventure. She even turned *me* down when I offered to go with her for part of it. She said it was destined to be a sacred—and solo—trip. That she couldn't find her own way in the world with someone holding her hand.

But apparently it's only sacred and solo until Trust Fund Ken invites himself to tag along after thirty measly seconds of conversation. Hurt slices through me.

I clear my throat and tap Emmy on the knee. "Hey, Em? No offense to Ben here, but you guys just met. Maybe traveling to a foreign country with a virtual stranger isn't the best idea?"

She snorts. "You're too cautious for your own good, you know that? You need to live a little, or you'll end up an old lady with only boring memories to keep yourself company."

Emmy could have pushed me overboard, and it would've shocked me less.

Ben laughs. "I don't think Hannah knows how to live any other way," he says, as if he knows me at all. As if he has any right to judge me in the first place. "Don't take it personally, but there are girls who live life to the fullest, and there are girls who read a lot and make friends with their teachers. Doesn't take a detective to figure out which one you are, Nurse Hannah."

Annnd the hits keep coming. Each word out of his mouth feels like a punch.

Emmy looks away. She knows that one struck home. Everywhere we go, in every friend group we find ourselves in, Emmy's always the fun one. She's always the one at the center of every "exciting" new plan, while I'm the one pointing out which parts of that plan are illegal or most likely to result in medical intervention.

If I had a dollar for every time I've been called "boring," or "mom," or "the babysitter," I could buy this boat with a briefcase of cash and give it a better name.

Nobody speaks, but I feel three sets of eyes on me.

I slide my sunglasses from the top of my head onto my nose, drop my full cup inside Bennett's empty one, and climb back to my feet. "Really glad I tagged along today. This is so fun for me. You two should get back to planning your trip and pretending you're not total fucking strangers."

I stomp back to the cockpit, weaving around ropes and vertical cables as the boat rises and falls over waves. I sit with my back to the bow and snatch up my water bottle from the seat. I take a long drink, grateful the water inside is still cold.

Captain Keith stops singing along to his mix to ask, "Everything okay up there?"

"Peachy."

"Sure looks like it." He grabs his own water bottle from the cup holder by the wheel and polishes it off. "Hold the wheel for a minute? I'm going to refill below."

I look from the wheel to him and back. Several times. "What?"

He waves me over. "Come on, it's nothing, really. Just hold the wheel steady. The wind isn't changing directions, and there's nothing out here for you to hit. I'll be right back."

"Um…" I stuff my water bottle in my bag and stand. I've barely wrapped my fingers around the metal wheel before he's bolting for the stairs. Almost as soon as his mustache vanishes below deck, Emmy comes flying around the side of the boat like an avenging angel.

I drop my head back with a sigh. Of course.

She skids to a stop on the other side of the wheel. "What is your problem, Hannah? And…what the hell are you doing? Where's Keith?"

I force a smile. "I don't have a problem. Go back to your boy and leave me alone. I'm steering the ship. The captain needed something down below."

"I'm not leaving until you apologize to Ben. You made him sound like a creeper. He's being nice. He doesn't want me to travel alone because he cares about me."

"Or because he found a hot girl naïve enough to travel with him," I suggest, my grip tightening on the wheel. "You're so damn trusting, Emmy. And that's fine when he's teaching you to paddleboard, but going off alone with him, thousands of miles from your family? You know nothing about this guy. Nothing. He could get mad and strand you in a foreign country. He could meet someone else and ditch you. He could take your passport while you're sleeping. He could go streaking through the streets of Venice. You have no fucking idea, because you *don't know him*. There's a reason your parents insisted Jackson come with us today."

Emmy folds her arms, and strands of blond hair billow around her shoulders in the wind. "I *do* know him. I've spent the last several days with him—"

"Days! You know what? I take it all back. You probably know him better than you know me. Carry on."

Jackson ducks under the boom and laughs out loud. "Come on, Hannah. Stranger danger is irrelevant when true love is on the line. Everybody knows that." He flops onto the bench seat beside me, arms propped along the backs of the cushions on either side of him. "While you're at it, why don't you try hitchhiking too? Wander a darkened alley? You know, since you're so determined to become a feature in the next season of *Unsolved Mysteries*."

The glare she unleashes on her brother is molten. "Ben is not some creep in a darkened alley. He's hot and rich and super nice."

Jackson slaps himself on the forehead. "Why didn't I think of that? *Of course* being rich means you can't be dangerous." He fake coughs, "Robert Durst...Phil Spector...Brooke Goodwin...the Murdaughs..."

"You're ruining this whole day," Emmy fumes. "I hope you're both happy."

She storms back to the bow, and I try not to laugh at the dramatics. She'll fume and rant and stomp all over, but she's very easily distracted. This will have little to no effect on her day.

Jackson stares after her with a sigh. "What are we going to do with her?"

We?

I lean to the right until I can see around the mast to the front of the boat. Ben stands behind Emmy on the bow, both of them facing the sea, arms extended. Having a full *Titanic* moment. She's recovered in record time.

I fully accept that I'm more cautious than she is. I also accept that Emmy's more likely to have fun in any given situation because she doesn't waste time worrying about what could go wrong. But one of these days, her impulsivity is going to put her in a situation that'll take something from her. She'll learn to be cautious in the worst possible way, and the carefree, wild, impulsive version of my best friend will vanish.

In this world, it's a matter of when, not if. Jackson and I won't always be around to prevent it. And jetting off to Europe with a stranger she trusts solely because he's been nice to her for a few days is an express lane to a dangerous situation.

Anyone can put their best foot forward for a couple days, or weeks. But the truth always comes out. No one can play the part of the good guy indefinitely if that's not who they are. When Ben's mask slips, I sure as hell hope the worst thing beneath it is an overinflated ego, or Emmy's grand adventure could quickly turn into a nightmare.

And there's not a damn thing I can do to stop it.

CHAPTER FIVE

Since the beginning, Emmy and I have always fought like volcanoes. We're both quick to anger, quick to yell, and then we cool down and lie dormant for a century or two. Before today, I think the last fight we had was at freshman Homecoming. Emmy got so caught up trying to curl her hair that she forgot to tell her mom I needed a ride until she was already at the dance. I had to walk a mile and a half in heels. I found her pacing in front of the school, waiting for me.

She shouted her apology across the parking lot.

I threw my shoes at her.

We were inside dancing ten minutes later.

Today is no different. Within twenty minutes we're giggling about Captain Keith's tattoo.

The rest of the morning is much less explosive. We watch whales jump from the water in the distance. We tan on the bow. Captain Keith teaches the boys the basics of sailing, each of them taking the *Be-Yacht-Ch* in wide circles near the mouth of the bay, the boom swinging from one side to the other as the wind catches the sail from different directions. Bennett spends his entire lesson boasting about the sailing camp he went to three summers in a row, and I roll my eyes because that's the most rich-kid thing I've ever heard.

Keith steers us to a cove and drags out a duffel full of snorkel gear. We spend the better part of an hour swimming and watching fish blink in and out of view around underwater rock formations. Ben swears he sees a sea turtle, but when we climb back on board, Captain Keith meets my gaze and shakes his head.

Liar, he mouths as I pass him, and I have to turn my laugh into a cough.

The day stretches on, and we eat the fruit, sandwiches, and snacks the resort packed for Ben until the entire "picnic" is reduced to a mess of wrappers we stuff back in his backpack. Our full stomachs and hours in the sun make us tired, but as the sun disappears behind the clouds, a pod of dolphins finds us and chases the boat. It's magical. By far the *best* part of the whole day.

I'm so unexpectedly relaxed that I almost forget about the storm.

A streak of lightning interrupts Emmy excitedly taking photos of us looking at the dolphins from the bow. It's so close, it makes all four of us instinctively crouch down. The answering clap of thunder is right on its heels, the sound ripping through the sky.

The dark storm clouds that have been hovering on the horizon are suddenly...not on the horizon anymore. They're practically on top of us.

"Um, I think we're done sailing," Emmy says, nervously wringing her hands in her cover-up.

Jackson stares up at the sky like it's about to drown us. "Yeah, this isn't good."

Even Ben looks worried. "Did that sneak up on us, or have we been heading into the storm this whole time?"

I frown. "What do you mean?"

He points at the ominous clouds. "We're aimed right at the storm, straight out toward the open ocean. Keith promised to keep us in the bay in case of bad weather."

Shit. *Shit.* I squint toward the mainland, but all I see is water—in every goddamned direction. I couldn't even tell you which way the mainland *is*, which probably means we're way too far out.

"Where *is* Captain Keith?" Jackson asks.

We turn toward the helm in unison. There's nobody behind the wheel.

"He was just there," Ben says. "I swear, he was at the wheel the last time I looked."

We scramble back to the cockpit. A stretch of rope is tied to the wheel to keep it steady.

Ben dives into the cabin first. "He must have ducked into the bathroom. There's no way he'd let his boat drift around under sail with a bunch of teenagers on board."

Logically I know Ben has to be right, but I'm almost positive I haven't seen him standing at the wheel while we've been watching the dolphins—and that's been at least twenty minutes. In fact, the last time I remember seeing him was when he let Ben take the wheel and the two of them spent a considerable amount of time pretending to be pirates. They even changed the music to a playlist of sea shanties.

There's no music now, and I can't pinpoint exactly when it shut off. The only sounds on the boat are the rush of the wind, the occasional snap of the sails, and the rhythmic splash as the hull cuts through the waves.

We follow Ben below deck as the panic builds. Ben's right: Captain Keith wouldn't leave the boat cruising for that long, especially knowing about the storm. This is his home. There's no way he'd be so careless with it...right?

The interior of the boat has a tiny kitchen alcove at the base of the stairs with a micro stove and a cluster of cabinets on the left. There's a small workspace beneath half a wall of radio and navigation equipment on the right. Beyond that, a U-shaped seating area wraps around a square laminate table. A long blue bench, presumably with storage underneath, runs along the other wall. The bin with all our shoes has fallen sideways into the walkway, likely from the last wave.

Three round portholes on each side let in weak storm-tinted sunlight. Two pocket doors sit in the wall ahead of us. The edge of the same rumpled mattress I spotted through the hatch on the bow is visible through the door on the left. The door on the right is closed. The bathroom, I'm guessing?

Ben rockets ahead of me and barges into the bedroom. "Not here."

I yank open the other door. Captain Keith is slumped inside the tiniest bathroom in the world, ass on the toilet, forearms braced on a sink that's approximately a foot in front of him, shorts bunched around his ankles.

"Oh my god, is he sick?" Emmy asks, peeking around me.

I shake his bare shoulder, and Captain Keith jerks upright, batting away my hand, but his eyes don't open. His leg kicks out, like a reflex, and something shoots past me. I twist as Ben emerges from the bedroom, and the four of us stare at the empty bottle of tequila on the floor.

"Isn't that yours?" Jackson asks.

Ben nods. "It was in my bag. But the last time I saw it, there was a lot more in the bottle."

We all look at Captain Keith as a wave rocks the boat. I fall into Ben. Jackson catches Emmy before she face-plants onto the table. The boat flops back a second later.

Ben steadies me, and we all turn to stare at our captain again.

I pinch the bridge of my nose and blow out a breath. "He's trashed."

"Yup," Ben and Emmy say at the same time. They sound almost amused.

I whirl on them. "The guy in charge is blacked-out drunk with his pants down, and we're aimed straight for a storm. How intensive was that sailing camp of yours, Ben? Do either of you know how to get us back to the marina in this kind of weather?"

Ben scowls at me. We both know the answer is no.

Emmy gestures toward the bathroom. "Just, like... wake him up!"

I start to say that's not going to do any good if he's downed half a bottle of tequila in less than an hour—never mind whatever he's been drinking from his water bottle all day—but Ben takes the suggestion to heart. "Out of my way."

He grabs Captain Keith by the forearms and hauls him to his feet, slamming him against the bathroom wall, and slaps him across the face.

The captain blinks, and his eyes widen in surprise. "Whaddya want?" he slurs.

"Pull up your damn pants!" Ben shouts.

For some reason, Keith listens and yanks his shorts and underwear up over his hips. Ben's stance in the doorway thankfully keeps the rest of us from seeing anything we don't need to see. When Captain Keith's righted, his button and zipper still undone, Ben takes him by the back of the neck and shoves him out of the bathroom. We move out of the way, parting to give him the aisle. Ben propels Captain Keith through the boat and up the stairs.

"What does he think he's going to do? Beat the guy sober?" Jackson asks.

Emmy rolls her eyes. "He clearly has a better plan than that."

But as she runs up the stairs, Jackson gives me a look that says he doesn't believe that for a second. Neither do I. We can't afford to let Ben take out his frustrations on the one person who knows how to get us out of here before the storm kicks our asses. We hurl ourselves up on deck after Ben and Emmy. The moment my head clears the cabin, a gust of wind hits me in the face. The sky is significantly darker than it was when we went below only a few minutes ago.

I step onto the deck, and a wave crashes into the boat and rocks us violently to the side, nearly knocking me off my feet. Fear blooms in my chest as I slide across the teak. Jackson catches me around the waist, but the force of the wave throws us both to the side. He grabs ahold of the lifelines, and we jerk to a stop. Frothy water washes across our bare feet.

Screaming cuts through the wind, and we spin toward the wheel.

Ben's shouting in Captain Keith's face at the helm. Emmy hovers anxiously at his back, dancing from foot to foot like she doesn't know what to do.

Ben's face is twisted with rage and his hands are balled into fists at his sides. Keith looks a little dazed, likely from the tequila. I'm not entirely sure how he's upright at this point. Ben's almost his exact height—and he's not trashed. Captain Keith doesn't have the upper hand if this gets violent.

The thought sends a chill down my spine that feels unnatural in this humidity. I pull Jackson toward me and shout to be heard over the wind. "If Ben's making the decisions, this could get out of hand really fast."

He nods and moves around the wheel. I'm a vibrating ball of anxiety following behind him, holding on to the lifelines to steady myself. I have no idea how he's planning to defuse this.

Just as Jackson reaches them, Captain Keith grins and says something. The words are lost to me, but Ben clearly hears it. His face turns bright red. His shoulders snap back. Every muscle in his back tenses, and I know what's coming before it happens.

Ben punches Captain Keith in the guts.

Emmy shrieks and scrambles along the bench seat to get out of the blast zone. "No fighting, you idiots!"

Ben hauls back for another punch but Jackson catches his elbow, and holds him away. Captain Keith dives forward and wraps his arm around Ben's neck, squeezing him into a headlock. He tries to drag Ben away from the helm but Ben grabs onto the wheel and the motion wrenches it in a half turn. The boom swings overhead with a groan. The boat tips, lifting my side high into the air so fast I'm scrambling to grab onto the lifelines again.

Ben and Keith land hard on the deck.

Jackson all but dives between them. He pries Keith's arm from Ben's neck, and when my side of the boat rocks back, he uses the motion to shove Ben against the wheel.

Captain Keith stays sprawled where he landed. He laughs at the sky. "Is that all you've got?"

Ben lunges for him again, but Jackson's between them this time, pushing Ben away with both hands on his chest.

Ben settles for screaming instead. "What the fuck is wrong with you, man? You said you'd get us back before the storm hit!"

Captain Keith snorts, propping himself up on his elbows. "And I will."

Ben jabs a finger at the sky. "Too late, asshole!"

Keith blinks as if he hasn't noticed the dark clouds. "Well, I'll be damned."

Once again, Jackson holds Ben back.

Captain Keith barks out a laugh, then another, until he's balled on his side in a fit of hysterics. "This isn't good," he all but wheezes.

Oh sure, just what you want to hear from the guy in charge. Anxiety rips through me and churns my already motion-sensitive stomach. These waves are not helping.

"Which way to the marina?" Jackson asks. "Maybe we can outrun the storm if we hurry."

"Nah."

That's it. That's the entire response from the captain of our fucking boat.

"Nah?" Jackson repeats. "What do you mean, 'nah'?"

Ben gets a leg in front of Jackson and sidesteps him in one fluid motion. He bends over Captain Keith and jabs a finger in his face. "Listen here, you frat-boy bitch: You're going to take us back to the marina right the fuck now, or you can kiss the other half of your money goodbye."

Captain Keith's jaw sets. "You're not gonna order me 'round on my own boat, you privileged little shit."

Ben pulls back his elbow to land another blow. Jackson tries to stop him again, but Ben snaps his arm farther back instead of forward and catches Jackson right in the nose. Jackson's head rocks back with the impact, and he staggers onto the bench seat beside his sister. Blood gushes from his nose and down his chin.

"Jesus, Ben. What the fuck?" Emmy crawls to her brother, dragging her pretty white cover-up over her head. She presses it against his face.

Captain Keith climbs to his feet. Ben is already charging at him, and as another bolt of lightning fills the sky, the two of them become a tangle of fists and elbows and grunts, staggering toward the side of the boat as the growing waves toss us from side to side.

I lunge toward them. I have no idea what I'm going to do or how to stop this, but if I don't find a way, someone's going to get seriously hurt.

Ben takes a hit to the side of the head and rolls against the lifelines.

I try to get between them. "Captain Keith, stop! You can't—"

He shoves me backward, and I trip over Ben's ankle. I land hard on the deck and stars dance in my vision. I can't make myself take a breath.

Jackson's bloodied face appears in front of mine. "Are you okay?"

I still can't breathe.

He places his palm beneath my collarbone and gently shakes my chest. "It's okay, Hannah. You just got the breath knocked out of you."

Yeah, no shit, Sherlock.

I want to shout it, but I still can't make my lungs work. The inside of my ribs feels more and more hollow with every second. Jackson takes my face in his hands, and even with the massacre of blood on his face, he seems calm as hell. Like he knows a breath is a second away.

And he's right. I gasp, and his shoulders relax. Emmy appears at my other side and the two of them help me sit up.

The idiots are still fighting.

Ben surges up, punches Captain Keith in the kidney. Keith returns a jab to Ben's ribs. They both grunt in pain and Keith shoves Ben away from him.

"I never should have taken you shitheads on my boat!" Keith screams over the wind.

Ben grins and lands a punishing blow to Keith's jaw. His head snaps back with the force of the hit. Almost in slow motion, Ben grabs Keith by the temples and yanks his head down as he lifts his thigh. Ben's knee connects with the captain's face *so hard*, I hear his nose break over the roar of wind and water.

Captain Keith drops like a rock, landing flat on the deck.

Jackson swears and steps over me. He loops his forearms through Ben's elbows and rips him away from the fight. Emmy and I roll to the side to let them pass, and Jackson drags Ben all the way back by the helm, commanding him to sit the fuck down. Emmy goes too, arms waving, mouth moving. I can't hear what she's saying, but it sure looks like she's ripping Ben a new one.

I crawl to the captain, relieved to find him conscious at least. He's lying flat on his back, cupping his nose with both hands. His knuckles are split and bloody. More blood streams down both of his cheeks, collecting on the deck. As I lean over him, he lets out a groan I can feel in my chest.

"Jackson, I need your shirt!" I shout over my shoulder.

He appears a moment later, dangling it in front of me, and I gently press Sherlock Holmes against Captain Keith's blood-geyser nostrils.

How the hell did we get here? We were watching dolphins and eating sandwiches, and now there's blood all over the fucking boat.

"I need you to sit up, Keith," I say, gently pressing my hand to the back of his shoulder. "The blood might make it hard to breathe if you stay on your back."

Not to mention if too much of that blood winds up in his stomach, he'll be throwing up blood *and* tequila all over the deck. We're in enough of a mess as it is.

Captain Keith follows my instructions, but the sound that comes out of his mouth as he rolls to a seated position is part whimper and part yelp. I carefully pinch the bridge of his nose, and he tries to bat my hand away.

"I know it hurts, but I'm trying to stop the bleeding," I tell him.

His eyes are bloodshot and angry, but he nods and mumbles a thank you, dropping his hands. He tries to lift his chin, but I pull it back down to keep the blood out of his throat. Beneath my fingers I can feel the deviation in his nose. His face is going to swell up faster than Ben's temper.

I find Jackson watching over my shoulder. "Can you try to find some ice?"

He nods. "On it."

Another clap of thunder shakes the sky, and the clouds open up, covering the deck with water in minutes.

Captain Keith swears under his breath. "We should have been back at the marina by now," he mumbles. "I didn't…I didn't mean to…"

"I know you didn't." I pull the T-shirt away to wipe his face, and I'm relieved to see the blood is significantly thicker. It's already clotting.

At the next strike of lightning, Captain Keith seems to run out of patience. He pushes my hands away and tries to get up. I drop the shirt and help him as best as I can, but he's much heavier than he looks. He takes a step toward the helm and sways on his feet.

I catch him by the elbow. "Be careful. The blood loss and the swelling might make you dizzy."

Half his mouth tugs into a smile. There's blood caked between his teeth and crusted in the hairs of his mustache. "You're a cool kid. I don't know how you got mixed up with him, but be careful. Nobody decent smiles while he hurts someone."

I feel the shock on my face. So I *wasn't* imagining the grin.

Captain Keith slowly shuffles toward the back of the boat, and I follow close behind in case he pitches to one side.

Jackson climbs out of the hatch. "I couldn't find any ice. Sorry."

Ben jumps to his feet, looking furious. "Don't apologize to him! He's the reason we're in this mess in the first place!"

Emmy grabs Ben's hand and tries to pull him back down to the seat beside her, but he rips out of her grip and takes the wheel. "I'll get us out of here."

Jackson grimaces. "*Can* you?"

"It won't be perfect, but I can do it."

"Twenty minutes ago the weather was too much for you, and now you're suddenly so capable?" I ask skeptically.

Ben scowls at me. "Twenty minutes ago I thought this idiot would do what I paid him to do. Now it's up to me to navigate us out of this mess."

I swear to god, his chest puffs up. It sounds like he's rehearsing for a press conference. I can see the headline now: *"Hero Saves Friends When Sailboat Charter Gets Caught in Storm."*

Keith barks out a laugh that turns into a painful wheeze. He grabs the lifelines to steady himself as he doubles over.

"What the hell are you laughing at?" Ben demands.

"An entitled shithead who couldn't navigate his way out of an infinity pool," he says, righting himself. He steps up to the helm. "Now get your hands off my boat."

Rain pelts the deck around us, falling faster by the minute.

Ben's jaw tightens. He looks Keith dead in the eye and unties the rope keeping the boat steady. "Fuck you. I'm in charge now."

Keith glares at him. "You can't fake it at sea. The ocean doesn't give two shits how many hundreds you wipe your ass with, and you don't know the first thing about sailing in a storm, Summer Camp. So for the last time, get your hands *off* my boat."

Ben glares at him, still gripping the rain-slicked wheel like he has no intention of moving. "I've got an idea: Why don't you fucking make me?"

Emmy climbs to her knees on the seat. "Benny, please? No more fighting."

"Yeah, *Benny*. Don't make this any worse for yourself," Keith mimics.

A wave pitches the boat to the side again. Jackson grabs at a lifeline. Keith trips over the back of the bench seat and lands ass-first on the teak walkway.

Ben turns the wheel so we coast over the next wave instead of being broadsided. The boom moves slowly over the top of my head, and I duck toward the hatch to get out of the way. Ben's gaze flickers to the sail and back to Captain Keith. "What the hell does that mean? Make what worse for myself?"

"It means when we get back to shore, I'm pressing assault charges," Keith says, pointing at his broken nose. He climbs to his feet. "Let's see you buy your way out of that."

Ben's jaw sets. "I won't have to buy my way out of anything. I didn't do anything wrong."

"I imagine the police will disagree with you, considering I have witnesses," Keith says.

Lightning splits the air above our heads. The answering thunder rocks the sky a fraction of a second later, making me flinch. Emmy squeals and slides lower in her seat.

Keith points to the cabin. "Get below deck, all of you."

Before anyone can move, a burst of wind hits, pitching me into the hatch frame. The sails catch, and the boat careens so far to the side that Captain Keith's feet dip into the ocean.

Emmy and Jackson look up at the sail. Captain Keith looks down at the water.

But I don't take my eyes off Ben, and *he* only has eyes for the captain.

One side of his mouth ticks up into a grin…and he very deliberately lets go of the wheel and throws himself back on the deck.

The wheel spins wildly out of control.

The boom rips through the air over my head, and Jackson dives out of the way with a shout. Captain Keith looks up at the sound, but it's too late. The boom smashes into the side of his head. His eyes roll back.

The momentum of the impact pitches him over the lifelines.

And Captain Keith goes overboard.

CHAPTER SIX

My brain tries to process what just happened. Blood splatters the boom, sail, and decking. The three of us stare at each other in shock for two or three seconds.

And suddenly, everything is moving too fast.

Ben shouts for Emmy to take the wheel and hangs over the railing, looking out into the water. Emmy's panic sobbing, frozen in her seat. Jackson races to the wheel and grabs it. I scramble to the side where Keith went over. The dark sky has turned the water into a churning mass of gray. We stand at the railing, barely breathing, as we zero in on the cluster of bubbles where he went under. I hold my breath.

He'll come up any moment now.

My lungs start to burn. The wind pushes the boat forward in the water. Ben and I slide along the railing, following the place Keith went under, waiting for him to pop up.

Nothing.

Shit. He's not coming back up on his own.

Ben turns to me with eyes so big, all I can see are the whites. "You're, like, a lifeguard or whatever, right? What the fuck are you waiting for?"

Shit. *Shit.*

He's right.

Work brain kicks on. I point up at the sails. "Stop this fucking boat."

I bolt across the deck, mentally making a plan as I go. I need something to get Keith back to the boat. I need to make sure I don't get carried out with the current. I need to make sure I can see him in the water.

I snatch a dive mask from the bag of snorkeling equipment on the deck and yank it over my face. The rubber strap tears strands of hair from my scalp. I ignore it and rip the emergency flotation off the back of the boat, hurling it as far out as I can.

I kick the back ladder into the water as I wrap one of the docking ropes around my waist.

"Hannah!" Jackson shouts from the helm. "Don't you da—"

I dive, gaze trained on where I think Captain Keith went under, one hand on my mask so the impact of the water doesn't knock it off.

The second I slide beneath the surface I know I'm not going to find him.

Warm currents rip at my body, and I feel myself flip beneath the waves, the force of it pushing me too deep. I fight my way back up to the surface and gasp. Salt water splashes into my mouth, and the rope tying me to the boat grows taut as the boat sails on.

I stick my mask beneath the surface and search for Captain Keith in the depths, hoping my prediction is wrong. That I'll somehow spot him. Some glint of his bare skin, a flash of his dumb tattoo.

He needs to be okay.

We need him to be okay.

I twist in the water, searching as far as I can see for any sign of movement as the seconds stretch on. There's nothing but churning current. Everything beyond my feet is a blur. I kick back to the surface, shouting his name over the waves. Jackson and Emmy join me. Their voices cut through the wind, but the way they're yelling in different directions tells me they can't see him either. Which means he likely didn't surface…

A large wave crests around the back of the boat, and I dive under to avoid it.

I'm so out of my depth—literally. I'm *literally* out of my depth. My lifeguarding course covered how to reach, throw, row, or go get someone in a lake or a pool. I spent the summers sitting in a tall chair, plucking floundering preteens from the deep end at the community pool. My training definitely didn't cover the steps required to locate an unconscious adult in the depths of the fucking Pacific Ocean.

I make one last desperate attempt to find him. I dive under and swim nearly straight down. The pressure of the water slams into my ears, as my body is forced back toward the surface, but I keep kicking. I look for a hand. For a leg. A wisp of hair. Anything to tell me which direction to swim. But I see absolutely nothing. Only blurry gray water that's playing tug-of-war with my body.

Defeat leaches into my chest.

He's been under too long.

He's not coming back. Captain Keith is going to sink to the bottom of the ocean in this fucking storm, and there's nothing I can do to save him.

My lungs catch fire, and with one final spin to look in every direction, I kick back toward the surface.

The current whips me around again, growing stronger. It tugs me to the side and flips me back toward the ocean floor, until the burn in my muscles matches my lungs. Another surge of water shoves me away from the boat, and the rope pulls tight around my waist.

I stare into what must be miles of seawater beneath my feet, and my pulse hammers in my throat so hard it *hurts*. In my mind, all I can see is something swimming up from the depths.

Snapping at my legs.

Dragging me under.

I wouldn't see it until it was on me...

I try and shove the thoughts away, but panic has already seeded itself somewhere vital.

The current shifts, releasing me to the surface. When I finally break through, I'm immediately hit in the face with another wave that mixes my first breath of air with rain and seawater. I choke it back out, struggling to catch my breath.

The rope pulls tight around my ribs. When I look up, Jackson is on the back platform of the boat, dragging me in. Emmy stands behind him, collecting the rope as he drops it on the deck. The life ring is already by her feet. They gave up on saving Captain Keith before I did.

I don't fight it or yell for them to let me keep looking. I'm desperate to get out of this water. I swim as fast as I can toward the boat, battling mental images of creatures sinking their teeth into my skin, tentacles wrapping around my ankles, mouths swallowing me whole.

Jackson helps pull me out of the water and boosts me up onto the main deck.

I collapse against the teak, gasping for air.

"Hannah, what the fuck were you thinking?" Jackson screams, angrily untying the rope from my rib cage.

I can barely hear him. My ears are ringing, salt water burns my nostrils, and I'm focusing very hard on all ten of my fingers splayed out beneath me as adrenaline pounds through my veins. I shove the dive mask off my face, close my eyes, and force air in and out of my lungs as the boat rocks over increasingly larger waves.

I've never been afraid of deep water before. This isn't even the first time I've been in the open ocean. But it all hits different when you're looking for someone in the water.

I imagine Captain Keith sinking into the depths on a loop I can't blink away. God, he didn't deserve this. A panicked sob rips from my chest, and I feel arms around me, but I don't know who they belong to.

When I finally sit up, I find Emmy on her knees beside me, arms like a vise around my shoulders. "You're okay...you're okay, Hannah," she says, and I get the feeling she's been repeating it for a while. Her entire body is shaking, but she's still trying to calm *me* down.

One of the striped resort towels is draped across my back. I pull it closer around me, even though it's soaking wet in the rain.

Jackson is crouched beside his sister, staring at me with angry, terrified eyes. "What the hell were you thinking, Hannah? If that rope untied or snapped, we wouldn't have been able to reach you fast enough in this current. You could have died."

I look away. "I know. I thought I could get to him, but—"

Ben's feet thunder across the deck, and he skids to a stop in front of me. The sail is down, and he seems to have secured the boom from swinging. The metal mast and support poles stretch up like skeleton fingers against the darkening sky.

He scans the deck around us, and the color drains from his face. "Where is he?"

The three of us exchange a look. Nobody wants to be the one to say it out loud.

"Hannah!" Ben yells. "Where's the captain?"

I flinch. "I couldn't find him."

Ben's eyes dart from us to the water and back. "Where the fuck is he?" he shouts again, like he didn't hear or can't process what I just said.

I grab onto the railing and climb to my feet. The towel slides off my back and lands in a heap on the blood-smeared deck. "I'm sorry," I say, louder this time. "I tried my best, but the current is too strong, and there's no visibility. If he was conscious, maybe he would have…"

I didn't think Ben could get any paler, but he does. He looks like the ghost of the sun-kissed boy we met at the resort.

"Fuck, fuck, fuck!" he shouts, dragging his hands through his wet hair and tightening his fingers in the roots. He turns on his heel and kicks the bag of snorkel equipment. "This can't be happening. He wasn't…"

We say nothing. The three of us watch as the reality of the situation sets in.

The only person who knew how to handle this boat in the storm is dead.

And our new friend Bennett killed him.

Emmy lets go of my shoulders and reaches for Ben. Jackson and I grab her at the same time to hold her back.

Ben clocks the movement and wheels on us. "It was an accident," he shouts over the storm, his eyes frantic. "You all saw that. The wheel slipped right out of my hands!"

My jaw clenches. That's not how I remember it. He can't rewrite history now that the consequences of his actions are starting to sink in.

He takes another step in our direction, and Jackson places himself between us and Ben.

Ben squares up to Jackson. "Oh, come on. You don't have to protect them from me. I didn't do anything! You all saw what happened!" he says again. Getting louder. "Let's not overreact."

"Listen," Jackson says, his voice steady and calm. "Let's get back to shore. Okay? You know how to operate a boat. Can you get us back in one piece? Can we motor in? We can figure out everything else once we're not stuck on a sailboat in the middle of nowhere. Can we agree that that's our biggest problem at the moment?"

Ben shoves him, and Jackson falls into me. "No, it's not fucking okay! I'm not going back to the marina until we're all on the same page."

Emmy lets go of my hand and scoots around her brother. "What do you mean? On the same page about what?"

"About what our story is going to be. We can say Keith got drunk and fell overboard. There was nothing we could do." He looks me straight in the eye. "Hannah tried to save him, but it was too late. He fell in and never came back up, and that's not our fault. That's the best version, right?"

"Let's just get back to shore," Jackson says again, his whole body tensed.

Ben turns to Emmy. "You saw what happened. You saw me lose my grip when the wave knocked me over."

Emmy nods, but I see the fear on her face.

"And you," Ben says, leveling a finger in my direction. "You were right in front of me. The storm ripped the wheel out of my hands, and the boom swung and knocked him over the side. You *saw* it."

His gaze drills into me like he's trying to force his version of events into my brain.

"I saw you *let go*," I snap.

"You didn't see shit," Ben seethes.

"You did it on *purpose*."

"Hannah," Jackson warns.

"Come on," Emmy says, her voice rising to an almost hysterical volume. "There's no way. Why would he do that? That's murder."

Ben's face turns ten different shades of red in quick succession. He backs up, throwing his hands wide as the wind slams into us, spitting rain and seawater across the deck. "Exactly. Why would I? Besides, he scrambled your brains when he knocked you against the deck. You're not exactly a reliable witness."

But I can see the glint in his eye even now. The same cold flash of hatred that was there before he released his hold. Three summers at sailing camp had to be enough for him to know what would happen next. How the boom would swing.

"How exactly does someone who knows *so much* about sailing lose control of the boat like that?" I ask. "And right after Captain Keith threatened to have you arrested for assault? What a coincidence."

Ben glares at me. "About as coincidental as the seasoned lifeguard who let his ass drown."

I step back like he slapped the hell out of me.

Jackson's hand finds mine, and he squeezes. "I didn't see you diving into the ocean, Ben."

"Listen, it sucks that he died, but let's be honest, he was a drunk nobody with a shitty boat. My only flaws are bad grip strength and terrible taste in boat captains," Ben shouts over the wind. "Jackson was right, we shouldn't have come out today, and that's on me for not taking no for an answer. But do you really think all of us should be blamed for a stupid accident?"

Emmy pushes rain-soaked hair from her face and frowns. "All of us? What did *we* do?"

It's the wrong thing to say.

All the anger leaches from Ben's face, and his expression becomes eerily calm. It's almost more terrifying than the thrashing ocean around us. He looks like a shark, poised to rip us to shreds.

The rain has plastered the white fabric of his button-up shirt to his body, and he plucks it away from his chest. "I have a life and a future to think about, and I'm not going to take the blame for this alone. So let me make myself clear: If I go down for this, I'm taking the three of you with me."

Anger races through me so fierce I shake with it.

But he's not done. "The smartest thing the three of you can do is keep your mouths shut. My family will never let me do time in some Mexican jail, and I'll happily throw you all under the bus." His gaze locks on Emmy. "I'm sure you understand. You wouldn't want one day to ruin your life either. He's not worth Italy, and nursing school, and your precious victim activism. United, we walk away from this. But if you turn against me, I promise that you'll be the ones who take the fall."

My mouth drops open. This boat is full of evidence of a brawl, and I bet Ben's blood is mixed with Captain Keith's in more than one place. That alone will contradict his version of the story, even without us saying a damn thing to the authorities. How can he possibly think he has any leverage here, no matter how rich his family is? It's three against one.

I cast a wary glance at Emmy. She's chewing her lip nervously.

I hope it's three against one anyway.

When none of us speak, Ben scowls. "Come on. It's not a difficult choice. Side with me, and your future is safe. Turn against me, and I'll ruin you."

I shake my head. "There's something wrong with you. Like, *seriously* wrong. Don't you think you should be more worried about surviving than saving your own ass? Look around, Benny Bear, your buckets of cash don't mean shit out here!" I shout, waving an arm at the miles of ocean around us.

Ben levels me with the same emotionless glare he gave Captain Keith before he let go of the wheel. The sight of it twists my stomach into knots, but before he can respond, a wave rises on the other side of the boat, growing bigger by the second.

"Brace yourself!" Jackson shouts, and we all scramble for something to hold on to.

I wrap my elbow around the lifelines. Jackson grabs Emmy and one of the wires tethered to the sails. Ben drops to his knees and grabs a vertical section of the railing as the wave crests and slams into us.

The force of it smashes my chest against the railing, radiating pain through my ribs. The boat rocks so far to the side, I think we're all going to be thrown into the ocean before it snaps upright again. The jarring motion loosens Ben's hold on the support, and he slides across the deck. Two feet of frothy water spill across the boat and drain back off the sides, leaving him spitting up salt water as he scrambles to his feet.

The boat rocks violently in the other direction, and lightning flashes. The sky beyond it is near black with pockets of deep blue and purple, and the water reflects that right back at us. The waves have grown so high, they're throwing us back and forth as we crest the top of one, only to tip the opposite direction down the back side of it. The storm's getting worse fast.

There's no way the motor is going to help us in this mess.

Jackson shoves Emmy toward the cabin. "Get inside! If we stay out here screaming at each other Keith won't be the only one swept out to sea."

Emmy nods and grabs at Ben's hand as she passes him. "Come on. Please?"

He doesn't move at first, instead staring at her hand like he's not sure if he's going to shake her off or not, but she steps closer, and when they lock eyes, his shoulders relax.

"Please Ben. Let's get inside where it's safer," she says.

And this time, he follows her.

Emmy, the asshole whisperer.

We stumble our way toward the hatch opening as another wave crests the side of the boat and washes over our feet. I'm not thrilled to be in a contained space with our resident sociopath, but they're right. It's not safe on deck anymore. We can deal with the fallout of Ben's actions after the storm.

Just outside the entry to the cabin, Jackson taps my arm and holds up a finger. He waits for Emmy and Ben to descend the stairs before he leans in close and says, "Are you positive Ben let go of the wheel on purpose?"

I narrow my eyes at him. "If you're about to pile on about how hard I hit my head, you better find something to protect your nuts."

He cracks a smile that quickly disappears. "I wouldn't dream of it."

"He *let go*. With both hands. At the same time. Then he threw himself to the deck *after* the wave rocked us," I say. "You should have seen the look on his face, Jackson. He was furious about Keith's threat. He did this on purpose."

"Emmy will have a hard time believing that."

"Do *you* believe me?"

He looks me straight in the eye. "Always."

I'm suddenly hyperaware that he still doesn't have a shirt on, and a blush crawls up my face. I turn and head down the stairs before I embarrass myself.

Again.

CHAPTER SEVEN

The boat creaks and groans around us as we descend the wooden steps into the cabin. My gaze goes straight to Keith's empty bedroom. He woke up in that bed this morning with no idea it was his last day on Earth. Or that he'd die at the hand of a vindictive dumbass.

I brace myself as I stagger through the kitchen, ducking to avoid a hanging mesh bag full of oranges swinging wildly above the counter. A smaller bag of onions and potatoes hangs beside it, but the potatoes have grown eyes that stick through the webbing like miniature tree roots.

Ben throws himself into the farthest seat on the pseudo sofa, back pressed against the bathroom wall. Emmy sits across the aisle from him, sliding into the bench seat that wraps around the table. I grab my bag, hugging it to my chest as if the familiar items will soothe me—even if it's only sunscreen and my clothes. I don't even know what happened to my sunglasses. I drag my jean shorts out of the bag and tug them on before I sit on the other side of the table, my back to the kitchen.

I fish out my water bottle and drink until the taste of salt clears from my mouth.

Jackson hovers in the aisle, adjusting his weight to compensate for the rocking of the boat. Everything about his body language says he's on high alert, and I'm not sure if he's more worried about the storm or the stranger in the cabin with us.

Wind howls through the open hatch. Emmy splays her hands across the table. "Can we please call a truce? Screaming at each other isn't going to get us out of here any faster, and I think we can all agree that calling for help is more important at this point."

"I can agree to that," Jackson says. He glances at Ben. "Can you?"

Ben scowls, but he nods.

He doesn't have much of a choice. He'll have no future to salvage if we aren't rescued.

I grab my phone out of my bag. It's still in the clear waterproof case. The time blinks at me from the home screen—it's almost 6:00 p.m. We should have been back to the marina already. I swipe at the screen, but as I suspected, I have no service. A low battery notification pops up. I'm at nineteen percent.

Everyone else is on their phones too.

"Mine's dead," Emmy says, pressing hard on the screen protector like that'll force it back on. I'm not exactly surprised. She's been on her phone all day.

Jackson pockets his with a frown. "I'm at fifty percent, but I don't have any service."

"We're too far from shore. We're going to have to use the radio," Ben says, flashing us his screen. It's open to the compass app, but I don't miss the red battery symbol in the upper-right corner. "We can use the coordinates on our phones to tell them where we are."

"Will that be accurate when we don't have service?" I ask, squinting at the little numbers at the bottom of the app. They shift as his phone moves.

He nods. "Yeah, the compass app uses different sensors. It doesn't need service. I have our latitude and longitude right here. We just have to call them in, and someone will come get us."

Something suspiciously like hope blooms in my chest. Once someone knows we're in trouble it'll be…what? An hour? Maybe two before we're on another boat headed back to the safety of the mainland. We can hunker down and muscle through for that long. Worst case, we get a little seasick, right?

Jackson moves to the workspace and runs his fingers along the controls of the radio system. He presses a few buttons, but nothing happens. None of the screens are lit up. Even the basic radio beside the receiver is dark. He presses various buttons, turns dials, and finally smacks the side of the system. The lights flicker on for half a second, then go out again. "What the hell is wrong with this thing?"

Ben leans forward in his seat to see what Jackson is doing, then reaches over to flip the light switch in the bathroom. It blinks and turns off. He sits back down and puts his head in his hands. "That Nickelback freak probably didn't give the start battery a fresh charge before we left. If that goes out, there's no power to the entire boat. He must not have expected us to be out long enough for it to run dry."

That explains why the music stopped.

I'm not convinced it's as simple as forgetting to charge a battery though. I think of Captain Keith musing about his boat. *With the cash I can make some much-needed repairs to my baby before our next adventure. She's been a little neglected lately.*

I wonder if the battery was one of those things he neglected.

Jackson laughs, and it's a harsh, sarcastic sound. He drops the radio receiver. The cord springs against the wall with a clatter. "Perfect. Just perfect. I love that we're all trapped because you and my sister don't know the meaning of the word 'no,'" he says, all but yelling the last part.

Emmy glares at him. "We had no way of knowing this would happen, Jackson. Obviously we wouldn't have come if we knew—"

"If you knew what, Emmy? If you knew it would be dangerous to take a boat into a storm that closed an entire marina? Or that your vacation fling would attack our captain? Which brainless, lack-of-common-sense move are we talking about here?"

"Why is this all on me? What about the captain who promised to keep us safe? Isn't this also his fault? He could have told us it was too dangerous instead of taking Ben's money."

"You know what, you're totally right, Em," Jackson says, tapping a finger on his chin with faux confusion. "And who was it that found the *one* boat captain in Puerto Vallarta desperate enough to overlook the obvious weather concerns once a bunch of money was waved in his face?"

Ben glares at him. "Go fuck yourself."

"Why? You've already fucked us all so thoroughly. Any other captain, any other boat, and this never would have happened."

Emmy jumps to her feet and jabs a finger at her brother. "Nobody made you come with us! You could have stayed at the marina if you were so worried."

"Oh, sure. Mom and Dad would have loved that. How would that have gone, exactly? *Sorry, the boat seemed sketch, so I bailed—but I let my little sister sail off onto the stormy seas with two random dudes after you explicitly asked me to keep her safe. Anyway, how was the fucking golf tour?*' That would have gone over like a ton of bricks."

For a moment, the only sound is the howling wind outside.

"I'm not going to apologize for living my life, Jackson," Emmy says. "I'm sorry I don't assume every stranger I meet is a threat and every boat is a safety hazard, but I'd rather hope for the best than worry about every single damn thing."

"Plenty of people go on vacation and have a great fucking time without stranding everyone at sea!" Jackson shoots back.

"This isn't my fault!" Emmy shrieks.

Jackson rolls his eyes so hard I'm surprised he doesn't fall over. "Really? Because we'd be safe at the resort if it wasn't for you and Sir Sails a Lot over there."

Ben jumps to his feet like he's about to charge at Jackson. I fling myself out of my seat and into the aisle to block his path. "Okay, enough! All of you, enough. We don't have time for this!"

As if the ocean agrees, a wave slams into the side of the boat so hard that I'm thrown through the air. Ben and Emmy crash against the portholes beside me in a tangle of elbows and knees. Jackson almost becomes one with the kitchen stove. The boat rolls until the porthole beside my face is completely submerged.

From the corner of my eye, the mesh bags of fruit and garlic dangle toward me instead of the counter, one almost kissing the ceiling. The boat screams in protest. The very air around us groans and creaks until a splintering crack cuts through the air, and we're all thrown back to the opposite side of the boat.

Emmy and I land in a heap on the floor. Ben ends up draped halfway across the sofa and halfway across my hip. Water rushes down the stairs. I scramble up off the floor and back on the dining bench to get away from it.

Ben grabs Emmy and hauls her onto the sofa.

Her panicked eyes race along the inside of the boat as she rubs the place where her head hit the bulkhead. "What the hell just happened? Is the boat going to sink? How are we supposed to call for help without a radio? I saw a movie once where a boat got stuck in a hurricane, and a wave the size of a building hit them, and they flipped. Are we going to flip over? Will it sink us?"

She's talking so fast, one thread of panic bleeds into the next.

Ben gently holds her face in his hands and presses his thumbs to her lips to make her stop. "Emmy, relax. Oxygen is good. Panic is bad. The waves have gotten big, but we're not going to sink."

"How do you know?" she demands.

"A sailboat is almost impossible to flip. It's designed that way. The keel will always right the boat—like it did just now."

"What's a keel?" Emmy asks.

"It's like a big metal fin stuck to the bottom of a boat. It weighs down the hull and keeps the boat upright in strong winds. Because of the keel, truly capsizing is rare, even in hurricane situations, and this isn't a hurricane. It's just a little wind and waves. I promise you we're not going to sink. The storm will pass, and we'll be fine... We just have to wait for help to get to us."

Wind and waves? Is he serious?

Emmy's eyes are wide as portholes, but she seems to relax, so I don't call him out on what a bunch of BS that is. This may not be a hurricane, but a *little wind* doesn't toss a boat around that hard.

Ben runs a thumb across Emmy's cheek, and she looks at him like he's the only thing keeping this boat afloat. Jackson shakes the water from his dark hair, his gaze laser focused on his sister. I understand, because I don't want Ben anywhere near Emmy either, but I'm grateful he knows what to say to keep her from having a high-seas panic attack.

I scoot around the table until the side of the boat is to my back—hoping for more leverage in case we roll again. Jackson watches me and moves in my direction.

"So that's our plan, then?" Jackson asks, slumping into the seat I just vacated. He props his elbows on the table and hangs his head. He's absolutely drenched. "Stay inside and wait?"

The boat tips again, in the opposite direction this time. I grab onto the table to keep from being thrown into Jackson, and when the boat rights itself, his hands are extended like he was braced to catch me.

"Unless that radio magically blinks on, I don't think we have any other choice," Ben says. "We have no way to reach the mainland, and I don't feel comfortable trying to handle this boat in the storm. Not until the wind dies down."

Alarm bells ring in my head. He was all confidence in his abilities when he was shouting at Captain Keith about being able to get us to shore, but now he doesn't feel comfortable? He keeps changing his story.

I catch his eye. "But you can handle it when it passes, right? As soon as the winds die down, you can get us out of this?"

He pauses long enough to stress me out, but he nods. "I can. It's a bigger boat than the ones I used at camp, but I can get us to shore. Or close enough to call for help. As soon as the storm dies down, I can do it."

I frown. He sounds a lot like a guy trying to convince himself he's not in over his head.

"We don't have to worry about any of that," Emmy says, staring out the porthole by her head. "Search and rescue will find us long before that. Someone from the marina will remember seeing us go out, and they'll notice when we don't come back. Besides, Mom and Dad will worry. Someone will come looking for us. Maybe they're already on their way."

That's a big maybe.

I nod, because I'm a terrible liar, and I'm not about to send Emmy into another spiral, but I highly doubt Nickelback Keith told anyone where we were going. It's even more unlikely anyone from the marina will remember us. The docks were practically deserted because of the weather. And how would anyone know where to look if they did remember us? Where would they even start?

Another wave washes over the top of the boat, and we all share a worried look.

"Right?" Emmy says, when nobody responds to her. "Someone's probably already coming to get us. *Right?*"

Ben reaches out and takes her hand, smiling far too wide. "I'm sure they are. It'll be a couple hours at most."

Jackson meets my eye and gives the briefest shake of his head.

Nobody's coming for us.

CHAPTER EIGHT

Captain Keith floats in the water beneath me, and I kick furiously, trying to reach him, but he sinks faster than I can swim, slowly fading from view until I can't see him anymore.

The desperation to swim faster, to reach farther, to grab and pull him from the tides is all-consuming. He was right there. I almost had him.

My lungs turn to molten fire in my chest. The surface shines above me, lit by the sun. I turn back for air. I've almost reached the surface when bubbles rush up around my face. Something wraps around my ankle and yanks. I sink deeper into the waves. I whip around to see what grabbed me, but I can't see anything. My feet have been swallowed by the darkness below me. Something is tied to my foot. I can feel it, but I can't get it off.

I thrash in the water, sinking deeper and deeper into the darkness until it closes around me like a mouth clamping shut. My lungs are an inferno, aching for oxygen that's just out of reach. The vise around my ankle tightens, and this time, when I look down, there's a hand wrapped around my foot. Captain Keith's smiling face appears from below, grinning from ear to ear—

"HEY!"

I jerk awake, almost head-butting Emmy on the other half of the dining bench. The seat creaks beneath me. Emmy groans, rubbing sleep from her eyes. The room spins and I clutch my head, trying to gather my bearings. I blink at the ceiling, and the last twenty-four hours intermingle with flashes of Captain Keith's face as he grabbed me in my dream.

It was only a nightmare.

Though our reality isn't much better.

The storm tossed us around all night long. Jackson did his best to keep the hatch door closed as waves spit water into the cabin, but the wind busted the latch. The waves were brutal. We all took turns hurling up our lunch in the bathroom—Emmy more than the rest of us.

She eventually fell asleep on my shoulder... but I don't remember falling asleep. I wanted to keep an eye on—

A loud crack echoes through the cabin, and I spin toward the sound. Jackson and Ben are behind me in the kitchen, and Jackson's hands are fisted in the front of Ben's wrinkled white shirt. He slams Ben's back against the useless radio controls a second time. "Are you out of your fucking mind?" he screams.

I jump to my feet and splash into nearly two feet of water. The entire cabin is flooded. The water's littered with stuff: Styrofoam cups, empty water bottles, loose oranges, trash, plastic bags, and microfiber towels. I blink, my tired brain trying to catch up to what I'm seeing—did this much water really come in through the hatch, or do we have a leak?—but I don't have time.

"I didn't do anything!" Ben insists, and I'm instantly on alert.

Jackson snarls and slams Ben into the wall again.

"Hey, hey. Stop!" I wade through the water as fast as I can, stepping on things I can't see with my bare feet as I go. "What's going on?"

"Get the fuck off!" Ben yells, trying to shove him away, but Jackson's right in his face, not giving an inch.

I try and wedge myself between them, but Jackson takes a step to the side and blocks the gap in the counter with his back. For a true crime nerd, Jackson's not as slight as he looks.

"What is going on?" I ask again, gripping Jackson's shoulder.

"He cut the radio wires," Jackson says through his teeth.

Emmy gasps and splashes through the water behind me. "Jack, let him go! He wouldn't do that!"

"He fucking did," Jackson says, glaring at Emmy. "I saw him."

"You're a liar. I didn't do shit," Ben says. "You were all asleep, and I was going above deck to check on the storm when he attacked me for no reason!"

Jackson's eyes narrow. "I'm not about to fall asleep with you roaming the boat—I stayed up to keep an eye on the girls. I stepped into the bathroom for *one* minute and came out to find you cutting the wires with the knife that's still in your pocket. Go ahead," he says, looking at me over his shoulder. "Check his shorts."

He moves to let me past him.

"Fuck you!" Ben yells.

Weak early-morning sunlight pours through the hatch opening and illuminates his panicked face. In that moment, I know I'm going to find a knife in his pocket before I so much as take a step in his direction.

Ben jerks his hips away and slaps at my hand, but Jackson grabs him by the forearms and pins him against the wall. I dive between them and slide my hand into the pocket closest to me before he can wiggle loose.

Sure enough, my fingers close around something. I yank it out and hold up a black folding knife with initials engraved into the handle.

B.T.A.M.

Of course he has two freaking middle names.

Emmy steps back, sloshing water in the process. "Ben. What...?"

My eyes trail over the controls behind him. Wires are sticking out of all the electronics—wires that were certainly attached when we fell asleep. They're all sliced clean through. Like he wasn't sure which did what, so he cut through them all just to be sure. Including the curly wire connecting the hand mic to the radio.

Ben's severed our only way to call for help.

"How could you do this?" I ask, my voice quieter than I intend as I stare at Ben's knife in my hand. Except that's not the right question. "*Why* would you do this?"

Ben fights against Jackson's grip, and I take a step back, forcing Emmy to as well. I hold Ben's glare until his shoulders go rigid.

"I'm not about to sail myself straight back to a murder charge," he spits. "I couldn't risk that battery blinking on long enough for you to call for help. Not before I'm positive you'll keep your fucking mouths shut."

Oh. My. God.

Emmy looks horrified. She reaches back for the bench seat behind her and slowly sinks onto it. I have the sudden urge to punch someone. He can't *possibly* be this stupid. Cutting those wires strands him out here too. Something's not right about this.

I rub at the stress headache forming in the middle of my forehead. "So let me get this straight. Your genius plan was to hold us hostage until we agreed to lie for you?"

"*No*. Until you agreed that what happened *was an accident*," he clarifies. "I'm the only person left on this boat with sailing experience, and now you have no other way to call for help, which means I'm in charge. Nobody's going home until we're all on the same page about what happened."

I wait for him to see the gaping holes in his plan, but he only holds my stare.

"What's stopping us from agreeing to cover for you, and then turning you into the police the moment we get to shore?" I ask.

Ben's eyes narrow.

"Or, what if we refused to lie for you?" I press when he doesn't respond.

Again, he says nothing. His mouth sets in a hard line.

Dread curls in the pit of my stomach.

"Answer the question, Ben. What if we refused to lie for you? What was the plan then? Were you going to let us float around until we all starved to death? Are you willing to die out here to cover up what you did?"

"I didn't do anything," he spits.

The terrible feeling in my gut grows. I hold up the knife. "Maybe you had no intention of helping the rest of us get to shore at all."

"Hannah, be serious," Emmy says.

"Oh, I'm dead serious," I say, still not taking my eyes off Ben. "What would have happened if Jackson took a bit longer to come out of the bathroom?"

The cold glint is back in Ben's eyes as he glances at the knife, then back at me.

I can see it so clearly—Ben creeping through the cabin, knife in hand. Killing us one by one, before we even knew we were in danger. Waiting outside the bathroom, ready to spring the second Jackson opened the door.

"I wasn't going to *kill* anyone," he says too late. And with far too little emotion to be convincing. "Don't be so dramatic. Maybe I shouldn't have cut the radio wires, but I panicked. You'd panic if everyone was accusing you of something you didn't do."

I wish I could believe him. I'd love to go back to thinking he's a dumbass who didn't think his plan all the way through, but goosebumps run down my arms because I'm right. I know that I'm right.

Bennett Mulholland is a psychopathic piece of shit, and if Jackson had fallen asleep last night, we wouldn't be alive to have this conversation.

"I *don't* believe you," I seethe.

"I don't care what you fucking believe!" Ben shouts. "I refuse to let you assholes make me into the bad guy."

Jackson slams him against the controls again. "You *are* the fucking bad guy!"

Emmy stands and sloshes through the water toward them. "Jack, stop. This isn't helping. Ben's not a danger to anyone."

"The hell he isn't!"

Emmy starts shouting at him, then Jackson starts shouting at her, and Ben starts yelling over the both of them, until the interior of the boat is a tornado of voices.

I set the knife on the table and sit with my head in my hands.

What are we going to do?

I don't even know where to begin. The closest thing we have to a sailing expert is a murderous, grade-A asshole, who more than likely wants us dead. The captain is gone. We can't call for help. We only know where we are as long as our phones hold a charge, and the chances of us teaching ourselves how to sail in the immediate future are slim at best.

Ben's knife glints on the table in front of me.

We need to secure Ben before he gets his hands on another weapon. It's a damn miracle he decided to take out the radio before he came for one of us. Shame seeps into my bones. I'm the one who saw him let go of the wheel—I knew what he was capable of. I let myself get distracted by the storm when the greater danger was sitting across from us in designer swim trunks.

Luckily Jackson was on it. I steal a glance at him over my shoulder, still screaming at his sister, and wonder how many other ways we're going to have to luck out to survive this.

Second priority has to be the boat. After we figure out what to do with Bennett, we need to see if the motor works. That would be the fastest way to get to shore. If it doesn't, then…we need to start a more long-term plan. Inventory our food and water. Search the boat for rescue supplies. Find the first aid kit. See if there's any way to get this water out of the cabin…

The list forming in my mind calms me quite a bit. That is, until Emmy's voice reaches a new octave, and I wince. Dog whistle screeches are officially where I draw the line.

Something bumps into my knee, and I find a swollen-looking orange floating beside my leg. I stand and stuff Ben's knife into the pocket of my shorts. I snatch the orange out of the water and hurl it at them. It hits the wall between Ben and Jackson's heads and explodes in a burst of salt water and pulp.

They all turn toward me in surprised silence.

"If the three of you don't shut up, I swear to god, I'm going to start singing *Hamilton* songs off-key at the top of my lungs until you're all suffering raging migraines. I'm trying to make a plan over here."

"You almost hit me with that," Emmy grumbles.

"What part of 'shut up' wasn't clear?" Jackson asks. He dodges the punch she levels at his shoulder and meets my gaze across the room. "We can't do anything until we deal with him," he says, rattling Ben against the controls. "I'm not about to watch my back every second we're trapped here."

"Jackson Cole, we can't throw him overboard," Emmy shrieks.

He gapes at her. "Why would I throw him overboard?"

"You said we have to deal with him. Like you're planning to off him or something."

"You've been watching too much *Yellowstone*. I clearly meant: *How are we going to keep this walking liability from doing more damage than he already has?*"

"He's got to be contained somehow," I agree. I tap my fingers against the table, trying to think. Maybe we can repurpose one of the ropes on deck and tie him to something up there? That would leave him in full sun though, at the mercy of the elements. There has to be a better option.

My eyes catch on the mesh bags hanging from the ceiling, and an idea takes form.

I wade through the water. "Throw him in the bathroom."

"What?" Ben and Emmy yell at the same time.

Jackson, on the other hand, doesn't say a thing. He just hauls Ben through the boat.

"Hey, hey, no!" Ben yells. He flails and kicks, splashing water in every direction. "No way!"

"You did this to yourself, dickhead," Jackson says.

I climb onto the bench and reach for the smaller mesh bag that held the sprouting potatoes—both bags lost their contents to the storm.

Emmy stands in the aisle beside me, hands on her hips. "This is going to come back to bite us in the—"

Jackson dumps Ben into the bathroom like a sack of rocks. He windmills backward and lands half on the toilet and half against the wall. Before he can get back to his feet, Jackson yanks the sliding door shut. I hop back into the water and brush past my still-protesting best friend.

"Hannah," Emmy squeals, "We can't just hold him hostage."

Watch me.

I twist the mesh netting until it creates a makeshift rope and slide it through the circular handle in the door while Ben pounds against it from the other side. Jackson plants his feet and presses his palms into the door, holding it shut while I drag the bedroom door closed and loop the other end of the "rope" through that handle too. I pull it as tight as I can and tie a quadruple knot in the mesh.

Jackson and I step back and wait.

Ben shouts something unintelligible on the other side, and the door rattles, but the rope holds.

"Hannah, we can't do this," Emmy says, appearing over my shoulder again. "He said it was an accident. I'm sure he didn't intentionally hurt anyone. We can't lock him in there."

I close my eyes and let out a sigh that weighs a thousand pounds before I look up at Jackson. "Make sure the rope doesn't start to come undone," I mumble.

"Open this fucking door!" Ben screams on the other side.

Jackson nods, and I lightly shove Emmy toward the kitchen.

She stumbles into the kitchen. "What the hell, Hannah?"

I step close and make her look at me. "I need you to hear me. Not just nod and smile and wait until it's your time to speak. Really hear me. Can you do that?"

Anger blazes in her blue eyes, and she looks like a furious Barbie in her hot pink bikini, but she nods.

"I love you to death, and most days I appreciate your happy-go-lucky 'everyone is my best friend' perspective, but not today. I need you to really think about what's happening here. A guy you just met at the resort convinced us to go out on a random boat because he didn't like that the licensed tours were docked because of the storm. The captain he hired got so drunk he couldn't stand, and Ben's first move was to drag him on deck and threaten him. And when that didn't work, Ben broke his nose. When threatened with assault charges, he intentionally knocked the captain overboard. There's probably still blood on the boom, Emmy. Ben *killed* him."

Emmy eyes fill with tears. "How do you know he did it on purpose? The waves were intense. He said he lost his grip. I saw him fall."

"I watched him let go."

"But—"

"I saw the look in his eyes, Em. *He let go* and threw himself to the ground. He knew exactly what he was doing."

The tears escape and stream down her face.

I take a breath. "And instead of showing remorse, Ben threatened all of us, because he's more concerned with his own future than the one he took away. He destroyed our only way to call for help, and I have no doubt he would have used that knife on us too. Ben isn't being treated unfairly. He's a danger, and I don't know what he'll do if we let him out of there. Do you?"

"He wouldn't hurt any of us," she practically whispers.

"He already did. Or did you miss him elbowing your brother in the face, or the *body* in the ocean? How many lines does he have to cross?"

Emmy folds her arms. "He might have a point, you know. You hit your head on the deck pretty hard. Maybe you didn't see what you think you saw."

I shouldn't be surprised that she's willing to believe a boy over her best friend, but I am. It takes me a second to banish the familiar hurt and meet her eyes. "I need you to decide who you trust more: Ben or me. Because I'm telling you right now that hitting my head didn't change what I saw. So either I'm telling the truth and the stranger you met a few days ago is a fucking liar, or I'm lying and making a terrible situation worse by locking up the only sailor among us for no reason. So which is it?"

Her tears are falling freely now. "Of course, I trust you."

"More than Ben?"

She hesitates but nods. I try not to take that personally. It's just the way she is.

"Then the best place for him is in the bathroom. As long as he's in there, we can focus on getting back to shore. We'll let him out as soon as help arrives, okay? But he can't be running loose after everything he's done, or we won't live long enough to get rescued. Do you understand?"

She wraps her arms around my shoulders and squeezes me tight. "God. How did we get ourselves into this?"

I don't point out the obvious. I hug her back. "We're going to figure it out, okay?"

She nods and steps back, looking past me. I follow her gaze to Jackson, who tugs one more time on the mesh rope holding the door shut. The door is still rattling, but it hasn't given way.

"I think it's secure," Jackson says, coming closer to us. He lowers his voice. "There isn't much room in there, and the door slides, so he doesn't really have the space to get the leverage he needs to force it open. The water is also working against him, I think. We should check the mesh every once in a while to make sure it doesn't stretch though. If he manages to get his fingers through a gap, he'll have a better chance of wrenching it open."

I turn to Emmy again. "Promise me you won't let him out of there."

Emmy sighs. "Fine."

A person less familiar with Emmy might accept that, but I've seen her wiggle her way out of one too many "fines" to let it slide. Especially where a boy is concerned.

"That's not a promise. I need you to understand why we put him in there, Emmy. Say it out loud."

"I get it, okay? We don't really know him. But I feel bad that he's stuck in that tiny space while we…"

I raise an eyebrow. "While we…what? Float around on a boat we don't know how to sail? Sorry, Emmy, but we're all in a shitty situation. Only one of us has consistently made it worse."

She sighs, and this time, when she nods, I feel like I've gotten through to her. Completely? Hell no. Will I have to watch her like a hawk if Ben starts crying in there? Yes. But in this moment, she's on board. Pun intended.

"You fuckers!" Ben screams from the bathroom. "You can't do this to me! My father will have your asses for trapping me in here. I'm a fucking Mulholland!"

"Yeah?" Jackson shouts back. "You're also a murderer, so sit down and shut the fuck up."

I bite back a surprised laugh. Emmy's directing an anguished look at the closed bathroom door, so I point up the stairs. "Come on, let's go check on the boat. Maybe we can figure out how to sail this damn thing on our own."

"Right, because we're suddenly going to know what each of those two hundred ropes does," Emmy says sarcastically, as we climb out onto the deck. Ben's furious shouts recede as we step out into the fresh air.

The waves have calmed considerably, but humid wind picks my hair off my neck and throws it around my face. After being cooped up in the cabin all night, it feels so open and spacious out here. I take a few steps toward the back of the boat. There's nothing but water and clouds as far as the eye can see, which is quite a bit farther now that the waves have calmed.

The horizon looks furious. The sky—and the ocean beneath it—are a deep bruise purple in the dawn. I can just barely make out where the sun lurks low behind the cloud cover. It turns the sky around it a lighter, almost wisteria purple with a red middle. It's as beautiful as it is terrifying, and I shudder.

I turn to point it out to the others and freeze when I see them staring at the front of the boat. They look terrified.

"What's wrong?" I ask, instantly on alert. I move closer, but my feet falter when I see what they're looking at. Or rather, what they're *not* looking at.

The mast is gone.

The sails and metal supports trail across the deck and into the water. The metal mast is snapped almost clean through right beneath the boom.

I feel like I'm going to be sick again as the enormity of what's happening sets in.

We're on a boat with no power.

The only person left on board who knows how to sail is locked in the bathroom.

The mast is broken, making sailing an impossibility even if we could figure out how.

The radio is useless.

The rescue we hoped would arrive in a couple hours is nowhere to be seen. Most likely because Captain Keith didn't tell anyone that he was taking a bunch of minors out into the Pacific in the first place.

We didn't board a tourist charter with tickets and a record of our names. We hopped on the *Be-Yacht-Ch* and vanished. Not a single person on shore knows what boat we got on or who we set sail with. Including Emmy's parents.

In the distance, a streak of lightning cuts the sky.

Jackson takes my hand, and I close my eyes.

"We are so fucked," I say.

CHAPTER NINE

We spend hours trying and failing to get the sailboat's tiny motor to start. It sputters once but doesn't turn over. Jackson searches the interior for manuals or gas lines or anything that might tell him how to get this hunk of fiberglass moving to no avail. The gauges on the dash are basically useless. The only one that seems to be working is for the water temperature, and it doesn't change our prospects to know the ocean is a balmy seventy-seven degrees.

The fuel gauge is equally unhelpful. The needle is on empty, but we have no way of knowing if it operates like a car and only rises to the right level once the engine is started. We could be out of gas, the tank could have ruptured in the storm, or we might have plenty of fuel and there's something wrong with the engine. We have no idea. Regardless, the motor won't be our salvation.

When that plan fails, we switch gears and attempt to drain some of the water from the boat. The sun is well hidden behind a thick layer of clouds, but I track its movement as we stand in a line, passing buckets we found in storage. Jackson scoops at the bottom of the stairs, passes up to me at the top, and I pass to Emmy, who dumps the water over the side of the boat. Over and over, we pass the same three buckets until my hands are raw and my arms are shaking.

It doesn't look like the water level drops more than a couple inches.

At least Ben's stopped screeching through the bathroom door.

Emmy dumps the contents of what's probably our two hundredth bucket over the side, then drops it onto the deck with a clatter instead of passing it back to me. "This is useless. I need a break."

Jackson's head pops out of the cabin, and he leans his forearms on the deck. "We can stop for a bit. I'm not sure it's helping anyway. We'd probably have to keep this up for a week to see the floor again."

I try not to look at him. He never put his shirt back on after we used it to sop up the blood from Keith's broken nose, and I've done amazingly well at not staring at him. The threat of death is an effective distraction. But now that he's helped lug gallons upon gallons of water out of the boat, he's glistening in sweat. He has no right to look so good when we're downright miserable.

Thanks to the storm, it's far more humid today than it was yesterday. Every exposed inch of my skin is sticky. My lips are chapped from the sun and my little dive in the ocean. My shoulders are uncomfortably pink, even with the cloud cover, and every few minutes some mysterious banging comes from farther up the boat, making us flinch.

Emmy peeks down the stairs and frowns at the water. "Are we positive there isn't a leak?"

This is the eighth time she's asked this since we started.

Jackson hangs his head. "Positive, Emmy."

"But how do you know? You're not a boat expert."

"I'm not, but I watched the waves come in through the hatch all night, and the water level is about the same as it was when that finally stopped. If the boat were leaking, the water would rise even without the waves. Logic strikes again."

"Well, *logically*, I'd say this can't be the first time waves have washed inside a sailboat. They must have something on board to pump the water back out. We should try asking Ben."

I roll my eyes. "Yeah, because that went so well last time."

When we couldn't get the motor started, Emmy asked for advice through the door.

Ben told her to fuck off.

"Yeah, well, if you two hadn't locked him up, he probably would have been a lot more helpful," she shoots back.

"Sure, sure. Maybe we'll also give back his knife, so he can slit our throats in our sleep. It'll be pretty difficult to worry about the water level when we're fish food," Jackson says, his voice dripping with disdain.

Emmy looks like she wants to throw something at him. "Whatever. I'm just saying that he probably knows an easier way to do this. Now move. I'm going to look for something to eat. I'm starving."

At the mention of food, my stomach lets out a low grumble, and I press my hand against it. We haven't eaten since yesterday afternoon. I didn't notice until now. It's hard to think of food when you're puking your guts out all night long.

Emmy gives me a pained smile. "I'll find something for everyone. Don't worry."

I nod, but I'm suddenly wondering what the chances are that Captain Keith kept enough food on board to feed himself for more than a day or so. He'd just arrived in Puerto Vallarta when Ben accosted him at the marina. It's not like he had time to stock up.

Emmy climbs over her brother, purposely throwing a knee into his ribs as she goes and disappears below. Jackson turns to follow her, and I wonder if he's planning to help or make sure she leaves Ben in his cage.

I sit at the top of the stairs while Emmy digs through the kitchen. I should help, but I don't move. Instead I take the rare moment by myself and use it to panic.

If we could get that damn motor running, we could head straight east. It's not exactly prime navigation, but even if Captain Keith's compass is off, we could follow the direction of the sunrise and hit land of some kind. Anything has to be better than the open ocean, and we could follow the coast until we reached a town or marina. But how the hell are we supposed to do that with no working motor or sails?

We're no better than a giant buoy floating aimlessly in the ocean.

How long can we stretch the food and water? Once we inventory everything, we'll have a better idea, but best-case scenario...a couple days? A week? What happens after that? Will some unlucky sailor stumble on the *Be-Yacht-Ch* in a few weeks and discover four sets of rotten remains inside the cabin?

Or maybe they'll never find us at all.

I can hear the true crime podcast now, picking apart the bloodstains on the deck while devising increasingly ridiculous theories about why one skeleton was found locked in the bathroom.

My hands start to sweat, and I rub them along the hem of my shorts.

I stare off at the darkest section of the sky to the west. The man at the marina said *storms*. Multiple. I hope to hell we're back on land before the next one hits, because if it's anything like the last one, I'm not sure how much more water this boat can take on before it starts sinking.

Emmy appears at the bottom of the stairs with a blue box. "Do you want the good news or the bad news?"

"Good news." I can't take much more bad news at this point.

"He's got a bunch of fruit snacks in here."

She tosses me a couple little bags, and I tear into them. The tiny gummy fruits sink almost painfully into my hollow stomach. "And the bad news?"

"That's about all he has. There're a couple cans in the cabinets, but it's...not a lot."

I hang my head with a sigh. Okay, so this isn't going to be one of those "survived three weeks at sea" types of adventures. We're going to have to find a way to get to shore sooner rather than later.

"We should dig around and see how much food we have to split between us," I suggest. "If we know what we're working with, we can ration it."

Emmy opens a cabinet that's empty except for a container with a dusting of dry oats in the bottom. "That rescue boat better hurry up."

I don't say a damn thing, and when Jackson opens his mouth, I level him with a glare. He snaps it shut again. There's no downside to letting her stay blissfully unaware of how bad the situation is. Once she accepts that nobody's coming, it's going to be significantly harder to figure out how to survive on this boat with her crying and carrying on.

Jackson pulls an orange from the water. "Do you think these are any good? Are orange peels waterproof?"

I shrug. "No idea. I guess we'll find out when we bite into it."

"Consuming more salt seems like a bad—" Something slams into the side of the boat again and he jumps. "What the *hell* is making that sound?"

That's a good question. I climb to my feet, trailing my fingers along the lifelines for balance as I move up the left side of the boat. The waves are much smaller, but we're still constantly in motion, rocking back and forth in a way that makes me miss standing still.

The broken mast cuts a line across my path. When it fell, it smashed through a portion of the lifelines, leaving behind a tangle of metal. I peek over the side of the boat and immediately clock the source of the sound. What's left of the boom is pressed against the side of the boat. The fiberglass is frayed and scratched where the metal rubs, and as I watch, another wave catches the sail and shoves the whole mess into the boat with a sharp crack.

Jackson appears beside me, and I jump out of my skin.

He sighs. "That's not good. If we don't detach that metal, it'll wear a hole in the boat."

"I know," I say, turning to study the broken mast and the dozens of ropes and snapped cables littering the deck. "But I don't think we can move it with the sail still attached. It's weighed down by the water. We'll have to remove it first."

"Okay, but how are we going to do that?"

I wiggle my fingers into my pocket and pull out Ben's knife. "With this."

He's shaking his head before I even finish speaking. "No way. You're not going back in the water."

"I don't see another option; do you?"

Jackson's hands ball into fists. "That's a terrible idea. The current is too rough."

I blow out a breath. I don't want to do this either, but I will if it means keeping this boat above water. "I'm the best swimmer. It should be me. Emmy can barely dog-paddle, so she's out. And I'll need you to pull me in if I get into trouble like last time."

He scrubs a hand down his face as I grab at the ropes on the deck until I find one long enough to reach the far side of the mast in the water.

"Fine, but for the record, I don't like this."

That makes two of us.

Memories of yesterday's panic in the water run through my mind, and I try to push them aside as best as I can. The ocean's not going to get any less deep the more I worry about what's in there with me. I can't pull Jackson in if we switch places, and if I can't get the mast detached, it's only a matter of time before we sink with the metal slamming into the boat at the waterline.

Getting freaked out about the miles of water beneath me won't save us. Detaching the sail might.

I kick off my shorts and tie the end of the rope around my waist again. Jackson pushes my hands aside to tighten the knot himself—like the control freak he is—and his fingers brush the side of my stomach. I look away so he doesn't see the blush crawling up my face.

Now is not the time.

"Okay. Free the sail as quickly as you can, and the second they're clear, wave, and I'll pull you back in."

I nod, doing everything in my power to not picture creatures coming up from the depths to drag me under. "Right. Got it."

His mouth presses into a grim line. "Please be careful."

I give him a two-fingered salute and try to smile. "I'll think about it."

His laugh sounds entirely against his will.

I throw my legs over the lifelines, tighten my death grip on Ben's knife, and jump before I have a chance to talk myself out of this. When I hit the water, it's so warm I almost feel no difference between it and the air. I kick my way to the surface and find Jackson anxiously watching me from the deck.

I flick the knife open and reach for the nearest section of sail, carefully cutting it away from the wires lashed to the broken mast one slice at a time. I methodically move farther from the boat and higher up the mast with each cut. As I go, Jackson keeps the fabric taut, giving me more tension to make it easier to cut.

Loose ropes twist and dance under the surface of the water, brushing my legs with every wave. Shredded tendrils of the sail trail up my thigh, and my mind is once again conjuring images of sharks and tentacles coming up from the depths. Last night's dream joins the party in my head, and the imagined tentacles transform into Captain Keith's puffy, waterlogged corpse grabbing at my ankles, my arms.

By the time I reach the farthest end of the mast, I'm damn near hyperventilating.

"You got this," Jackson calls. "You're almost done."

I am. I'm almost done. A few more slices, and the sail will be free.

There's nothing in the water. There's nothing in the water. There's nothing—

Something brushes my leg, and I clench my teeth to keep from screaming.

There's nothing in the water.

I have to dive under to reach the next portion. The top of the mast is at such a downward angle, it's a good three feet beneath the surface. Cutting through the fabric underwater is taking forever. I surface and tuck the knife into the front of my bathing suit to free up both hands, then start yanking the last few feet of sail off the mast. Jackson's braced on the boat, ready to pull me back the second I'm done.

A wave hits the opposite site of the boat. With a loud groan, the *Be-Yacht-Ch* rocks toward me, pushing the mast deeper into the water. Jackson almost goes overboard and barely windmills himself back onto his heels. I watch, frozen in place, as the stretch of mast between me and him bends. The base lets out a loud, grating creak as the boat rights itself, and the mast snaps off completely.

The whole mess slides off the boat and plows into me. I'm shoved beneath the water before I can take a breath.

Something tugs around my waist and drags me down. The wave folds a portion of sail up over my body, and I thrash around, trying to free myself. All I can see is the canvas cocooning me, taking me under with the mast.

I'm dragged…

Down.

Down.

Down.

Into the sea.

CHAPTER TEN

I press both hands against the mast and try to heave it off me, but it only forces me deeper. My lungs start to burn in my chest. I frantically try to figure out what I'm caught on, walking my hands down the mast. At first all I feel is a jumble of wires and metal and sail. Finally my fingertips slide across a jagged piece of steel that's hooked on the rope around my waist.

My emergency "don't drift out to sea" line is trying to kill me.

The water gets darker as I'm forced farther from the surface. Pressure builds in my ears, getting worse the deeper I go until my eardrums feel like they're going to burst.

Salt water burns up my nose.

I try to flip myself feetfirst toward the surface to dislodge the rope, but even when I'm eye level with where it's caught, it won't budge.

My lungs are screaming for air.

The rope around my waist pulls tight without warning. I don't know if Jackson has the other end or if I've sunk as far as the rope will allow. I almost grab for the knife in my bathing suit, but I can't risk dropping it into the ocean. Instead I press my feet against the mast, grab onto the section of rope between me and the snag, and pull with all my strength, yanking from side to side. I imagine the jagged edge of the steel like a big serrated knife slicing the rope one thrash at a time. The tension shifts in my grip, and I can only hope that means it's working. I close my eyes and heave.

With a great snap I can feel in my teeth, the rope severs.

The mast slides away from me, and I kick up and away before anything else can hook me. The sail floats in the waves above me. I kick as fast as I can, carving through the water to get to the open space between them and the boat.

When I finally break the surface, I gasp in a lungful of air and saltwater. Arms close in around me, and I almost scream that breath right back out until I realize it's Jackson. I twist in the surf and throw my arms around his neck, filling my lungs so fast it makes my head swim.

"I've got you," he says.

"Is she okay?" Emmy shouts above us.

I try to tell her I am, but all that comes out of my mouth is a croak.

Jackson slides the emergency ring under my arm, then grabs onto the rope and uses it to pull us closer to the boat. He swims us around to the ladder at the back. It takes a great effort to unlock my arms from the float and his neck, but I force myself to grab onto the metal rungs.

My lungs ache. My legs ache. My chest hurts. Salt water burns my eyes.

Jackson tightens his grip on me. "You first. I'll help you."

I genuinely don't know if I have it in me to pull myself out, but Emmy appears at the top and grabs my hands. Between her and Jackson pushing from below, I spring from the water. Once again, I find myself collapsed on the deck. Emmy drops down on one side of me, and Jackson barely clears the top of the ladder before he lands on the other side. All three of us are breathing hard.

Jackson rolls onto his back, still gripping the emergency float. "You're not going in that fucking water again, Hannah," he says, pressing his fists into his eyes in a way that looks painful.

Emmy brushes hair from my face and busies herself untying the useless frayed rope from my waist. When it comes away from my skin, we both look down and find an angry line of friction burn around my middle.

Emmy winces and tears her eyes away. "For once, I agree with the devil spawn. I thought you were never going to come back up. The weight of the mast yanked the rope right out of Jackson's hands. He couldn't pull you in."

Her voice shakes, and she chucks the rope overboard like it personally offended her. I sit up so I can hug her. She clings to me like I clung to the life preserver. "It's okay. I just got caught for a minute. It looked worse than it was."

Probably.

My throat feels like I've swallowed a mouthful of sand, turning every word into a scratchy, clipped version of my normal voice.

Emmy pulls away. "I'm going to get you some water. Don't move."

She sprints toward the cabin and disappears inside.

The moment she's gone, Jackson lets out a sigh and drops his fists from his eyes. He rolls toward me and sits up, letting the life preserver fall to the deck. He grabs my hand and holds it tight between his, but he doesn't say anything. He stares down at where our skin touches with an expression that looks a lot like fear.

When he looks up at me, his eyes blaze. "I thought that was the last time I was going to see you. I can't deal with you dying right in front of me, Hannah. I can't."

I squeeze his hand, still breathing hard. "I'm fine," I croak. "It was just a little swim."

It's meant as a joke, but he doesn't smile.

He leans forward until his forehead presses against mine. I think I stop breathing again. "That's not funny. Not even a little bit."

"I know."

"Promise me you won't go back in the water."

I take a shaky breath. "I won't go back in the water…unless there's no other choice."

Jackson pulls back to glare at me.

I clear my throat again. "We're stranded out here. Who knows what we'll have to do to get back to shore. But I promise not to go back in if I don't have to."

"If we need to go back in the water for any reason, I'll do it."

"But—"

"No. No buts. I don't care if you can't pull me back in. I don't care if it makes more sense for you to do it. I only care about you being safe on this godforsaken boat. Okay? I need you to be safe, Hannah."

I sit in stunned silence for a beat too long.

"Promise me," he says.

I give him a shaky nod. For a moment, I'm living half in the present and half in long-banished memories of winter break. Hot chocolate and fingers in my hair. My stomach twists, thinking about what happened next. What *he* did next.

The look on Jackson's face makes me wonder if his thoughts went in the same direction.

"Sorry," Emmy shouts, coming back up on the deck. "Yours was empty, and it took me forever to find an unopened water bottle…"

We spring apart, and she stops short, furrowing her brow.

My heart pounds in my ears. A lie forms on the tip of my tongue, ready to brush this off as nothing. Because of course it *was* nothing.

But Emmy blinks and hurries across the boat, holding out a water bottle without saying a single thing. I take a long drink and hand it to Jackson when I'm done. He shakes his head and pushes it back to me without looking up. His gaze stays on the deck.

Emmy cups her hands over her eyes and looks across the ocean. The sun is making a real effort to peek through the clouds, but only a few sad stripes of sunlight make it. The air is so warm that I'm already drying, but my hair is plastered to my head. I attempt to wring it out as Emmy continues to inspect the horizon. Her lips press into a thin line.

When she sits, she sighs deeply. "What the hell are we going to do?"

Everyone's silent until Jackson climbs to his feet. "We're going to make a plan, that's what. We have to get to shore somehow. We can't wait to be rescued, and floating aimlessly in the ocean is a death sentence."

"How do we know which direction takes us to the marina?"

He frowns. "I think we need to lower our expectations a bit, Em. We have no idea how far the storm blew us. If we can reach dry land of any kind, that's going to be a win. We can worry about finding civilization from there."

"What about the jungle? Captain Keith said the mainland has whole stretches of wilderness. How would winding up on shore be any better if we're in the middle of nowhere?"

"There's better potential for food and water, and flagging someone down with a signal fire," Jackson says.

Emmy interlocks her fingers, and her knuckles get a little whiter from her grip. "I guess you have a point. How are we supposed to get to shore?"

"*That* is the question of the hour," he says, looking toward the front of the boat. "For now, Hannah made sure the mast isn't going to sink us while we figure it out."

It nearly sunk me though.

I pull myself to my feet. A portion of the sail is bunched by the broken section of the lifelines, with a swath of them trailing into the water. "Let's pull the sail back on the boat. If we're out here when the second storm hits, we might be able to use it to prevent more water from getting inside. Or to create shade here in the cockpit while we figure out how to make the cabin usable again. There has to be a way to get the water out of there."

Emmy tilts her head to one side. "What second storm?"

"Do you ever listen?" Jackson asks, sounding exhausted. "The guy at the marina said there's more than one storm rolling in. Which means we don't have time to mess around. We have to figure out a way to get moving."

"Okay...but whether we get moving or not, we have barely any food," she says. "We'll run out today or tomorrow, and then what? We die on some abandoned stretch of beach?"

Jackson tugs her into a hug. She wraps her arms around the back of his ribs like she's hanging on for dear life.

The next time he speaks he's completely calm. "You aren't going to die, Em. We'll find a way to get back to shore, or someone will spot us trying. We have options. Okay? We just need to be smart."

She nods against his chest, and I shuffle off toward the sail to give them a moment. Not for the first time, only-child jealousy rears its ugly head. Those two bicker like it's an Olympic sport, but I've watched them drop everything to help the other dozens of times. No matter what, Jackson and Emmy have each other's backs.

Like last fall, when Emmy snuck out to surprise her boyfriend while his parents were out of town—and caught him making out with a sophomore instead. After Emmy stormed out of his house, her piece of crap car wouldn't start, leaving her stranded five miles from home after midnight. Of course Tanner The Cheating Asshole wouldn't give her a ride.

Jackson was home for the weekend to do laundry and caught me not so stealthily pulling my extremely loud Volvo out of the driveway to rescue her. The moment he found out where I was going, he got in the car. It didn't matter that it was the middle of the night. If Emmy needed help, Jackson was always right there, even if it meant helping me jump-start her POS in the dark.

It's only ever been me and my dad. I barely remember my mom. Having the Coles next door gave me the closest thing I'd ever have to a sister, but it's not the same as what they share.

I start dragging the wet canvas over a portion of the lifelines, and another pair of hands appears next to mine. Jackson starts hauling it in too, only he's much faster than me.

Emmy moves past me and starts dragging the end of the sail toward the bow of the boat to make room. She raises an eyebrow at me. "What's with your face? You look like you're plotting something."

I smile. "I was thinking about Tanner's poor PlayStation, actually."

Emmy grins.

While we were jump-starting her car, Tanner *might* have yelled something rude about Emmy out the front door. And I *may* have taken offense on Emmy's behalf. What happened next was hardly my fault. If he didn't want me to run into his house and rip his PlayStation out of the entertainment center, he should have locked the door.

Allegedly.

Jackson barks out a laugh. "I'll never forget the look on his face when he came running out after you. I thought he was going to pass out when you smashed it against the curb."

"He's lucky you have little arms, or he might have lost his Xbox too," Emmy says.

"I couldn't grab the Xbox before he made it around the sectional," I admit.

"You would have smashed both?" Jackson asks, hauling another armload over the railing.

"Are you kidding? After what he did to Emmy? I would have smashed both *and* the TV if I'd had the time."

"Remind me never to piss you off," Jackson says. "Or at least give me a head start to pack up my game consoles before I run for the hills."

He winks at me. A full-on flirtatious wink.

Before winter break that one little gesture would have made me swoon right off this boat, but now all I feel is a stab of annoyance. One that grows into a full flare of anger when the words *run for the hills* settle into my brain.

I should keep my mouth shut, but it's been a long ass twenty-four hours—I'm sleep deprived, probably dehydrated, the boat is broken, I almost drowned, and I'm *sick to death* of making myself smaller to better suit Jackson Cole.

I yank another section of sail toward Emmy and glare at him. "Run for the hills? Interesting choice of words…though I suppose that is your specialty."

He freezes and looks back at me with a furrow between his

eyebrows. I clock the exact moment he makes the connection—and that furrow morphs into one hell of a scowl. "If you have something to say, Hannah, I'd prefer you just say it."

"Since when?" I snap.

Jackson takes a step closer and lowers his voice. "If this is about winter break—"

"Hey, is everything okay?" Emmy calls back to us.

I hold his angry stare and answer without looking at her. "Yeah, we're fine."

"Yeah. Fine. Sure," he mumbles.

I grab for more fabric, but he bats me away and moves to my other side.

"I've got this on my own," he says.

"Right. Jackson Cole, ladies and theydies. The guy who never needs anyone."

He whirls on me. "If you think for one second that I wanted to—"

I watch his gaze catch on something behind me, and whatever else he'd been about to say dies on his lips. I whirl around and see smoke billowing from the cabin. Dark, cloying smoke as black as the water was during the storm.

For a second I can't process what I'm seeing. Smoke in the middle of the ocean? My brain conjures images of the forest fires back home, of orange-red hell skies and iPhone alerts about unsafe air. Of acres of Oregon forestry burned to the ground, leaving nothing but charred black earth in their wake. There, fire is an inevitability.

Out here, surrounded by water, it feels impossible.

How does a boat dripping with water catch on fire?

"Oh my god," Emmy shrieks. "Ben!"

Almost on cue, gut-wrenching screams ring out from inside the boat.

CHAPTER ELEVEN

I reach the stairs before Jackson does and throw my arm over my nose and mouth to block the smoke pouring from the hatch. It smells like burning paint and plastic. Emmy comes to a screeching halt beside me. All the color has leached from her face.

Jackson bodychecks his sister out of the way. "Emmy, stay away from the smoke. We'll get Ben. Stay here and help him when he comes up."

I have no idea what she thinks of this plan; I'm already jumping the last two stairs and splashing into the water. Jackson's right on my heels. With my first breath, I'm coughing. I crouch down to get below the smoke in order to see my way forward.

The kitchen isn't the source. It's coming from a crack in the bathroom door. Black smoke streams out of the opening, and Ben's screams fill the cabin.

My god. Is he burning alive in there?

"Hold on! We're coming" I shout.

I fish Ben's knife from my bathing suit and start sawing at the mesh bag holding the door closed. The knife cuts the cheap mesh way easier than the sail. I glance behind me and find Jackson rummaging through cabinets. With a victory shout, he stands, brandishing a fire extinguisher, and barrels toward me.

Please, let that be one of the things Captain Keith kept up-to-date on this death trap.

I free the handle. Jackson steps up, aiming the nozzle toward the bathroom, and I shove the door open with both hands.

A rush of smoke and heat blooms into the boat cabin.

And something slams into me. Hard.

I fall back into the water, and the knife goes flying. A blur of white and tan jumps over me, and I spot the source of the smoke right inside the open door. Three rolls of toilet paper are covered in flames in the basin of the small sink. The fire licks at the wall behind it. The plastic frame around the mirror sags under the heat.

That fucker set the boat on fire.

Rage wells in me, and I lunge down the aisle after him, wrapping my arm around the first piece of Bennett Mulholland I can get my hands on. Turns out to be a knee. I lock my arms around him and hold on.

"You dick!" I shout.

Ben charges forward, dragging me halfway up the stairs before he pauses to shake me off.

I splash back into the water, and Ben scrambles onto the deck.

I chase after him. Behind me, the whoosh of the fire extinguisher is music to my ears. Jackson has the fire handled. Slimeball Ben is all mine—and I'll break more than his PlayStation when I get my hands on him.

I race onto the deck and spin in a circle, looking for him. *And* Emmy. She's not at the top of the stairs anymore.

I sprint along the side of the boat. One side of the loose sail has blown up and over what's left of the mast, creating a partition blocking the front half of the boat from sight. I trail my hand along the top of the lifelines for balance as I run. I kick a heap of sail out of the walkway and finally see a flash of blond hair blowing in the wind. Emmy faces a furious Ben, his back toward the front of the boat.

Emmy's between us, hands held up in front of her like she's trying to calm him down. I breathe a sigh of relief when I clock the four feet of space between them.

I come to a stop at Emmy's side, as she shouts, "I'm trying to see if you're okay!"

"Of course I'm not fucking okay!" Ben yells back. "You three locked me in a tiny bathroom like some common criminal!"

Emmy glances at me, and everything in her expression says, *I told you that was a bad idea.*

I wave a hand toward the wisps of smoke still trailing from the hatch. "Did you really set the fucking boat on fire because you didn't like being stuck in the bathroom?"

Ben glares at me. "You gave me no other choice."

My mouth falls open, and I snap it shut again. The absolute stupidity of this boy. "You're out of your damn mind. What if we didn't let you out? What if Jackson didn't find the fire extinguisher in time? What if we didn't have a fire extinguisher at all? We all could have burned to death!"

"Calm down, it was a couple rolls of toilet paper. I knew you wouldn't leave me in there if you thought I was in danger. Besides, the boat's half full of water; it's not like it could have spread very far. It was just a little sink fire."

"Fire *climbs*," Emmy says.

Ben blinks at her and frowns, like he didn't consider that. "Yeah, well... actions have consequences. Maybe next time you'll think twice about holding someone hostage."

I lunge for him, but Emmy wraps her arm around my elbow and holds me back. "Hannah, no. We can't start this again."

I ignore her. "Hostage?" I shout. "You killed someone! What else were we supposed to do?"

"I didn't kill anyone, you fucking liar!" His face turns even more red.

Emmy's grip tightens on my arm, like she knows I'm *this close* to beating him to death with my bare hands.

"Okay, stop!" she shouts, "The boat didn't burn! Ben is out of the bathroom. We're no worse off than we were twenty minutes ago, right? Maybe Ben can help us get back to shore now?"

It sounds like a desperate plea.

With a final glare, he shifts his attention to Emmy. "As long as I don't have to go back in the bathroom, I'll help. Sure."

"Like we can trust you," I snap.

"What other choice do you have?"

Oh, I'm going to punch him in the face.

"I knew you'd help us," Emmy says. "I told them not to lock you in there."

Okay, now I want to punch them *both* in the face.

"So much for trusting me," I say, ripping out of her grip.

Her face falls, but we're interrupted by Jackson storming around the curtain of sail. Soot coats his face in heavy streaks, and he's still carrying the fire extinguisher. Fury radiates off him as he closes the distance between us in a few long strides.

He points a finger at Ben. "You!"

I feel a sharp tug on my hair and stumble backward. Pain crackles down my scalp. Ben's arm folds around my neck, and my back slams into his chest. He brings his other arm up to lock around his wrist and squeezes. My air cuts off completely.

"Back off, Jackson," he growls.

I scratch at his arm, trying to pry him away from my neck, but he only squeezes tighter.

Emmy's eyes widen. "Ben! What the *fuck*? Let her go!"

I want to scream *I TOLD YOU SO*, but that would require air.

"Not until you call off your guard dog. Drop the fire extinguisher," Ben says.

My nails dig into his forearm. I scratch at his skin. I try to twist my head to the side. I reach back and claw at something fleshy—maybe his neck?—and still he doesn't let go.

Jackson's eyes are locked on mine.

"Put it down!" Ben shouts. "Or she can join Captain Keith at the bottom of the ocean."

Emmy is frozen in place.

Jackson very deliberately drops the fire extinguisher on the deck. "There. Let her go."

"Kick it off the boat," Ben says. "You're not attacking me with that thing as soon as I let go of her."

The look Jackson gives him makes me think he doesn't need the fire extinguisher, but he does as he's told and kicks the fire extinguisher through the lifelines.

It lands in the ocean with a splash, and Ben's forearm finally loosens enough for me to take a breath.

I gasp in air and, on the exhale, wheeze, "I hate your guts."

Ben leans in close to my ear. "I'm not about to be mauled by your overprotective boyfriend because some drunk went overboard and you're all mad about it. And I'm certainly not going to be a prisoner on the boat I fucking paid for."

I twist my head to the right, enough to see his face. "Why don't you use all that family money to hire a good defense lawyer and leave us the hell out of it? And he's not my boyfriend."

Ben's answering laugh is sharp and bitter. "Could have fooled me."

"Let her *go*," Jackson says, taking a step closer.

"Aww," Ben whispers. "He looks so worried…"

Jackson takes another step. "I'm not fucking around, Ben. If you don't let her go—"

Emmy smacks her brother in the ribs and steps around him. "Ben, listen. I know you're freaked out, but we're on your side. You don't have to go back in that disgusting bathroom—"

My glare should vaporize her. "The hell he doesn't!" I shout.

I want to say more. I want to ask what has to happen for her to turn on this boy she's only known for a few days. Why it's so easy to have his back at the expense of mine. I don't get a chance to say any of it though, because Ben tightens his grip on my neck, and I can't breathe again.

My ears start to ring, and I'm distantly aware of Emmy shouting. Of Jackson stepping closer. Ben squeezes, and black dots dance in my vision. He's not going to let go until I'm unconscious. Maybe not even then.

My teeth grind together, and I take a quick step to the left. Ben shifts to follow me, but not fast enough. I drop my shoulder and snap my arm back. I hit him square in the nuts.

Ben folds over on himself, dropping me in favor of the family jewels. He makes a sound like a cat coughing up a hairball.

He doesn't even see it coming.

Jackson takes three long steps and punches him in the face. Ben rocks back and flips off the front of the boat. His yelp of surprise cuts off with a splash.

Emmy gasps, and I follow her to the side. We stare down at the mass of bubbles below us, waiting for him to resurface. I'm hit with an overwhelming sense of déjà vu. I'm sure there'd be some kind of universal justice in Ben being swept away like Captain Keith, but I don't have it in me to watch this happen a second time.

Emmy grabs my hand. Our eyes don't leave the water.

CHAPTER TWELVE

Ben breaks the surface with a dramatic gasp, and I practically sag to the deck in relief. "Thank god." I turn to glare at Jackson. "Can we please stop dumping people into the ocean for fuck's sake?"

He folds his arms and looks away. "Yeah, fine."

Ben shakes water from his face and looks up. "You're all out of your damn minds. I should have known it was waste of time being nice to a bunch of low-class resort pests. Look where it got me!"

The three of us exchange a glance. After everything he's done since we left shore, he still thinks he has the moral high ground? Why? Because we had the good sense to keep him away from us? He was in the bathroom for a few hours, twiddling his thumbs, while the rest of us tried to get us out of the mess *he* created.

What a fucking baby.

"I take it back," Jackson says. "Dumping him in the ocean is the best thing I've done all day. He can drown for all I care."

I frown. "You don't mean that."

His gaze trails to my throat, and I press my hand against the skin there. It's warm to the touch, and I can feel bruises beginning to form.

"I mean it more than I should," he finally says.

Splashing draws our attention back to the water. Ben is swimming toward the back of the boat. Jackson narrows his eyes and speed walks to head him off.

Emmy and I follow, nearly tripping over a mess of ropes on the deck.

"What are you going to do?" I ask.

"Same thing I've *been* doing. Keeping you both safe." He kneels down, flips the ladder up, and locks it in place. Far out of reach to anyone unlucky enough to be in the water.

"Don't be ridiculous! Put that back down," Emmy hisses, trying to knock it from his hand, but Jackson positions himself between her and the ladder.

"He's not coming back on this boat."

She pales. "What do you expect him to do, swim for shore?"

"Don't know, don't care."

I cover my face with my hands. Stress courses through my veins. He can't be serious. Letting Ben slowly drown is no better than what he did to the captain.

I tug at Jackson's wrist until he looks at me. "We can't let him die."

"Toss him a life jacket." Jackson looks me dead in the eye. "It's better than what he deserves after the stunt he just pulled."

I shake my head. "What will we deserve by the end of this? Not much, if we make choices the way he does," I say, pointing at Ben as he comes around the side of the boat.

Jackson won't meet my eyes, but his grip on the ladder is white knuckled.

Ben reaches up and grabs for a rung but finds nothing but air. He wipes his face and scowls at us. "Hey, shit stain, quit fucking around, and drop the ladder."

Right, because insulting the person standing between you and safety is a genius move.

Jackson props his arms against the swim ladder. He looks so casual. "Nah, I don't think so. We're significantly safer when you can't get to us. Enjoy the swim."

Emmy looks over at me and mouths, *What is he doing?*

I shrug. I honestly have no idea.

The waves and the wind carry the boat away from him, and he swims to catch up with us. "Okay, very funny. Now put it down."

Jackson doesn't move.

"Jack, come on. At least throw him the emergency flotation," Emmy says. "We can tie the rope to the back of the boat and tow him along so he doesn't get swept out to sea."

It's not a half-bad idea. "I'm also Team Flotation."

Jackson still makes no move to lower the ladder. I stare at the side of his face, trying to understand how far he plans on taking this. He can't want him to drown? Right?

Panic creeps into Ben's expression as he looks around. The expanse of open ocean is unsettling from the deck, but I know firsthand how much worse it is from the water.

A wave crests the top of his head, and he comes back up sputtering. "Please! I was only trying to get out of the bathroom!" He locks eyes with me. "Hannah, I'm sorry. Okay? I'm really sorry. I don't like small spaces, and I freaked out. I didn't mean to hurt—"

Something moves in the water, and my heart stops.

Ben freezes mid-sentence and whirls in a circle. "What the hell was that?"

Emmy digs her nails into Jackson's arm. "Jack?"

Ben slaps the back of the boat. "*Please* let me up!"

Something glides through the water again, this time from a different direction…and much closer. It coasts behind him, a darkened oval beneath the surface that quickly disappears into deeper water. Ben must feel the motion at his back, because the screech that comes from his mouth is almost inhuman. He kicks for the ladder like he can propel himself into the air by sheer will alone. When that doesn't work, he claws at the fiberglass, trying to find purchase that doesn't exist.

"*Please!*"

"Jackson. He's the only one who knows how this boat works," Emmy says. Fear makes her voice higher. Her words clipped. She tries to force the ladder out of Jackson's hands, but he's stronger than she is. "We can't let him die in there."

He peels his sister's fingers off his arm and pushes her back a few feet before turning to Ben. His face is deadly calm. "We're not letting you get away with murder, so you have a decision to make: Would you rather be arrested or eaten by whatever's in there with you?"

All I can see are the whites of Ben's terrified eyes. He doesn't even look like himself anymore—down in the water, afraid for his life, he looks years younger. *Helpless.* I don't know how I feel about Jackson using a real threat in the water to force Ben to comply. It feels a little bit like psychological warfare.

"Arrested!" Ben shrieks. "I'll turn myself in. Whatever you want. No more escape attempts. No more fires. Just let me back on the fucking boat!"

Jackson unhooks the ladder but doesn't let it drop. "And you'll help us get back to shore?"

Whatever's in the water makes another pass. This time it comes out from beneath the boat and grazes Ben's leg. "Yes!" he screams. "I'll help you! I'll help you!"

"And how do we know you won't turn on us the second we let our guard down?"

"Tie me to the fucking mast if that makes you feel better! Just let me up!"

Jackson drops the ladder. Ben is halfway up it before I can blink. He flops onto the deck, chest heaving. His face has lost nearly all its color, leaving it a bloodless shade of pale unique to terror. And corpses.

Emmy folds herself onto the deck by his side. I expect her to hug him or something else that'll piss me off, but she surprises me by keeping her distance. "You're okay, Ben."

He doesn't react; he simply stares unblinking at the gray sky, trying to catch his breath.

Emmy glares up at her brother. "What the hell is the matter with you? He could have died."

"Unlikely." Jackson lazily leans against the back railing. An amused smirk spreads across his face. The sight of it turns my stomach.

I'm missing something. I must be. There's no way he's entertained by the thought of Ben's demise, right? That's not the Jackson I know.

"If you don't wipe that smirk off your face, I'm going to kick you in the nuts so hard, they'll turn inside out," Emmy says.

Jackson only smiles wider as Ben struggles to sit up.

Something moves out of the corner of my eye, and I look down at the ocean. This time three figures move under the water. A few seconds later, they crest a wave and dive back under, and all the muscles in my body relax.

"I'm no marine biologist, but I'm pretty sure even rich sociopathic assholes are safe from dolphins," Jackson says dryly.

Ben and Emmy turn in sync, first looking at Jackson, then the water.

"Dolphins?" Emmy says.

Ben winces. "Not a shark?"

Jackson folds his arms. "Nope."

Sure enough, several more leap from the ocean. A whole pod of them seem to have found the boat. Maybe even the same ones from yesterday.

"Did you know it was dolphins the whole time?" I ask.

The look he sends me is half surprise and half hurt. "Of course. Do you think I'd leave him in there if I wasn't sure it was safe? Jesus, Hannah."

Shame heats my cheeks. I did think that. Only for a second, but I did. "I'm sorry. I wasn't—"

"Whatever, it doesn't matter." He scowls and nudges Ben's knee with his foot. "Get up. You can catch your breath from the mast. Having your unpredictable ass loose on the boat is raising my blood pressure."

Surprisingly, Ben climbs to his feet and walks straight for the broken mast without protest. I guess I'd make the same choice if the alternative was floating in the open water. Again, I expect Emmy to hover close to Ben's side, but she hangs back and lets Jackson nudge him across the boat.

Jackson finds a loose section of rope and follows it as he goes, clearly puzzling out what it's attached to. "Hannah, where's the knife?"

He won't meet my eyes.

"Um...somewhere below. I'll grab it."

I wait for a nod or a sign he heard me, but he keeps inspecting ropes until I duck into the cabin. Inside, I'm immediately hit with the stench of damp wood, smoke, and something that smells like rotten seaweed. It's disgusting. I hold my breath and wade through the water as fast as I can while still being careful not to cut my bare feet on anything sitting on the bottom. Long black smoke streaks stain the ceiling by the bathroom. I sink my hands into the disgusting cabin water just outside the door and drag my fingers along the cabin floor. It takes a few minutes, but I find it. The second I have it in my hand I'm back on my feet, shaking the disgusting water off my hands, and hurry back to the fresh air.

We need to get that water out. It's dirty and probably contaminated with oil, gas, and boat chemicals. No way that's healthy to breathe, and if we're about to get hit with another storm, we won't be able to stay above deck for long. I look toward the darkest part of the sky. The sun has moved up over our heads, but the clouds are getting so dark I can barely see it. The wind is picking up again too.

We don't have much time.

I find Jackson standing guard over Ben, who looks to have made himself comfortable against the mast, his long legs stretched out in front of him.

Emmy's dug up one of the blue and white resort towels, and she drapes it around his shoulders. "Here, this should help keep you from burning."

Ben smiles at her. "Thank you, Em. I appreciate it. Especially after...everything."

"We all do stupid stuff when we're scared, right?" She pats him on the shoulder with an almost unnatural smile. "I'll look for some sunscreen too."

Oh sure, why don't you make the murderer a cheese plate while you're at it?

I all but slam the knife into Jackson's palm while I glare at Maritime Romeo and Juliet over there. He cuts the section of rope free and gets to work securing Ben's hands behind his back.

Ben turns his attention to me. The wind blows a strand of wet blond hair across his forehead. "You have every right to hate me, Hannah," he says, misunderstanding the reason for my anger. "I crossed a line, and I'm really sorry. I totally freaked out. I get so claustrophobic in small spaces, and it felt like the walls were closing in on me."

I don't know where to start. If I say I don't believe he's sorry, it'll provoke him. And I'm certainly not going to pretend it's okay. I also don't fully buy the claustrophobia excuse. If that small bathroom really scared him, he would have yelled *that* through the door instead of screaming hateful shit and cursing our very existence.

Maybe it's unfair of me to pick apart his response. Panic makes people react differently, but that's the ultimate problem with Bennett. He's so good at the upstanding-guy act, but when he lets the mask slip, he is seriously dangerous. He's proven that over and over again.

"We know you're sorry," Emmy says, speaking for me when I don't respond. "I would have freaked out if someone locked me in a small room too."

I roll my eyes so hard it hurts. Emmy hasn't been claustrophobic *a day* in her life.

Jackson loops the remaining length of rope around Ben's chest a couple times for good measure. When he's finished, he studies his knots, tugging on them a few times to make sure they're secure before he stands. "First things first: It's time to cough up whatever you used to set the boat on fire."

Ben nods toward his left leg. "The lighter's in my pocket."

I'm closest, so I kneel down and wiggle my fingers into his pocket for the second time. I pull out a gold square of metal, and my stomach sinks. I *knew* he had this. I watched him play with it on the dock until the clicking threatened my sanity. Why didn't I check *both* of his pockets?

I roll the little lighter around in my palm, and water leaks from the cracks in the lid. I flip it open and try the flint, but it doesn't work.

Jackson takes it from my palm and taps the edge against his shorts to shake out the water. "We should hold on to it. My dad used to have one like this, and he dropped it in a lake once. He took it all apart, left it in the sun, and when he put it back together, it lit right back up. These metal lighters are no joke. Might be useful later." He holds it out to me.

"I'll put it in the waterproof sleeve with my phone."

A cooler breeze cuts across the back of the boat and throws my hair across my face. We all turn at the same time. The dark clouds on the horizon have crept closer. We probably only have a couple hours before the water gets rough again.

If we're going to survive this next storm, we need a plan.

"We can't leave him tied to the mast when that storm hits," Emmy says.

Jackson pushes hair out of his face with a sigh. "We need to get the water out of the cabin if *any* of us are going to have shelter from the storm. Do you know how to do that, Sailing Camp?"

"There should be a system to pump out the water, but the pumps usually kick on automatically when water is detected. So either it's broken, or the boat doesn't have enough power to run it." Ben pauses, still staring at those dark clouds. Emmy leans forward like she's hanging on his every word, and my hands ball into fists at my sides. "He might have a manual one? It would probably be under one of the bench seats or in one of the easy-to-reach compartments inside."

"I can look for it," I say, turning away and heading for the hatch.

"While you're at it, a food and water inventory might be a good idea," he adds.

Emmy nods enthusiastically, like it's the most profound idea she's ever heard. Which is particularly annoying considering I already suggested the same thing earlier.

"It won't matter if we're dry and warm if we starve to death," Ben says, watching her carefully. "I hate to say it, but if we haven't been rescued yet, it's probably safe to assume that nobody's coming."

Emmy wrings her hands together.

"Or that they don't know where to look yet," he adds quickly. "We might be on our own here for a little while."

Emmy lays her head on his fucking shoulder and takes a deep breath. "You don't have to tiptoe around me. I know things are bad. But we're all in this together, right?"

Ben leans the side of his head on the top of hers. "Absolutely."

I see red.

"I'll go see what I can find," I say, desperate for some distance before I punch the trauma bond right out of her. I point at Ben as I pass. "Jackson, keep an eye on them...and the storm."

Jackson nods and plops down heavily beside Ben. They promptly begin a glare-off that might outlast us all.

I can't keep my eyes off the darkening sky as I hurry toward the hatch. The shift from *wait for rescue* to *survive as long as possible* is almost palpable.

A small part of my brain wonders if there's any point to drying the cabin, gathering food, rationing drinking water. Any of it. Ben called the last storm "a little wind and waves," but it snapped our mast and tossed us around like marbles in a tin can. I've watched way too many of those "Yooo, ho" sea shanty videos of cargo ships navigating monster forty-foot waves to underestimate the ocean.

If this second storm is any worse than the last one, we might not live to see tomorrow.

CHAPTER THIRTEEN

I duck into the hatch and slide down the stairs. My feet splash through the water, and things immediately tangle in my toes and bump into my knees. I wade through to the table, grab the waterproof phone holder from my bag, and tuck the lighter inside before I get to work looking for food and a water pump. Before I put it back in the bag, I hold the power button down to turn the phone back on. I don't have high hopes for a cell signal, but it doesn't hurt to try.

The dead battery symbol blinks at me instead of the Apple logo. I groan.

Emmy's phone was already dead yesterday and Ben's had even less of a charge than mine did. If we can somehow manage to get closer to shore, Jackson's our last hope to call for help.

I make sure the waterproof zipper is firmly sealed on the phone holder and toss it back into my bag. When I step back into the kitchen, I see something that looks like a yellow flashlight floating at the surface, and bend to fish it out. It turns out to be a soggy banana and I fling it back. "Eeew."

"You should know better than to touch anything in that water. Who knows what that grubby captain had in this boat," Emmy says behind me.

I jump and whirl around. I didn't even hear her feet on the deck.

She's crouched in the hatch opening. "There could be used condoms floating around."

Oh. My. God.

I turn my nose up toward the fresh air tempting me through the hatch. "That's disgusting."

"No puking. We're already low on food. Keep those fruit snacks where they belong." She drops down into the kitchen beside me.

"What are you doing in here?" I ask. I start digging through the kitchen cabinet beside the stove. Inside is bare except for two cans in the back. Condensed tomato soup and sliced peaches. I stack them both on the counter.

"Helping," she says "Ben suggested we find a duffel bag or something to put the food in. To keep it all in one place."

I roll my eyes. "Oh, did he? What a novel idea. And here I was hoping to store it all in the ass cheeks of this bathing suit. What would we do without Ben's invaluable advice?"

She taps a pink nail on the box of fruit snacks on the counter with a frown. "I was hoping we could get some work done before this part, but okay."

"I don't know what that means." I open another cabinet and find a can of expired…butter? I didn't know that even existed. I hold it out to Emmy. "This is the grossest thing I've ever seen. And it's six and a half years old. I vote we feed it to your psychopath boyfriend. With any luck it'll kill him."

She snatches it out of my hand and throws it into the water. "Clearly you and I need to have a conversation. You've been glaring at me all day, and it's starting to piss me off."

I'm pissing *her* off?

It's so absurd I laugh into the open cabinet in front of me. "I can't even begin to tell you how little I care about pissing you off right now. But I'll make you a deal: I'll stop glaring at you as soon as you stop making excuses for a murderer."

The next cabinet has the remains of a cardboard frame from a case of water bottles, but there are only two left. I add them to the pile on the counter.

Emmy grabs my shoulders and turns me around to face her. I expect anger—or maybe some argument about why I should be more understanding of Ben's claustrophobia or whatever else she's using to excuse this shit—but she doesn't look angry. She looks devastated.

"Hannah, are you kidding me? I'm not making excuses for that bag of dicks!" she hisses. "He *choked* you."

I can feel the confusion on my face. I bat her hands away from me and point toward the deck. "Yeah, and then I watched you cover his precious little shoulders with a towel and flutter around him like some pathetic groupie."

Now I get some of the anger. "I didn't see what he did to the captain, and maybe I didn't want to believe that the guy who was so nice to us this whole trip could be that fucked up, but I watched you *stop breathing*, Hannah. You turned fucking purple, and he smiled the whole time. I wanted to cheer when Jackson knocked him off the boat, and I'm beyond fucking offended that you'd think I could watch any person on this planet lay a hand on you and not hate their guts."

"I don't understand. What was all that crap about the sunscreen and *we're all in this together* and cuddling up to him on the deck?"

Tears stream down her face, and she wipes them away. "I figured he'd have more incentive to help us if he thought he still had someone on his side. He might let something helpful slip while he's trying to convince me to untie him."

"You're pretending you still like him to gather sailboat survival tips?"

She shrugs and wipes away another tear. "I may not be built for manual boat labor or fixing broken noses, but I can manipulate a stupid boy better than anyone."

The last hour is suddenly making a lot more sense. Emmy's the one who suggested we leave him in the water and drag him along behind us. She only argued for letting him back on board once the "sharks" showed up, and even then it was about saving his *sailing* skills—not him specifically.

I was so busy feeling betrayed, I completely missed what she was doing.

Apparently it's my day to underestimate members of the Cole family.

I pull her in and wrap my arms around her. She hugs me back so hard it hurts, but I don't mind. Relief floods every inch of my body. "Thank god, Emmy. I thought you went to the dark side."

She pulls away. "We're all stressed the hell out, so I'll give you a temporary pass on not giving me the benefit of the doubt, but I reserve the right to be mad about this later. Maybe on the flight home."

I laugh. "That's fair. So long as I reserve the right to make fun of you for your terrible taste in boys."

She holds out her hand, and we shake on it, grinning like idiots.

I *missed* her.

"Okay, how about I look for food, while you look for the pump thing?" Emmy suggests. "If Jackson's up there too long with that fucker, one or both of them might end up in the ocean."

She has a solid point. I move into the main part of the cabin and start lifting the seats around the table to get to the compartments beneath them. "What the hell does a water pump even look like?"

"That's a good question," Emmy says, dropping another can of peaches onto the pile I started. "Something with hoses?"

The first compartment is packed full of soggy junk. Clothes, ruined magazines, extra snorkeling masks, one solitary flipper, a stack of books, and a tackle box that leaks water from the cracks when I lift it up. Nothing with a hose. I move to the compartment on the other side of the table.

Emmy makes a triumphant sound and holds up a jar of peanut butter and a mostly empty bag of bread. She adds both to the pile. "The peanut butter is almost gone but a win is a win. And maybe if I make Ben a sandwich, he'll help us brainstorm how to make the engine turn over."

I dig through the next compartment. It's full of soggy towels, two bright-orange life vests, a fluorescent-green bag holding an emergency raft, and what looks like a first aid kit in some sort of waterproof bag? "I'm not sure pretending to be on his side is the best idea, Em. Look at what he did when Captain Keith turned on him," I say, chucking the two life vests on the table. Leave it to Frat Boy Keith not to have enough for everyone on board. "Could be dangerous."

She adds a container of tuna to the pile. "It's only dangerous if he finds out. Which he won't. Think about it, if you were on a boat with three strangers who all wanted you to go to jail, would *you* want to help them? He's lied about so many other things; what if there's an easy way to get to shore right here, right now, and he's keeping it to himself so he doesn't go to jail?"

I close the compartment lid and move to the sofa-style bench on the other side of the aisle. "How is pretending to be Team Ben going to help if that's the case? What are you going to do, offer to testify on his behalf?"

"I'll say whatever it takes. Then when we're safe on land, we'll turn him in to the cops as planned. He'll get locked up, and we'll go home."

"Emmy," I sigh. "What if it doesn't go down like that? What if you trick him this whole time, turn on him later, and then his parents get the charges dropped? What if he finds you in Italy? He's already proven he's unstable."

She shakes her head. "He's only doing all this because he doesn't want to get in trouble. If the charges get dropped or they choose not to charge him at all, he'll run back to his life in Miami without looking back. He wouldn't gain anything by coming after me once everything's out in the open. But if it makes you feel better, I'll start my trip in another country, and I'll make sure to block him on social media so he can't see where I am."

"Your parents went to the same college as his parents. He knows your name and where we're from. He could find you in twenty minutes if he tried."

Her jaw tightens.

"I'm not trying to make you mad, Em. I'm only pointing out that this might not be the best plan. He's cooperating because he's strapped to the damn boat. It's in his best interest to help us to shore, or he'll go down with the boat too. Why poke the bear when we're not absolutely sure it's necessary?"

Emmy stands up straight and starts aggressively stacking the meager supply of cans and water bottles. "Is it a natural impulse to shoot down every idea I have, or do you have to work at it?"

"What's that supposed to mean?"

She looks like she's about to say something, but she shakes her head. "Nothing, never mind." She sloshes toward the hatch. "I'm going to make sure the two idiots aren't spitting on each other; you've got this on your own, right?"

"Em, hold on," I say. "I'm not trying to shoot you down—"

She stops at the bottom of the stairs. "Not intentionally, but that's what you're doing. I promise I can pull this off. If he's keeping anything from us, I'll trick it out of him. You just have to trust me."

I pinch the bridge of my nose and yank the sofa compartment open. "I *do* trust you, but when you're done with a guy, you say it with your entire body. He's going to figure it out. You're a terrible liar. Which is a good quality, by the way. You're the most genuine person I know, but it means he's going to see this coming a mile away."

Emmy's eyes narrow. "Maybe I should take some tips from you then. Or are you going to tell the truth about what's going on between you and my brother?"

The compartment lid slips from my fingers and slams shut before I even see what's inside. I spin toward her, schooling my features. "Nothing is going on."

It's not a lie, but it's not the whole truth either. The guilt sinks its teeth into me, and I fight to keep it off my face. Unfortunately she can smell a half-truth like a bloodhound.

"Are you sure about that? Because he dove in after you without a moment's hesitation when the mast took you under."

I open the compartment again and use it to hide my face. "He thought I was about to be *Captain Keith: The Encore*. I would have done the same if it were you. Or Jackson. Or even Ben."

"And that's all it was? Saving you out of obligation?"

My stomach twists into a knot. "What else would it be?"

"No idea, but the fact that you won't look me in the eye when you say it speaks volumes."

"I'm trying to find a way to get the water out of the boat."

"No, you're trying to find a way out of this conversation," she says. "I just don't understand *why*. You tell me everything. I thought you were over him?"

I flinch. "I *am* over him."

"Then you might want to start acting like the smart, independent badass you are and stop staring at him with those 'please love me' hearts in your eyes."

Jackson lowers himself to a crouch at the top of the stairs and raises an eyebrow. "Interesting time to come check on you two."

My cheeks flush, and I turn away from both of them.

"Em, Sailing Camp is asking for you," he says.

"We're not done here, Hannah," she says, before stomping up the stairs and along the deck. I catch a flash of her legs through the portholes.

Jackson clears his throat. "Ah, Hannah?"

"Yeah?"

"Do you need any help...or...?"

My head is still half buried in the compartment, and I'm not too proud to admit I'm hiding from the tsunami of embarrassment coursing through my veins. "Nope. I've got it handled, thanks."

The stairs creak under his weight. "Are you sure? I can help you figure out the—"

"Nope!" My face flames hotter when I hear how high-pitched that comes out. I try again. "I've got it. Besides, your sister is determined to play undercover girlfriend to trick our resident murderer into coughing up useful sailing tips, so you'll be needed up there when that plan goes to shit."

He sighs, and when I look up again, he's gone. I groan at the smoke-stained ceiling. I don't think I've ever been this embarrassed in my life, and the fact that I give a single shit about this in the middle of a survival situation only makes me feel even more pathetic.

I should have said no to this trip. I should have gone with my gut and made some kind of excuse. I could be home in my own bed right now…

Far from two of the people I love most in this world, while they're in danger.

My throat gets tight at the thought of them out here with Ben while I enjoyed a blissful spring break from the safety of my couch. Probably rewatching *Grey's Anatomy* for the hundredth time when the call came in that they were missing.

My dad has probably gotten that same call about me.

Tears sting in my eyes. I've never met someone more professionally capable in my entire life. At the hospital, he's a well-oiled machine, and everyone relies on him to keep his department running smoothly. But at home? When it's only me and him, he's a walking bag of worry.

Finding out I'm missing, lost somewhere at sea?

This will break him.

I swipe a tear from my cheek and blow out a breath.

Nope. I can't do this.

If I crumble, it's all over. We need to get off this *Be-Yacht-Ch*.

I force my attention back to the storage bin. I have a task. Get the water out of the boat. That's much more productive than drowning in guilt or what-ifs.

I fully flip up the bench seat this time, and bingo. This one is full of mechanical-looking stuff—the most promising one so far. There're a bunch of tools and wires, zip ties and clamp-looking things, pieces of PVC piping, electrical tape, and hardware. But after digging through the contents, I don't see anything that looks like a pump apart from some kind of coiled clear ribbed hose. If there's a pump in here, I'm not seeing it. Sure would have been great if Ben hadn't spent the day proving we can't trust him. He might actually recognize what some of this stuff is for. The thing I need could be right in front of me, and I wouldn't even know what I'm looking at.

Time for a new plan.

I snatch up the hose and unwind it. It's about two and a half inches wide and maybe twenty feet long. I dunk the hose in the water, until it's fully submerged. I slap my palm over one end to keep the air out and fling it out the open hatch, making sure the other end stays in the water. The first time, the hose falls back in the cabin. The second time, I walk the covered end up the stairs to maintain the suction, but I slip and almost smack my face, losing my grip on the hose altogether. The third time I get the hose up on the deck and over the side of the boat.

Water starts pouring from the hose and I throw both hands into the air, victory style.

And they say the internet is rotting our brains. Guess who would be shit out of luck today if she hadn't spent enough time doomscrolling to see a video about a dude draining his aboveground pool with a spare hose? This girl right here.

As long as there's no air in the tube and the draining end is lower than the water you're hoping to remove, it'll siphon right out.

I look back to see if anyone witnessed my victory, but they're all on the other side of the propped-up sail. Oh well. It's a victory just for me then.

I poke my head back inside the cabin to make sure the other end of the hose is fully submerged and pluck a soggy hardcover from the water to hold the hose in place. The interior end is only about nine or ten inches below the surface, but that'll drain at least half of what's in the cabin, and at this point, anything is an improvement. Water is heavy as hell, and we can't afford to sit any lower when the next storm hits.

Stretching my avoidance to its limits, I grab the loaf of bread off the counter, hastily make two sandwiches with a scrape of peanut butter, and cut them in half. None of us have eaten anything but fruit snacks since yesterday afternoon. We have to make the food last, but we're also going to need energy to make it through this next storm, and we should eat the bread first, before it starts to mold.

I stack the halved sandwiches in a pile, grab the water bottle Emmy brought me earlier, and make my way back to the others.

Ben is still latched to the mast. Emmy is so close to his side, she might as well be in his lap—clearly committed to her role. And she's leveling Jackson with a death glare.

I'm apparently interrupting sibling argument number five thousand.

Jackson sits a few feet away on one of the flat sections of decking in the middle of the boat, shaking his head. "That's not how it works, Emmy."

"Why not? We have the compasses on our phones. We can use them to see our current coordinates," she says, ignoring my arrival.

Emmy's never been one to tolerate being left out; I'm not exactly shocked at the silent treatment.

"And what exactly are we supposed to do with our coordinates?" Jackson asks.

"Use them to figure out where we are."

"Do you by chance know the correct coordinates for Puerto Vallarta? Or what that random jumble of numbers even means? We're not sailors. We don't even have a map."

She scowls at him but says nothing.

"Not to mention, we might not have access to our current coordinates anymore," I say, handing Jackson a sandwich and dumping two in Emmy's lap. I'll leave her to feed the hostage. "My phone is dead. Emmy's is too. So unless either of you happen to have a charge…"

Ben shakes his head. "Mine died last night."

Jackson leans to the side and fishes his from his pocket. He presses the button but nothing happens on the screen. "I was at twenty percent when I checked for a signal this morning, but it went in the water with me when I dove in to help Hannah."

Shit.

Emmy stares daggers into the side of my face. "Didn't even stop to take his phone out of his pocket first. *Interesting*."

I clear my throat. "The *point is*, we can't use coordinates we don't have. We'll need another plan."

It's silent for a long moment as we all stare at our food. As if we're collectively thinking about how hungry we are. I take a bite first. The bread sticks to the inside of my dry mouth, but I don't mind. It's nice to have something other than fruit snacks in my stomach.

Emmy eats her sandwich in tiny gopher bites. Like she thinks the more she chews, the more filling it'll be. She holds Ben's sandwich to his mouth, and he eats half of it in one bite. His is gone before Emmy's finished with hers, and I see him eyeing it. I stop eating, ready to smack his face if he tries to guilt her into sharing her ration, but she finishes her meal in peace.

When everyone's sandwich is gone, I drink a quarter of the water left in the bottle, swishing it around the inside of my mouth. I hand it to Jackson, who does the same. Emmy drinks her quarter and pours the rest into Ben's mouth.

We have two full water bottles left, which won't go far, but at least there's some food and water in us.

Jackson brushes the crumbs off his shorts. "How do we get this boat moving, Ben?"

He grimaces. "That's a complicated question. Without a sail or a working start motor, we're at the mercy of the tides and the wind, with little to no way to get us moving in a specific direction." He adds, "Even if we could get the engine going, it's unlikely we'd make progress with the water in the cabin weighing us down."

They all turn to me.

"There wasn't a pump, as far as I could tell, but I figured out a way to drain it with a hose. It won't get all of it out though. The hose isn't long enough to reach all the way to the cabin floor and still drain overboard at the same time."

Ben raises his eyebrows. "You made a siphon out of a spare hose?"

They're still staring, and I shift uncomfortably under their attention. "Yeah?"

"Hannah's always been the smart one," Emmy says, and absolutely no part of that sounds like a compliment. She grins at her brother. "Wouldn't you agree, *Jackson*?"

Oh, for the love of—

"I'm...going to go check how much drinking water we have," Jackson says.

And he flees, like a coward, and I'm left to stare down Emmy's smug face all on my own. I'm going to have to tell her about winter break. She's like a dog with a bone; she'll never let this go. I'm just not ready to talk about it yet.

So I deflect.

"Is the water from the sink safe to drink?" I ask Ben.

I can feel Emmy's glare. I ignore it.

He shrugs. "Depends on how long it's been in the holding tank. If it's been sitting for a long time, probably not. But Keith lived on board and frequently sailed long stretches at sea, so he probably wasn't drinking only bottled water. He'd have to refill the tank often and change the filters, or he'd be sick as a dog."

So as long as the tank has enough water—and the storm doesn't kill us—we might be okay until we're rescued. The thought is oddly comforting. Dying of dehydration is slow and ugly.

A gust of wind blows the sail off the top of the broken mast. When Emmy doesn't get up to fix it, despite having shoulders almost the same color as her bathing suit, I get up to do it. She watches me cross the deck with a scowl. I fling the sail back over them like a tent, dragging it to one side so that their legs are fully shaded, but when I'm done, I stay on the bow of the boat rather than rejoining them.

The wind seems to have spun us in a half circle. The mass of angry storm clouds is ahead of the boat now. It seems like it creeps closer every time I blink, dragging the higher winds along with it, which in turn blow the weather in faster.

I have a bad feeling about this second storm.

Ben's voice carries to me through the other side of the sail.

"...could really do a lot more to help if I wasn't tied up," he says. "I think I could get a secondary sail strung up, with a little help. But I doubt I could talk the three of you through it. You don't know what anything is called, and I'd have to spend half a day teaching you how the boat works before you'd understand my instructions."

I roll my eyes. How does he expect to get this miraculous secondary sail up without a mast? He's so full of shit. He's been tied up for a half hour, and already he's trying to weasel his way to freedom. Figures he'd go the "I'm the only one who knows how to sail" route.

"Is there a place an emergency sail would normally be stored?" Emmy asks.

"Depends on the boat. I could help you look, but Hannah and Jackson don't trust me anymore. I really want to help get us home, but my hands are quite literally tied behind my back."

Emmy laughs. "Maybe I can change their minds. We can't leave you up here in the storm anyway. If we can get the boat moving, I think they'd be a lot more open to it."

Ben's answer is barely above a whisper. "You're the only reasonable one on this boat."

Emmy laughs again. "I'm going to catch Hannah now, while Jackson is down below."

Ah, FML.

"Divide and conquer?" Ben asks.

"Exactly."

I move away from the sail. I know my friend, and there's absolutely no chance she's getting up to talk to me about Ben. I cross all the way to the bow so Ben won't overhear us.

I wait until Emmy has a good grip on the lifelines beside me before I say, "I know it's killing you, so get it off your chest."

Her lips purse together like she's trying to hold back. I can practically see everything she wants to say spinning behind her eyes. "It's probably not the time."

"It's *definitely* not the time, but I don't see a better one showing up anytime soon."

"I just…" And the dam breaks. "I don't understand why you'd tell me you were over him if you're not. He's not telling me anything either. It makes no sense. If something happened, if you two have feelings for each other—"

I shake my head to stop her. "Jackson does not have feelings for me."

"What's going on then? Because there are weird vibes between the two of you. It's like the awkward six months after a couple in the friend group breaks up."

I scrub a hand down my face. I don't want to lie, but I don't have it in me to explain either. "Em, I'm not ready to talk about this yet, okay? It's embarrassing enough having a crush on someone for a decade, and then piling what happened on top of it? It makes me want to fling myself into the ocean."

"But something did happen between you two?"

"Yes."

That much, I can give her.

"But you won't tell me what it was?" she asks, sounding hurt. "Since when do we not talk about things like this?"

"I don't know, Em. I guess since now."

Emmy's silent, and when I look over at her, she's glaring at the storm. "It's been different between us since you got your Linfield acceptance. You're distant and critical of my travel choices. Now you're keeping secrets too."

"Whoa, I am not critical. I'm worried about you and your personal safety. I just want you to be more careful."

Emmy turns her glare on me. "You've *never* supported my travel dreams. You or my parents. Nobody takes what I want to do seriously. I'm sorry I don't want to settle down and be a nurse or teacher—"

"Nobody's asking you to become a different person! I'm asking you to not take strange men with you overseas. I'm asking you to travel with a friend. I'm asking you to be a little more wary of your surroundings, so you don't die in a ditch in the Maldives!"

"Like I said, *critical*."

Someone clears their throat, and we both spin toward the sound.

Jackson's standing behind us. A half-filled gallon jug dangles from the tips of his fingers, and his mouth is set in a grim line. "Sorry to interrupt, but tiny problem: The boat's out of water."

CHAPTER FOURTEEN

I stare at the jug in Jackson's hands like it's a bomb about to blow us all up. It feels about that dire. We'll be dead in a couple days if that half jug and two water bottles are all we have to share between the four of us.

Like I said, death by dehydration is a bitch. Once we run out of water, we'll slowly get weak and confused. Our bodies will divert energy and blood flow to essential organs, until eventually our kidneys will start to fail. Waste will build up in our bodies, and our livers, our brains, and eventually our hearts will stop.

Systematic organ failure.

My dad treated a kid for dehydration a few months ago. He was medevaced in from Eastern Oregon after he and his dad got lost during a hike. They ended up wandering the desert for almost a week before they were discovered, and despite medical treatment on the ground, en route, and in the ER, he died soon after he touched down in Portland.

He was only seven. His dad survived.

When my dad got home, he gave me a long lecture about how easy it is to die of dehydration if you get lost on a hike—not that I've ever willingly gone for a hike in my life—or worse, anywhere dry and hot.

So now, I know way too much about multiple organ failure and—

"Hannah!"

I jolt. "What?"

"I said your name ten times. You checked out," Jackson says, and I'm surprised to find him right in front of me. I automatically take a step back to put some space between us. He clocks the movement with a frown, but I don't need to give Emmy anything else to comment on.

I slip around him. "I'm going to go check that the hose is still draining," I mumble.

"I was just back there. It was fine—" Jackson starts to say, but Emmy cuts him off.

"Let her go, Jack."

A wave hits the side of the boat as I'm going down the stairs, and I all but fall into the kitchen. I catch myself on the countertop and hang my head. Rage, frustration, and impatience war for the top spot in the hierarchy of my emotions, and I honestly don't know which one is going to win out in the end. It seems like every hour on this boat is worse than the last.

I check the water level to distract myself, and I'm relieved to see it's dropped significantly. The siphon is much more productive than our bucket train. It still has a ways to go, but at least one thing is going right. I peek out the porthole in the kitchen, and the boat is definitely sitting higher in the water with all that weight removed. I don't know if it's enough to keep us afloat if the storm gets really bad, but that elusive hope starts to build in my chest again.

It *could* be enough. Which is more than we had before I found that hose.

Too bad we're going to die of dehydration.

I sink down on the bench seat and hug my knees.

I hear footsteps on the stairs, and I know it'll be Jackson before I even lift my head. He sits on the top step, gallon jug still dangling from his fingers, and frowns. "Do you want to talk about it?"

Nope.

I spot a bucket on its side in the water and kick it toward him. "Do you want to make another line and see if we can get more of this water out?"

He ignores that. "What happened with you and Emmy? I heard you yelling on the bow."

I'm not about to admit the part about *him*. "She said I didn't care about her travel plans, and it all went downhill from there. Because apparently worrying about her getting murdered by a stranger makes me *unsupportive*."

"I don't think too much worrying is the problem, Hannah."

"Then what is?"

He jumps down into the water and places the gallon jug on the counter. "It doesn't take a psychology degree to notice that the more excited you get about Linfield, the more she talks about her trip."

"That's not true. Emmy's been planning that trip forever."

"Planning, yes. Obsessing? No. She's always had a Pinterest board of destinations, and I don't know how many times she's barged into my room to show me some new travel video of an obscure town in Romania or Japan. But it's always been... I don't know. Hypothetical. A collage of ideas rather than an actual plan. When you got your acceptance, she went all in. Start dates. Possible hotels in different cities. Bus routes. Which flights are easiest and cheapest. The works."

An uncomfortable itch works down my spine. I didn't know any of that.

"So? She needs a plan if she's going to make this trip happen. Graduation is right around the corner."

"I just find it funny that the more steps you take toward your future, the more she seems to panic-plan her own. And she's not getting a lot of support. As long as you've wanted to be a trauma nurse, she's wanted to see the world. But she watches your dreams get celebrated while she gets lectured about 'wasting too much time wandering around.' My parents are the worst offenders. They keep calling it a 'gap year' or a 'pitstop' while she figures out what she wants to do in life. Everyone's being a little rude about her plans, honestly."

"I've never been anything but supportive of Emmy's travel plans."

"You've also sent her links to pickpocket-proof bags, insisted she take self-defense classes, and lectured her about how dangerous it is to wander foreign countries by herself. While also jumping down her throat when she invited Ben to go with her. I'm not saying you were wrong for that—going alone would be safer than traveling with that guy—but Emmy already feels like none of her plans are ever good enough. I think she's really struggling with everyone constantly wishing she'd choose a safer, more conventional dream."

I feel a little sick to my stomach. When I got my Linfield acceptance the Coles threw me a party. With themed decorations and a banner and everything. They did the same for Jackson when he got his acceptance. I was at their dinner table when Emmy announced her travel blog idea. All her mom said was, *Oh honey, there's no way to make a living doing that. Are you sure you don't want to fill out a couple college applications?*

When I don't respond, Jackson says, "She wants everyone to take her choices seriously too. Especially you. And underneath it all, she's terrified of being left behind."

I feel myself deflate, and the rage, frustration, and irritation lose a bit of steam. I almost don't want them to. That mix of emotion is armor. Without it, we're just two girls who are equally afraid of losing the other.

"It hurt my feelings when she asked Sailor Dick to go to Italy with her instead of me. It felt like being replaced in real time. Like I was nothing."

"Even if they took that trip together, he could never replace you. You're not exactly easy to leave behind, you know."

I tilt my chin so he doesn't see me roll my eyes. Oh, the irony.

He sighs and sloshes over to sit next to me. A gust of wind howls against the boat, and we rock forward and back again.

He clears his throat. "Okay. I think we need to talk about this."

I become very interested in the scrapes on my knees. "Talk about what?"

"About what happened between us."

I knew he was going to say that, but hearing it is still jarring. It was his idea to keep things quiet. Why bother digging up the past?

"We've done a great job pretending nothing happened. No reason to stop now."

He laughs softly. "Yeah...I don't think we're actually that good at pretending."

"*You* are."

"I'm shocked you think so. I can't even park at my parents' house without thinking of you up on that ladder surrounded by Christmas lights."

As a general rule, I do not allow myself to relive that night. It's too embarrassing. But one sentence out of his mouth, and it all rushes back.

I stood in my driveway groaning into the night. Roughly half of our Christmas lights were on the ground. My dad was on the tail end of a twenty-four-hour shift, and I'd gone to pick up some brownie ingredients to surprise him with dessert to kick off our Christmas Eve together.

The lights were decidedly *up* when I left the house.

I didn't want my dad to come home after a long shift and have to rehang them, so I postponed my baking and trudged inside to get a ladder. We always hung the Christmas lights the same way: stretched back and forth from the trees to the house in a giant *W* pattern. The wind had ripped out the hooks above the front door and in one of the trees.

Armed with new hooks, the one over the door was relatively fast to reattach, but the one in the tree was being a little shit. Every time I sunk the screw into the trunk, the tension of the lights pulled it back out again. On attempt number six, I was ready to chop down the entire tree.

"Need help?"

I startled and dropped the hook. It landed right between a pair of familiar white sneakers.

Jackson bent to scoop it up. "I'll take that as a yes?"

I blinked at him like a fool. I knew he usually came home from college for the holidays, but I'd somehow missed him over Thanksgiving, and there'd been no sign of him since winter break started. I think I'd convinced myself that he'd already come and gone. The last place I expected to see him was standing in my yard.

The butterflies were immediate—and a little nauseating.

I held my hand out for the screw. "That's okay. You probably have a million things to do with your family. I've got this. Thanks though."

He shook his head. "Get off the ladder, Hannah. My mom will kill me if she looks out and sees you up there while I stand around doing nothing to help."

"Then go inside."

He rolls his eyes. "You know my mom. She raised helpers; that won't fly."

He was right, of course. But the embarrassment of him seeing me in my *Bob's Burgers* PJ pants was more than I could take. "I won't tell her if you don't. Besides, I'm almost done."

He frowned, and the next thing I knew, there was an arm around my waist, and my feet left the rungs on the ladder. I laughed in surprise, and Jackson set me down beside him. He was halfway up the ladder with the strand of lights before I could protest.

And worse, he had them reattached in less than ten seconds. I folded my arms at the audacity of it all, and he laughed as he jumped off the last rung.

"You were trying to sink the hook too high. The lights were too tight. About a foot lower, and you wouldn't have needed my help at all."

"Oh." I looked up at the tree. "That makes sense. Thank you."

He smiled at me, and my stomach did several profound flips. It should be illegal to be helpful and kind and attractive all at the same time. I thought him going off to college would diminish my crush, but the second he reappeared, I found myself right back where I started, hopelessly drooling after him.

I cleared my throat. "Well, I have some brownies to make before my dad gets home, and a mug of hot chocolate with my name on it. I've been out here a lot longer than I want to admit."

I started for the front door but only made it a couple steps before he asked, "Are you making it from scratch again? With the chocolate chips?"

I turned. "Of course," I said, mildly offended. "There's no instant hot chocolate in this house."

He grinned. "What are the chances you'll make me a mug? Since I so gallantly helped you with the lights and everything."

I raised an eyebrow. "You want to come inside and have hot chocolate with me?"

"Yes, please."

"*Why?*"

"Why wouldn't I?"

Then we were in my kitchen, and I was sliding a mug of hot chocolate toward him, and we were...talking. I told him I was worried about Emmy going overseas and not seeing my best friend every day. He told me his fall semester was more stressful than he expected. I shared my anxiety about getting into Linfield, and he shared a story about someone letting a goat loose in the dean's office that almost made me snort hot chocolate out of my nose.

"College is not *all* studying," he said. "You'll find out next year."

It felt oddly normal. As if we hung out, just the two of us, all the time.

I smiled and put our cups away in the dishwasher. "I don't know how many loose goats are in my future. That sounds like more of an Emmy thing. She's always in on the shenanigans; I'm usually the one worrying about getting caught. I'm a bit more comfortable being the invisible one."

He walked around the island and came to a stop in front of me. "You're not invisible."

I laughed. "That's very nice of you to say, but it's okay. I don't mind. I'm not a fan of the spotlight—not the way Emmy is, anyway. I definitely don't want to trade places with her."

His eyebrows pulled together, and his gaze dropped to my mouth. "What *do* you want?" he asked.

My pulse thundered in my ears.

I could only think of one answer.

You.

I blink, and I'm no longer in my kitchen. It's not Christmas, and Jackson is definitely not looking down at me like he wants to kiss me. He looks a little angry, actually.

"I know it was my idea to not talk about winter break, but that clearly wasn't the right call if we keep biting each other's heads off every time we talk for more than ten minutes."

"Maybe the solution is less talking then."

"I understand you're mad, Hannah. But I'm getting tired of the little jabs."

I stand and snatch my coral bag off the dining bench. "You're in luck then. If we ever get out of here, I'm off to Linfield, and with your sister traveling, you and I will have fewer reasons to run into each other. You'll finally be free of me and my *jabs*," I say, throwing the canned food and two water bottles into the bag.

He stands too. "I don't deserve this. I did the right thing."

I zip the bag and chuck it back on the counter before I turn to glare at him. "What the hell does that mean?"

He curls his hands into tight fists. I can feel the exasperation radiating off him. "It means that night got away from me. I had no intention of kissing you when I walked into your house, and once I did, I definitely didn't expect to *keep* kissing you. I sure as hell didn't expect we'd almost get caught making out in your kitchen by your dad."

My face heats at the memory of Jackson tearing out the back door with his jacket and shoes in his hands as my dad came in through the garage door.

I open my mouth to tell him I don't need to hear this, but he holds up both his hands.

"I also didn't expect *my* dad to catch me trying to stealthily close the gate to your backyard. I must have looked guilty because he guessed what happened in about three seconds."

One of those moments passes where I know, with complete clarity, what he's going to say next. Our families have been joined at the hip for a decade. I know exactly what Mr. Cole would say if he thought Jackson and I were about to cross a line.

My body goes numb.

"He reminded me that I was older than you, that I was away at college, and that you...had a bit of a crush."

Dear god, someone sink me to the bottom of this ocean.

"I knew how you felt! It never bothered me," he says in a rush. I wonder if I look as mortified as I feel, because he starts talking faster. "I didn't think much about it to be honest. You were Emmy's kind, dependable other half. But then Shithead Tanner called Emmy a whore, and you stormed out of his house like a PlayStation-destroying avenging angel who reduced him to tears in his own driveway before I could even lift a finger to defend her myself.

"After that...I don't know. It was different somehow. You were still kind and helpful and friendly to every person you talked to, but I noticed other things about you too. The way you stood up for other people, the way you took care of your dad—you weren't *just* the kind friend, you were strong as hell, constantly taking care of everyone around you. Kissing you almost seemed inevitable after that. Like you figured out your feelings before I did, but I'd finally caught up. You know?"

I nod, but I can barely hear him over the pulse in my ears.

"But when my dad pulled me onto the porch, he was furious. For *you*. He said if this ended badly, it could cause problems with our families too. Emmy would be furious if we went there and it didn't work out. Things would be uncomfortable whenever I came home. He said you might even stop coming by whenever I wasn't at college. Our families are *so* close. He told me point-blank that if I was going to go there, I better make sure it's worth the risk. And...and I..."

I take a step back as the boat rocks again, and I almost lose my balance. He reaches out to steady me, but I jerk out of his reach.

"And it wasn't. Worth the risk," I finish for him.

He levels me with a haunted expression, and I know I'm right. I've spent the last three months wondering how I could have gotten everything so wrong. Trying to understand why he backpedaled so hard. But learning the truth now only makes me sick to my stomach. Ignorance really is bliss, sometimes.

"I avoided you like a coward for the rest of break. The next time we saw each other, you had your early action acceptance from Linfield and my parents were throwing you that party. I'd almost completely convinced myself that my dad was full of shit, until I walked into your party and saw it firsthand. Out of everyone cheering you on that day, the only family you had there was your dad. Ninety percent of your support system is *my* family, and if something went wrong between us, you'd lose more than I would. It scared me shitless, because I didn't know if I had it in me to not mess up with you. We'd only kissed—we've never been on a real date. I thought maybe I could take it back without too much damage. So I asked you to take a walk with me the next day."

I hold up a hand to stop him. I remember every detail about that shitty afternoon. Of the "walk" that only lasted half a block before he pulled me to a stop to tell me what a mistake Christmas Eve had been. *I never should have kissed you. I didn't mean to lead you on, but I don't think this is a good idea.*

I told him not to worry about it, that it was one kiss, and we didn't need to be awkward about it, but what else was I supposed to say? *That kiss meant everything to me; please don't take it back?* I'd beg for him over my dead body.

I don't even remember walking home. Only feeling blank and frozen, like I'd shut down. My dad was working, so I locked myself in my room. It took almost a full day for the tears to start. By then, our last semester of high school was in full swing, Emmy was making all kinds of senior year plans, and it was easier to pretend I wasn't interested in any of it because I was stressed about school than to admit her stupid brother ruined hot chocolate for me.

A week later, Emmy's parents invited me on this spring break trip from hell. Because apparently, I kicked a witch or gave cholera to a saint or something in a past life.

Jackson watches me carefully.

I take a deep breath that smells like mildew, smoke, and extinguisher chemicals. "I don't know why you're telling me all this. It changes nothing. If anything it makes what happened worse, because now I know you and your entire family were aware of my pathetic crush. I really could have done without that information."

"It's not a pathetic crush—"

"What I don't understand is what you thought this would accomplish. You did the right thing? Congratulations. What do you want, a pat on the back? How's this: Thanks for leaving me out of decisions about my own life. Thanks for not talking to *me* about any of this, and talking with your dad about things that should have stayed between us." I reach out and tap him on the shoulder twice. "Good job, pal. You did the right thing. Gold star. How does it feel?"

"Like shit!" he explodes. "It felt like shit talking to my dad instead of you. It felt like shit watching the light and excitement in your eyes go out. It felt like shit watching you avoid me this whole vacation. I hated every minute."

"So? Get over it!" I shout back.

He rears back. "Get *over it*?"

"Yes! Get over it. Deal with the guilt on your own, and leave me the hell out of it. I already feel stupid enough. You kissed the wrong girl and panicked. Stop making that my problem."

He stares at me. "I don't feel guilty for kissing you. I feel guilty because I had a chance to tell my dad to fuck off and mind his own business, and instead I ran away."

The butterflies come back full force, but I imagine them flying into a bug zapper. "You're only saying that because we're trapped on this stupid boat. I'm not Emmy. I don't do meaningless vacation flings, and if that's what you're proposing, I'm not interested."

"That's not what I—"

"You clearly ran for a reason," I insist. "And you've been perfectly content to ignore me up until now, so why don't we go back to that? All this can be a funny story we tell at Thanksgiving in ten years."

He steps closer. "I haven't been ignoring you. Not at home, and certainly not here. Why do you think I'm always reading in the same spot by the pool? You have to walk by me anytime you leave the beach for smoothies or food or the spa. I sit there like a loser, flipping pages of a book I can't focus on, hoping to catch a glimpse of you. Or I try to think of a normal way to tell you I love your new bathing suit. And that color on your nails. I notice everything you do, and it's torture. When

I saw Ben flirting with you at the resort, I practically threw my book into the ocean."

I can feel the shock on my face.

"All I do is think about you, and that was true long before we got on the plane. It's been killing me to pretend I don't care. I don't want to do it anymore."

His hands cup my face. I don't push him away.

"Wow, sounds like you might be the one with the pathetic crush," I breathe.

"Definitely."

Then he's kissing me, and for that one minute, I care a little less that we're stuck at sea, and that Emmy's fake dating a murderer, and that I'll probably get eaten by a shark out here. I'll care about all that later. Right now, there's a painful hole in my heart that's being filled for the first time since I left him on that sidewalk. A momentary reprieve from weeks of feeling like a lovesick idiot with a one-sided crush.

He threads his fingers in my hair, breaking away to whisper, "I'm sorry it took me so long to quit being a coward."

"Nobody's perfect. But if you tell me tomorrow this kiss was a mistake, I'm going to feed you to the man-eating dolphins," I say, dragging his face closer to mine.

His laugh ghosts across my skin. "Noted."

He runs his thumbs across my cheeks and kisses me again.

"What are you two—"

We break apart half a second too late. Emmy's frozen halfway down the stairs.

Her eyes ping-pong between us and slowly narrow into slits.

"Aw, crap," Jackson mumbles.

CHAPTER FIFTEEN

"My bad. When the yelling stopped, I thought you two might have killed each other down here," Emmy says. "So sorry for interrupting you and your *secret* kissing. When you're done stabbing me in the back, I'll be on deck."

"Stabbing you in the back?" Jackson says. "Could you be any more dramatic?"

"You're really going to say that to me after what I just saw?" she shouts, climbing down the stairs. Her voice echoes the inside the boat. "How long has this been going on?"

"A couple months," Jackson admits at the same time I say, "Three minutes."

Emmy folds her arms. "You two need to get your lies straight."

I frown at Jackson. "It hasn't been a couple months. We kissed once at Christmas and then again now. Nothing in between."

Jackson's jaw clenches. "I wouldn't say *nothing* in between. But you're technically correct."

Emmy looks like her head might blow straight off her shoulders. "Christmas?! You've been keeping this from me since Christmas?"

She doesn't look at her brother. Emmy's furious gaze is all for me.

My mind goes blank. I don't even know where to begin explaining this mess. I should have told her the truth when she first asked me about it, but I didn't have the words then either.

"That's my fault," Jackson says, steadying me by the shoulders when the boat pitches to the side again. "We kissed, and then I put on the brakes. I asked her not to tell anyone."

"I'm not just *anyone*," Emmy says.

"No," I say. "And I should have told you, but I felt like an idiot. Keeping it to myself meant I got to wallow in private and pretend it never happened."

I can feel the weight of Jackson's gaze. The boat rocks again, and this time it throws Emmy fully into the kitchen.

Emmy rights herself with a groan. "Well, you're clearly done with the denial, since you're down here sucking face instead paying attention to the storm." She throws herself up the stairs and out onto the deck without another word.

The regret is not only instant, it also consumes my entire body.

"Emmy, wait!" I shout.

Jackson groans and follows me up the steps after her. I don't know what I'm going to say, but an apology is a good start. She's right; I should have told her about Jackson. Shame or embarrassment be damned. I kissed her brother and lied about it.

I catch her by the wrist halfway along the side of the boat, but before I can say anything a teeth-rattling clap of thunder splits the sky. All three of us duck, and when we look up, the sky above our heads is a churning mass of black.

Emmy meets my stare. "Pause?"

"Pause," I agree.

"Yeah that's a solid idea," Jackson says.

A fresh crackle of lightning fills the sky.

Shit. These ocean storms move *fast*. The deck is already coated in a sheet of rain, and as we watch, the wind catches the sail tent and flings it off the boat and into the ocean where it drags behind us. Ben cowers at the base of the mast and bellows for help.

"We have to get him off that metal mast before he gets electrocuted," Emmy yells over the wind.

"I'll get him." I push her toward her brother. "There're two life vests on the table; each of you put one on. I'll be right behind you."

"No, I can help," Emmy says, moving back toward me.

A wave slams into the side of the boat, and she almost goes flying.

I lock eyes with Jackson, and he plucks his sister right off the deck and carries her toward the cabin. "Don't let her come back up here!" I shout at his back.

He nods and disappears below deck.

Another wave crests the top of the boat as I reach the mast. It nearly knocks me off my feet this time, and I cling to the twisted, broken metal until it recedes.

Ben spits salt water from his mouth. "Fuck! I've been yelling for you idiots for ten minutes! Get me off this thing!"

I drop to the deck behind him and start yanking at the knots around his wrists.

The boat rocks. We tip sideways over the top of one wave and slide down the other side of it, only to be pitched back up into the air by the next one.

"Hannah!" Ben yells, sounding more frantic now. "Please tell me you're making progress! I'd prefer not to die out here!"

I cast a worried look at the rising waves and yank on another loop. "I'm working on it."

"Work faster!"

Another wave tosses us up, and it feels like I've left my guts in midair. My knees lift off the deck, and I'm airborne for a second before my kneecaps take the brunt of the fall. I grit my teeth and yank another loop free, but Jackson did a good job with these knots. It's taking too long. The sky dims further as a particularly dark cloud moves over top of us. The ocean reflects it back, the waves turning almost black.

The waves seem to be getting taller by the minute.

My fingernails start to fray and splinter against the ropes.

Something comes down over my head, and I almost scream before I realize it's fluorescent orange and slightly scratchy against my cheek.

Jackson tugs the life vest into place around my chest.

"Is Emmy okay?" I shout over the wind.

"She's down below. Where you need to be."

I tug at the life vest. "This one was for you."

He scowls. "Over my dead body, Hannah."

He reaches into his pocket and flicks open Ben's knife, quickly slicing through the bindings on his wrists, and I sag with relief.

"Thank god someone's thinking!" Ben shouts, untangling himself from the ropes.

"And just like that I regret helping you," I shout.

But he's not listening. He's staring in horror over our shoulders. We spin around. A twelve-foot wall of water surges toward us. I hear Ben scream, and Jackson grabs my arm, but then my head is underwater.

Something slams into my shoulder. Pain radiates down my arm, and I gasp in a mouthful of seawater. My head clears the surface, and I spit it back out. I half expect to find myself adrift in the ocean when I open my eyes.

Instead I see Jackson.

His eyes are closed, and his face is pinched with effort. My right side is pressed against something hard, and I'm shocked I'm still on the boat. One of his arms is wrapped tight around the mast, and the other... around me.

He opens his eyes, and they fill with relief. Ben is pressed sideways against the lifelines, like a fish sputtering in a net, but he's still here with us.

Jackson points toward the back of the boat and yells over the wind. "Get below!"

Ben nods, but he wobbles toward us, which is the wrong direction.

Safety in numbers, maybe?

A gust of wind hits the same time as another wave and sends Jackson stumbling ahead of me. He reaches back for my hand, but a high-pitched scream echoes inside the cabin. Jackson's eyes widen, and he looks toward the hatch.

"Go!" I shout. "I'll grab Ben. I'll be right behind you."

Jackson keeps his weight low and scrambles to check on his sister.

Ben clings to the mast like he's genuinely in danger of being blown right off the boat. He looks absolutely terrified.

I reach back for him. "Come on! I'll help you."

He takes my hand, but instead of letting me pull him toward the cabin, he yanks me backward.

"What the hell—"

He grabs at the buckles on my life vest. "I need this! Give me your vest!"

I try and twist away from him. "What? No!"

Ben releases the top buckle and tries to rip the life vest over my head without unfastening the others. I curl my arms to my chest to keep it from slipping off, and his yanks get more frantic. "I need this, Hannah!" he shouts. "I need it more than you. You're a better swimmer!"

I gape at him. "Like that will matter out here!"

"I deserve it more!" he screams.

The sailboat groans and careens down the back of a wave, and suddenly we're falling, the deck practically vertical. I slide until I hit the set of lifelines on the opposite side of the boat. One of my legs shoots between the metal wires. The skin at the back of my thighs rips open. My feet dunk into the ocean through the railing. Ben grips the mast and screams at the top of his lungs.

The boat rights itself, and I'm thrown sideways onto the bow. Ben lunges for me. That cold glint is back in his eyes, all of his focus trained on my life vest, like it's his only salvation. Like I'm the only thing standing between him and basic survival.

I grab one of the lifelines for balance and plant my foot in his stomach, sending him sprawling back. I race along the opposite side of the boat, screaming Jackson's name. I'm only four feet from the doorway to the cabin when I'm tackled to the deck.

Ben presses my cheekbone into the soaked decking until I feel my skin split. "I'll take it from your corpse if I have to," he shouts. "One way or another, that life vest is mine."

Ben pulls his fist back—and I roll my head to the side. He punches the deck beside my face, and I hear the crack of his knuckles over the storm. He rears back with a scream, holding his hand to his chest. A blur of pink and orange grabs Ben by his wet hair.

Emmy, clad in her bright-orange life vest, twists her fingers into fists and yanks at his scalp with both hands until Ben is screeching and clawing at her hands. She slams his temple into the side of the cabin, and he drops to the deck with a groan, gripping his skull.

Jackson's standing outside the hatch, one arm extended toward us like he was in the process of helping before his sister beat him to it.

Emmy lets out a screech of frustration. "God, I really do have the worst taste in men."

I gape at her and bark out a surprised laugh.

Jackson shoves us both toward the hatch opening. "Get the fuck in the cabin!"

I hesitate. Ben's in a crumpled ball on the deck, one wave away from never being seen again, and I can't make my legs move. I may be the smasher of PlayStations, but I'm not *him*.

Jackson grabs my face. "Hannah, I need you to get below before I lose my fucking mind. Do you understand? You're getting out of this even if it kills me."

"What about him?" I ask, pointing at Ben. "Nobody deserves to die like this, Jackson."

The boat pitches up the side of another wave, and Jackson swears at the top of his lungs.

"I'll tie him to something. Get below."

There's no time for that.

I spot the emergency flotation on the deck and make a split-second decision. I lunge over the back of the seats in the cockpit. I don't dare look at the water. We're moving across it so fast, rocking left and right at angles we certainly never did during the last storm. These waves are bigger. The wind is stronger. And I don't know if the water I drained from the boat is going to be enough to keep us afloat this time.

I rip the emergency flotation off the back deck and run it to Jackson.

He levels me with a punishing glare but slams the flotation over the top of Ben's head and yanks one of his arms through it. "Here you go, asshole. Good fucking luck."

Ben grabs at Jackson's arm, screaming for help, but Jackson shakes him off. Emmy pulls me toward the cabin, and I reach back for Jackson, creating a human chain headed for safety.

Movement to our left draws my attention up.

And up.

And *up*.

A wave bigger than a bus comes out of seemingly nowhere, and it's the scariest thing I've ever seen in my life. I hear someone scream. It might have been me. Maybe it was Ben.

We're not going to make it into the cabin. I lock eyes with Jackson. Without saying a word, we both reach out at the same time and shove Emmy back through the open hatch. She tumbles into the boat. I feel Jackson try to shove me in too, but it's too late. The water surges toward us, and I know, without a doubt, that I'm about to die.

CHAPTER SIXTEEN

Something tickles the side of my face by my hairline. It moves away. Returns.

There must be a fly in the hotel room. I turn my head to shake it away. I'm too tired to do anything else about it.

The tickle resumes. I crack my eyelid open, slowly becoming aware of the rest of my body piece by piece. Sunlight sears painfully through the back of my eyes, and I lift my hand to shield my face, but it gets caught on something near my hip. My other hand clenches onto something soft with an abrasive surface. My legs are out in front of me, and when I move my ankle, I don't feel the back of my foot press into a mattress or slide across a blanket. It drops down below me with no resistance.

I'm in the water.

My eyes snap open. For a moment, all I can see is blinding, brilliant sunlight against the bluest sky. I lift my head, trying to understand what's happening, and there's nothing but water as far as I can see. I try to twist for a better view, but there's a rope tied around my waist.

Why is there a rope tied to my waist?

I untangle myself and flex my hand. The muscles in my palm and down my forearm ache when I move, and the rope left long burn marks around my arm. I grab the rope and use it to turn myself around...and pause.

The *Be-Yacht-Ch* is on its side behind me, half under water.

I wait for that to shock me, but I feel numb as I stare at it.

It's leaning so far forward that it looks one stiff breeze from flipping completely. The fiberglass bottom reflects the sunshine, curved like a beached whale. The cabin looks almost entirely submerged. Only a couple of the porthole windows remain above water. The back sticks up a little higher than the front, but conservatively about seventy-five percent of the vessel must be beneath the waves.

I have the weirdest sensation of being outside my body. I'm staring at the boat and cataloging everything that's wrong with it, but it feels like I'm watching myself bob in the water. Like it's not happening to me. Our boat is slowly sinking, I'm alone in the water, but I feel nothing. My insides are hollow. I blink over and over at the wreckage, trying to understand, but there's no understanding this. There's just destruction.

Something digs into the skin under my arms. I raise my elbow, and the sight of my skin, rubbed raw from the life vest, shakes loose some whisper of urgency.

You have to get out of the water.

I grab the rope from the surface and tug until it pulls tight somewhere on the boat. I haul myself in little by little, sliding over wide swaths of the detached sails hovering just beneath the surface.

A few feet from the boat, the stub of the snapped mast flickers in and out of sight below me. I release the rope and clumsily swim the rest of the way. The life vest makes moving my upper body awkward,

The hatch and the wheel are both underwater, but the benches on one side of the cockpit are still above the surface. I scrabble for purchase against the now-vertical decking, trying to haul myself out of the water, but it's too slippery.

I grab the railing along the back end of the boat and try using it like a ladder. Time and time again, I pull myself partway up only to fall back in the water when the muscles in my arms give out. Each time I fail, my muscles scream in protest, and the salt water stings my cracked lips and my scalp until those too go numb.

The fourth or fifth time I drag myself out of the water, I somehow manage to get my upper body up over the side of the boat and lean forward far enough to keep from falling again. Barnacles dig at my skin. I kick myself through a gap in the railing until I'm sitting half on the boat's side and half on the bottom.

My lungs burn. I sit there for what feels like a long time, letting my muscles relax and catching my breath.

I don't know what to do now. I stare down the fiberglass bottom of the boat and frown. The whale tail thing Ben said would keep us upright isn't there. A bunch of rusted out supports mar the bottom where it likely should have been attached, surrounded by a hundred thousand more barnacles.

I stretch my legs out in front of me and examine them like they belong to someone else. They're covered with cuts and bruises, but I got up on the boat without screaming in pain, so nothing must be broken.

I guess that's good.

What's left of my sunset red pedicure winks back at me like a bad joke.

I feel like I'm forgetting something, but all I can do is stare at my toes.

Eventually the life vest starts to hurt. I unbuckle it, and my shoulders ache as I slide it off. The muscles inside don't want to move, and the skin outside stings and splits as I rip open raging red sunburns with each shift of my arms. My left elbow has an almost-black bruise wrapping around the bottom that throbs when I bend it. There's a gash on one of my knuckles. I look down. The bruises continue across my ribs, and there's a cut in the hip of my bathing suit, but it's otherwise still holding together.

My hair falls over my shoulder in a stiff, salty mass, and that tickle on my forehead has returned. My fingertips dance along the edge of my scalp and catch on a slimy three-inch patch of skin that's been almost completely flayed from my skull, leaving it to flap freely in the wind.

That's not good.

The feel of my own scalp between my fingers, slick with blood, sends a burst of panic through my body. My hand falls to my lap, and I stare at the crimson stain on my fingers, at my position on the half-submerged boat, at the rope still knotted around my middle.

And the mental lights come back on.

My breath saws in and out of my raw throat. My hands start shaking, and before I know it, I'm puking over the edge of the boat as the previous night rushes back to me. The wave. The wind. The boat pitching on its side. Hands on my ribs. Screams. Being swept off the boat and then…nothing.

I whip around, staring at the eerily flat ocean around me.

Oh my god.

Where are Emmy and Jackson?

I yell their names. I even yell for Ben. Nobody answers.

I rip off the rope I don't remember tying to myself and crawl along the side of the boat. The fiberglass is so hot under the sun it burns my knees and the palms of my hands, but I ignore it. I grip the base of the lifelines like a horizontal ladder and drag myself along, screaming their names over and over and over.

I don't know how many times I call for them, but I shout long after my voice cracks and my lip splits open again. I'm met with more silence.

Dread creeps up my body. I peer over the side into the portholes, but the interior of the boat is silent. I roll to my knees, screaming again for my friends, but the only thing making any sound out here in the middle of the ocean is *me*.

I blink, and I'm sitting on the side of the hull again. I don't remember when I started crying, but tears are streaming down my face, and I can barely breathe. I stare out at the sun glinting off brilliant blue water, and I slowly slip back into the numbness.

Shock. I'm going into shock.

Or I've been in shock this entire time, maybe.

When blood starts stinging my eye, dripping from the wound on my forehead, I lie back and allow gravity to draw it away from my face. Pain burns through my chest, part physical and part all-consuming grief, as the reality of my situation sinks in.

Everyone's dead.

I'm stranded out here alone.

I never thought surviving something like this could feel like the worse outcome, but I suddenly wish I hadn't been wearing my life vest. That last wave would have taken me out. It would have been a quick death. With my friends.

Now I'll die alone.

Tears slide down my temples as I sob up at the sky. Did Jackson die quickly? Will they find his body, or is he at the bottom of the sea with Captain Keith? With Ben?

I roll the frayed friendship bracelet between my cracked fingertips.

What about Emmy? She had a life vest, but the size of those waves... I can't imagine how she could have survived that. Will some poor fisherman find her floating corpse? Will she wash ashore? What will be left of her when she does?

I think I'm going to be sick again.

I sit up to puke and hear a thump from somewhere beneath me. I ignore it and hang over the side until the nausea passes. There's nothing left for me to throw up anyway. When I sit back up, I hear it again.

Three knocks, this time.

Some of Captain Keith's things must be rattling around inside. I crawl over the top of the lifelines and slide down to the porthole closest to me. Water laps at the other side of the glass.

The sound comes again.

Three knocks.

Long pause.

Three more knocks.

Another pause.

My eyes widen. Loose items floating in the water wouldn't be that regular. There's no way. I press my ear against the side of the cabin and wait. Three more knocks. I crawl a couple feet toward the front of the boat.

The knocks are quieter.

I crawl back the other way, frantic now to prove to myself that I'm not hearing things, that this is real. That someone's still here with me.

Please, please. I can't do this alone.

Press my ear to the cabin.

Louder.

Hope blooms in my chest. "Jackson?! Emmy?!" I scream.

Three more knocks.

I scramble back, listening every foot or so for the sound, until I come to the last porthole. I cup my hands around my eyes and peer into it, surprised to find air on the other side.

My eyes adjust to the darkness inside.

And an eyeball blinks up at me.

CHAPTER SEVENTEEN

"Emmy!" I scream. Her blond hair is plastered against the glass and tangled in the shoulder of her life jacket.

She doesn't react. Her eyes are open, and she blinks, but she looks straight through me. Her middle knuckle taps against the glass three more times, and then her hand falls.

I rap my knuckles against my side of the glass, and her eyes focus on me for a second before she stares through me again.

"I'll get you out!" I yell, shoving myself back onto my knees with a much-needed surge of adrenaline. It clears my mind so quickly I no longer care that I'm battered, bruised, and burned.

I need to get Emmy out as fast as possible. There's no way to know how long this boat will continue to float, and when it sinks, her little pocket of air won't save her. She's been in there all night. It's a miracle she hasn't passed out from lack of oxygen or drowned yet.

The portholes don't open, and the hatch over Captain Keith's bedroom is completely submerged. Swimming through the main hatch is my only option. It's a significantly more *dangerous* option, but Emmy doesn't look like she can get herself out of there. I scramble back through the lifelines and wrap the rope around my waist again with shaking, painful fingers. The moment the knot pulls tight, I pencil dive back into the water. The loose skin on my scalp burns so badly, I break the surface with a gasp. I swim toward the submerged opening of the hatch. It's hard to tell how far down I'll need to swim to get through, but the opening is probably two or three feet underwater.

I don't have a dive mask. I'll have to feel my way to the air pocket.

I take several deep breaths, expanding my lungs in case I get turned around. I'm about to dive under when a thought stops me in my tracks.

Where was Jackson when the wave hit?

Ben was still on deck.

Emmy was clearly inside.

But where was Jackson?

Wasn't he by the hatch? Could he have gotten inside the boat before the wave hit?

Am I about to swim into his dead body?

I think of Emmy's unseeing gaze and shake the thought away. Whatever I find in there doesn't matter. I can't let it matter, or I'll lose her too. With one last deep breath, I dive under the water.

I kick down and pull myself through the doorframe. Inside the boat is eerily silent. Only the sound of my arms cutting through the water breaks up the stillness. The boat leans so far to my left that the little kitchenette is almost entirely below me now, and the destroyed navigation desk is above my head. The depth of the bow forces me to swim down at almost a thirty-degree angle to get farther inside. Something bumps into my shoulder, and I hold back a scream. Images of waterlogged corpses materialize in my mind, but it's too small to be a person. Some shapeless possession of Captain Keith's drifts aimlessly around in the remains of his kitchen.

Emmy's pocket of air is right by the first porthole, which is now the very top of the inside of the boat. I use the wide flat edge of the counter to drag myself through the rest of the kitchen and shove off it, toward the patch of light above me as my lungs begin to burn.

I spot something in the water that looks a lot like a blurry leg.

My heart thuds painfully in my chest.

Please be Emmy. Please be Emmy. Please be Emmy.

I can't bring myself to grab onto the ankle in case it's not. Instead I swim up to the pocket of light, bracing myself for the worst. I break the surface with a gasp and hit my head on the porthole.

Emmy's wedged into a small triangle of air, her life vest still securely strapped to her chest. Her face and right hand are pressed against the porthole glass. Her pink friendship bracelet is still wrapped tightly around her wrist.

She turns her forehead away from the window, eyes closed, and one side of her mouth tugs up into a smile. "Knew you'd find me."

I burst into tears and wrap my arms around her. She doesn't respond, but I cling to her anyway, pressing my face into her salty hair.

"God, I'm so sorry, Emmy. For every single fucking thing."

"Me too… Thought you were dead," she mumbles.

"I thought *you* were dead." I pull back, trying to inspect her injuries through the water. "Are you hurt? Is anything broken?"

"Where's Jack?" Emmy whispers.

The pain almost takes my breath away. I've purposely ignored the fact that it's only Emmy and me on this boat, but she's brought his glaring absence to the front of my mind.

He's not here.

Jackson didn't survive the second storm.

Grief slices clean through me until I'm choking back another sob we don't have time for. I pretend I didn't hear her and probe her scalp with my fingers, looking for cuts or swollen patches.

"Do you think you can swim out of here?" I ask, my throat thick with tears I won't let out.

She shrugs one shoulder but doesn't speak. When I touch the space around her temple, she groans and pulls her head away from my hands. "Stop," she mumbles.

"Does your head hurt?"

She doesn't answer me.

I cup her face in my hands. "Seriously, Em, what hurts?"

She pauses for so long, I think she's passed out. Then, "My arm."

"Which one?"

She nods toward the shoulder farthest from me. Grateful for the distraction, I swim around to her other side and carefully pull her arm from the water. I see the source of the pain before her skin breaks the surface. The light from the porthole falls across her forearm, illuminating a wrinkled white gash from the back of her wrist to her elbow. The saltwater has seeped into the edges of the gash, turning the skin almost clear. Her flayed muscle yawns open all the way to the bone. As I watch, a bubble of pus the color of earwax seeps from the wound.

"Shit."

Shit, shit, shit.

It's deep. I'm not sure how it stopped bleeding on its own, but based on the corpse-like pallor of her face, I'd bet she's lost a lot of blood.

I visualize the placement of the benches beneath me. There was a first aid kit in there somewhere. And the emergency raft. She's got her life vest to keep her afloat; if I could leave her here for a few moments, I could find—

The boat lets out a heart-stopping creak.

Nope. Never mind.

Now is not the time. I need to get her the hell out of the cabin. I can come back for the rest. The first aid kit won't help us if we're dragged to the bottom of the ocean.

I reach for the buckles of her life vest. "I have to take this off to get you out of here, okay?"

She grunts, and that's good enough for me.

The snaps all come loose, but right before I shove the vest off her shoulders, I see a strip of coral-colored fabric across her chest. I thumb the material and follow it to a bulge by her hip.

My mesh bag is draped across her body.

"Holy shit. Emmy, is that all the food?"

Her mouth quirks up. "Guess my plans don't *all* suck."

I laugh in surprise. She was stuck inside this little air bubble all night long. That strap had to have dug like hell into her shoulder, and she still kept it safe.

"Emmy, you might have just saved both our lives."

She smiles, but then her head lolls to the side like she's too tired to hold it up.

I don't think she has it in her to swim out on her own. I'll have to drag her. The boat creaks around us again, and my blood pressure rises until my heartbeat pounds in my ears. Moving quickly, I untie the rope from my body and tie it to Emmy instead. Then I pull my bag over the top of her head and slide it over mine.

I grab the porthole frame for support with one hand and Emmy's chin with the other. "I know you're tired, but I need you to do one thing for me, okay?"

She blinks and nods.

"I'm going to drag you out of here by the rope, but I have to swim to the hatch first. When I tug twice, you need to get the vest off and take a deep breath. Okay?"

She nods again.

"I'm going to need more than that, Emmy. I need you to be awake enough to do this. Can you take the vest off the rest of the way?"

"Yes," she mumbles. "You tug. I vest. Deep breath."

Uncertainty barrels through me. "I'd be more confident if you could talk in complete sentences."

She smiles, but says nothing.

I don't have a choice. Pulling her out is the fastest way. "Okay, I'm going. I mean it: Two tugs, get out of the vest, take a breath. I'll drag you out as fast as I can. If you can kick to help me, that would be great."

Her head lolls to the side. "I'll do my best."

Thank Poseidon. A full sentence.

I don't wait; I take a breath and dive under, not wanting to give her the chance to fall asleep or lose consciousness while she's waiting for me. The weight of the cans in my bag pull me down, and I let it until I'm level with the hatch opening again. I grab the counter and propel myself toward it, careful not to touch the rope so she doesn't mistake it for a tug. I clear the opening, and when I break the surface, the overhead sun is searing. I race to toss the bag up over the side of the boat with a groan of pain as my shoulders protest again.

It lands with a loud thunk, and water pours through the mesh bag, but the cans settle and stay put. Just in case, I loop the strap around a broken piece of the lifeline before I swim back to the hatch. With my luck, Emmy would go through the trouble of protecting the food all night and it'd end up at the bottom of the ocean five seconds after I got my hands on it.

I swim back to the hatch, pull the rope until it goes taut between me and Emmy, and give it two hard tugs. I count the seconds, mentally running through the time it would take her to remove the vest and fill her lungs. When I'm sure she's had enough time, I dive under, plant a foot on either side of the hatch opening, and pull with everything I have.

Right away I can feel the resistance of her body moving through the water. She's getting closer. I haul her out, trying not to imagine her smashing her head into something, or breathing water into her lungs because she'd passed out before she could take a breath. I pull faster, my heart slamming into my ribs.

What feels like hours later, I glimpse a hand in the water. I pull her through the opening and kick toward the surface. She breaks through a second after me, and I wrap my arm around her ribs.

"You did it, Em,"

She spits out water and takes her first breath of fresh air in probably half a day. "The food?"

I push her toward the back of the boat. "It's up there. I've got it."

By the time I get her to where I climbed up earlier, she's practically gasping for air. Rattling, angry breaths saw in and out of her lungs, and she looks more green than pale.

"You just have to get up on the boat, and then you can rest, okay? You've got this."

She grits her teeth and nods. I hook my arm in the railing and use it to push her up above me. Her knees wobble, but she gets one of them up on the side of the boat, and I'm right behind her, nudging her along the side of the boat toward the cabin. Once she reaches the portholes, she collapses on her side, chest heaving.

I crumble beside her.

For a while, all we do is breathe. Every muscle in my body feels like it's been punched. My eyes sting from the salt, even when they're closed. The blistering sun makes quick work of drying us, and a slow itch begins to crawl the length of my body, but I'm alive. Emmy's alive.

"Thank you," Emmy whispers.

I throw my arm around her and pull her close, fighting back tears again. "Can't let you die on our perfect BFF trip."

The ghost of a laugh escapes her lips.

Her gasping wheezes continue long after I've caught my breath. I sit up and check her face, her pulse, and the wound on her arm. Now that she's out of the water, the pus is building up. It looks awful.

And infected.

I press my hand to her forehead. She's hot to the touch.

Fuck.

I scramble back to where I stashed my bag and drag it to her. There're only four cans of food inside—condensed tomato soup, two cans of peaches, and a small can of tuna in oil—but both water bottles seem to be sealed. I open one and lift the back of her head, trying to get her to drink, but she spits out a whole mouthful before I can get her to swallow any.

I allow myself one mouthful before I put the cap back on. It tastes like salvation, but it scratches all the way down my raw throat. I zip the water back into the bag.

"Jack?" Emmy mumbles.

Grief slices through my chest again, somehow stabbing and burning at the same time. I have to tell her he's gone. That we're here alone. But I can't find the words.

How do you tell your best friend that her brother is dead?

"The...one at the..."

I look down at her. "What?"

She shakes her head. "The cold one."

"Em?"

The next thing out of her mouth isn't even English. It's an incoherent scramble of consonants and long pauses. The fever is making her delirious. I have to go back inside the boat. I need to find something to clean out that wound. Which means...leaving her up here by herself.

How can I leave her when she's barely aware of where she is or what she's saying? What if she falls into the ocean while I'm rooting around inside? I can put my life jacket on her, but I can't tie her to the boat, because I need the rope to get myself in and out of the cabin.

I ball my hands into fists.

I don't know what to do.

Emmy groans and shifts to face me, whispering Jackson's name over and over, and I turn to look out in the distance, so she doesn't see the tears pooling in my eyes.

If Jackson were here, he'd know what to do. He always does.

Did.

A light breeze drifts across my face, and I close my eyes against it. Maybe there's no point in treating Emmy's wound. What are the chances we'll make it out of this anyway? Things were dire when the boat was *upright*. When we had shelter. When there were four of us to figure out what to do together. Now we're dying in slow motion.

Maybe it's mercy to let the fever claim her in her sleep.

Could I do that? Could I sit here and watch her die?

I open my eyes and swallow against the tightness in my throat. I don't think I can get us through this on my own. I don't know enough. I'm not *strong enough* to do it alone.

Emmy groans behind me.

Strong enough or not, I can't let her suffer.

I just can't.

I grab my life vest and ignore her protests as I roll her back and forth to get it on her. She needs it more than I do. At least this way, I know she'll be safe up here. I loop the bag strap around Emmy's head, and when I sit back, something in the water catches my eye.

Directly ahead of the sunken bow of the boat.

I cup my hands over my eyes, watching something flicker in and out of sight in the bright light about three hundred feet in front of us.

What in the hell is...?

As I watch, an arm lifts into the air, and my brain pieces together what I'm seeing. It's a person. Clinging to the boat's emergency flotation.

Only the hand waving at me isn't attached to a blond sociopath.

It's attached to a mop of dark hair.

"Oh my god."

Jackson's *alive*.

CHAPTER EIGHTEEN

Before I know it, I'm in the water. I don't remember tying the rope around my waist again, or diving in. One second I'm standing on the boat, and the next I'm frantically swimming toward Jackson. I expect it to be exhausting, but the current must be working in my favor because before long, he's right there.

When I reach his side, he automatically releases an arm from his death grip on the flotation and wraps it around my back. I cling to the ring, my chest heaving.

"Where the hell did you come from?" I gasp.

His eyes are bloodshot, and his lips are peeling and split. A painful looking sunburn races across his forehead and down his nose, but he smiles. "I could ask you the same," he says, his voice hoarse. "I thought I was lost to the ocean for sure."

I lean my head against his, and this time, I don't hold back my tears. "God, I thought you were dead. What happened?"

"I was tied to the boat at one point," he says, as he nuzzles his face where my neck meets my shoulder. "But it came loose. I was trying to conserve energy in case I spotted land, but I'd pretty much given up hope."

I keep expecting him to disappear, for this all to be a mirage or something, but he smiles at me, and this is exactly what I needed. I needed Jackson to be okay. I needed his level head to help me figure out what to do next. I needed *Jackson*.

I lean in and kiss him.

When he breaks away to take a ragged breath, he's smiling from ear to ear. A rare Jackson expression.

"How's Emmy? Where is she?" he asks

My stomach sinks. "She's on board, but she's not good. Come on. She's been asking for you."

Together we swim back toward the boat. He's way more energized than Emmy. That's not surprising, considering he doesn't have a fever or a disgusting oozing wound, but he's been adrift in the ocean probably close to eighteen hours. When he said he conserved his energy, he wasn't kidding.

At the boat, he waits for me to climb up first, but the moment we're both out of the water, he goes straight for his sister. I hang back to give them a minute to gush over their mutual survival, but Emmy's not very responsive. She mumbles incoherent answers to his questions.

She needs more water.

I grab the one I opened from my bag and try to hand it to Jackson, but he shakes his head.

"Give it to Emmy. She needs it more than I do."

It's as hard as it was last time, but we finally get her to sit up long enough to drink a few mouthfuls before she lies back down.

"Do we have a plan or are we still in 'glad to be alive' mode?" Jackson asks.

"We're in 'need a plan but don't have one' mode."

"Right on schedule, I see."

I sit beside him and check Emmy's temperature again. Her cheeks are more flushed, and I don't know if that's from the sun or the fever, but I dig through my bag for the sunscreen and slather it all over her. She doesn't react at all.

I can't stop looking over every inch of Jackson, even his nerdy Sherlock shirt. How in the hell did all three of us survive this?

"What happened during the storm?" I ask.

He pauses before he responds. "The wave came out of nowhere. If it was ahead of us, we might have had a chance, but the second I saw it coming from the side, I knew it was bad."

A shiver races down my spine. I'll probably have nightmares about that wave, climbing impossibly high, for the rest of my life.

"I did the only thing I could think of. I grabbed you and held on. The wave hit so hard. I think my shirt got caught on a broken portion of the rail, because the water cleared and I was still on the deck, with you under me. You had blood running down your face, and you weren't responding when I called your name, so I grabbed the nearest rope and tied you to a metal support as tightly as I could. I barely finished tying the knot when another wave hit, and the next thing I knew, I was in the ocean with that flotation ring. I'm not even sure how I got it."

That makes two of us.

He points at my loose piece of scalp. "That doesn't look great."

I shrug. "Better than Emmy?"

"Barely."

We both turn to stare at her. She's still on her side, and from here, she looks so vulnerable, curled into the fetal position. Her injured arm is stretched out in front of her, baking in the sun. I got sunscreen all down both her arms, but I didn't want to get it too close to the wound. Pus and sunscreen don't exactly mix.

"So what do we do now?" I ask.

"You tell me."

One comment, that's all it takes for the relief of finding him alive to be replaced with annoyance. "*Me*? I'm not in charge here. You're the idea man."

"I'm fresh out of ideas. I think it's your turn." He gestures to the boat. "This thing is like an hourglass, slowly leaking the last of the air keeping it afloat. If you don't want to go down with this ship, you need to make a plan."

I scowl at him. "I know that, Jackson. I just don't know what to *do* about it."

He nods thoughtfully. His sunburn looks impossibly red, but he doesn't complain. He watches me and waits.

I wrap my arms around my knees. "There's an emergency raft in the boat."

"Can you get to it? Safely?"

"Maybe. As long as the hourglass doesn't run out of sand while I'm in there. But what good will it do us if we're still out in the middle of the ocean?"

Jackson takes a deep breath and blows it out through his nose. "Not sure, but it's better than being in the water."

"Well, aren't you buckets of help."

"We haven't even covered the possibility of you not being able to find the raft. Or it being too heavy to drag up here."

I groan and climb to my feet, carefully working my way toward the back. "Are you trying to make this seem more hopeless? I promise you don't have to. I'm aware we're probably going to die. I don't need you to confirm it."

"I'm not confirming anything. I'm pushing you to make a plan."

"Why?"

"Because you'll be dead for sure without one."

"Ugh! How can I be so happy to see you one minute and so sick of you the next?"

Jackson lets out a laugh that makes my stomach flip. "It's one of my many talents." Then he sobers. "What's the most pressing problem?"

I make a mental list and prioritize until there's a clear winner. "Emmy's fever. And the infection in her wound."

"So, step one, get her medical attention. Lucky for her, that's sort of your specialty."

"I'm not a nurse—yet. I was only raised by one."

"Which makes you the most qualified person to keep her alive. Of those left on this boat, anyway."

Ben's face flashes in my mind. I'm acutely aware that he's not only missing, but also that nobody's asked about him. He made his bed, but I feel a little bit bad about it anyway.

Right up until I remember him trying to rip the life vest from my body to save himself. If he'd been successful, I'd be dead. Without a doubt.

That takes care of the guilt pretty fast.

I shake my head. "Okay, so medical attention for Emmy. I think there's a first aid kit in the boat. There should be something in there to keep her wound closed and covered at least. Then... we need a way off this boat. If the raft is still on board, I can grab that too. There were extra snorkel masks in the storage benches around the table. That'll make it easier to find everything. The tricky part is what comes after that. How are we supposed to get to shore in an inflatable raft if we couldn't make it happen before the boat flipped?"

"A raft is easier to maneuver than a damaged sailboat we don't know how to operate," he points out. "Besides, we're fresh out of other options. We can't stay out on the ocean like this. We're too exposed. There's not enough food, not enough water. And the *Be-Yacht-Ch* is not long for this world."

I turn in a slow circle, scanning the hazy horizon. He's right again, and he's not saying anything I don't already know, but the idea of maneuvering waves in a tiny inflatable is downright terrifying. Not that there's a single cloud in the sky at the moment. But the memories are there. I don't think I'll ever look at lightning the same way again.

I look up at the sun, slowly moving through the sky toward the bow. "Fine, but we don't leave the boat unless we have no other option. That or we have something to aim for."

"Hannah."

I pull at the knot around my waist, making sure the rope is still secure. "Yeah?"

"I think we have something to aim for."

My head snaps up. In the distance, a sliver of green lines the horizon. I blink a dozen times, absolutely sure I'm hallucinating. But no matter how much I rub at my eyes, it's still there.

"Oh my god... Is that...?"

Jackson turns to me with wide hopeful eyes.

I'll take that as a yes.

The wind is to our back and the current is taking us straight toward that sliver of green.

"Mainland or island?" I ask.

"Does it matter?"

Nope.

I grab his hand and squeeze it as we stare wordlessly at our salvation in the distance. The longer we stare, the wider the sliver of green becomes until I'm almost positive we're staring at the mainland. As horrifying as it was, that second storm had its benefits. All that wind must have pitched us closer to shore.

Reluctantly I let go of Jackson's hand. "Okay, same plan but in high speed: we need the first aid kit and the raft, and we need them before the winds or currents change and we're swept farther out. Can you hang on to the other end of the rope? If I need help, I'll tug on it, and you can pull me back in?"

"Of course. I've got you."

That's all I need.

Jackson leans forward and presses his forehead against mine. "Be careful, Hannah. If this boat goes under, and you're still inside it, you won't survive."

The fear should be familiar by now. I should be able to block it out easier, but it churns my stomach. But once again, I have no other choice.

I place my hand on his cheek and smile. "I'll be right back."

He holds the rope steady. "You better be."

I take a deep breath and jump back into the water, hoping with everything I have that the raft is still on board, or I don't know what we're going to do.

This time, I get into the cabin and up to the air pocket in a flash. The air is stuffy and thinner, but it'll do. Jackson's face appears on the other side of the porthole, and I give him a thumbs-up. I refill my lungs and swim down to the table. Loose items float around my face as I go deeper.

I maneuver down to the compartments around the table and get ready to move fast. I don't want everything else to escape when I open the lid, or it'll make searching the rest of the space a nightmare. I lift the lid and wiggle my arm inside to the bicep, twisting to reach down far enough. My fingers dance around machinery parts, and all kinds of plastic and foam textures that are decidedly not a dive mask, until I run out of air. I snap the lid closed and push back to the air pocket.

I only stay long enough to take another breath, and then I'm right back where I started, shoving my arm back into the storage space but on the far side. Almost the second my hand gets near the bottom, it closes around something smooth and flat, with a nose piece.

Yes!

I snatch the mask out and swim to the air pocket. The dive mask feels like gold in my hands—there's little to no chance I'd be able to find what I need without it. Not before this boat sinks anyway. I dump the water out of it and—very carefully—slide the mask over my face without ripping that loose piece of scalp clean off my head.

This time when I dive under, the true state of the boat is clear. There's stuff *everywhere*. Plastic bags, socks, waterlogged cardboard, the now-empty plastic bin that used to hold our shoes, pot holders, plastic plates, and hand towels. The new "bottom" of the boat is littered with broken dishes and coffee cups. Almost all the kitchen cabinets have been knocked open.

Blankets from Captain Keith's bed are drifting through the door from his room. I knock items away from my face and swim down to the compartment on the other side of the table. With the mask, I spot the first aid kit right away and kick back to the surface for air.

One more item, and I'm out of here.

The boat lets out the kind of creak that makes my entire body cringe. I pause to see if it's going to flip. After the longest moment in my life, it doesn't.

I make sure the first aid kit is completely sealed inside its bag, slide my arm through the handle to free up my hands, and dive straight back to the storage compartment housing the raft. This time I don't bother being careful with the lid. I throw it open and go straight for it. The fluorescent green bag is impossible to miss. I drag it out, batting away all the other stuff that floats out with it, and lug the heavy case toward the hatch opening. Lifting this thing is like pulling a small kid out of the deep end.

I'm not going to be able to haul it up on my own. It's too heavy. The weight will drag me down with it.

I set the green bag inside the hatch opening and kick to the surface. "Jackson!"

I wait, but there's no answer. I call for him again and tug on the rope but there's no movement or tension on the other end. I can't see him on top of the boat either.

The boat lets out another groan, and I swear under my breath. Emmy must have needed something. I'm going to have to do this myself until he gets back.

I dive back down, make sure I have a good grip on the bag's handles, and kick off the boat. I break the surface and the added weight tries to drag me right back down. I struggle against the waves. Everything burns—the saltwater up my nose, my arms with the effort of holding onto the raft, my legs from trying to kick hard enough to keep me above water. The handle of the first aid kit even yanks at the rope burns on my forearm until my whole arm is on fire.

Jackson doesn't return.

Finally I reach the back railing, breathing hard. I climb back-first up the railing, dragging both the raft and the first aid kit behind me. Water streams from the bags but they don't get any lighter.

"Jackson!" I gasp.

He still doesn't appear. Biting back a plume of frustration, I take a breath and heave both items the rest of the way to the top. They land half on the lifelines and half on the fiberglass with a wet thud. I turn to rip Jackson a new one for leaving me high and dry, but my frustration dissolves into panic when I find him crouched over Emmy.

"Help her!" he begs while his sister convulses against the deck. "I don't know what to do!"

Shit.

Emmy's having a seizure.

CHAPTER NINETEEN

I scramble across the boat to get to her.

"What do we do?" Jackson asks.

"Move!"

I grab Emmy's shoulders and turn her on her side. The foam building in her mouth runs down the side of her cheek, but her airway clears. Her eyes have rolled back into her head.

"How long has she been seizing?"

"I don't know. Not long."

I start counting seconds in my head. The foam had just started building up in her mouth, so I add an extra thirty seconds. It's not a scientific way to measure what's happening by any means, but there's a time limit on seizures. Anything over five minutes is bad. Like, classified as a medical emergency, "could totally fry your brain and deprive you of oxygen for so long that you don't wake up again" bad.

The seconds pass like hours. Every time Jackson tries to talk, I shush him and keep counting. At the 139 mark, the convulsions start to slow. She shakes one final time, then slumps. I wipe the foam from her mouth again and slowly set her on her back.

Her seizure lasted about two minutes and nineteen seconds, including my thirty-second buffer. Nowhere near the five-minute mark. I think she'll be okay.

I brush my fingers down her face, and she blinks up at me. Her chest rises and falls normally. She's coming around.

"Hannah, what the hell was that?" Jackson asks anxiously. "What just happened to her?"

"She had a seizure," I say, finally pulling off the dive mask. I don't rip my scalp with it, but several strands of hair are yanked from my head.

"Why?"

"I have no idea, it could be a lot of things. She could have hit her head when the boat rolled. It could be the fever. High temperature spikes can sometimes bring on seizures. Or maybe low blood sugar? Without tests and people who know a hell of a lot more about medicine than me, there's no way to know for sure."

"Is she going to have another one?"

"If we don't stop whatever's causing it? Probably." I rip open the first aid kit but the only things inside are a bottle of calamine lotion, a plastic container of knuckle Band-Aids, a packet that says "sting relief," and a single-serve packet of Tylenol. No bandages. No gauze. Not even an ice pack. At least I can give her the packet of Tylenol. "Can you grab the open water bottle from my bag?"

He sits back and sinks his hands into his hair. "But we don't know what's causing it."

"Correct," I say, nodding toward my bag.

"So what the fuck are we going to do about it? And why are you so calm?"

For the love of... I get up and get the water myself. When I return to her side, I try not to snap at Jackson, because I know he's scared. "Freaking out won't help her, will it? All we can do is get her fever under control, get some food and water into her, and hope that addresses the problem, but we have no hope of cooling her down on this boat with no shade."

"So we have to get her to shore."

I nod and help Emmy sit up so she can take the two little pills. "As fast as possible. This Tylenol might lower her fever for a few hours, but we need a longer-term solution for keeping her temp down."

I don't bother mentioning that if she has a head injury, there's nothing I can do for her—here *or* on shore. We stand a much better chance of signaling for help if we can light a fire, so getting to the mainland is still the best plan, but if Emmy has a serious brain bleed, she'll be gone before anyone finds us. Maybe before we reach the shore.

Emmy lies back with a sigh. I stuff the empty water bottle in my bag in case we need it later and turn my attention to the life raft. Inside the fluorescent green bag, the raft itself is encased in a white hard-shell case with instructions printed on the side. Pictures too.

I read them three times. I can't mess this up.

Tie the "operation line" to something strong. Unhook the safety that's keeping the release closed. Toss the backpack shell into the water. Pull hard on the operation line until the CO_2 canisters inflate the raft. Inflation should take between fifteen and thirty seconds.

I lug the case up to where the water laps at the front of the boat and quickly tie the operational line to the railing. I follow the directions to the letter, and when I yank on the cord, a bright green octagonal raft unfurls with a hiss. It's about eight feet across, with a fluorescent canopy that pops up automatically, filling the inside with the first bit of shade I've seen since I woke up floating in the water.

Jackson comes up behind me and nods toward the growing line of trees in the distance. "How far do you think it is?"

I wring my hands together. "I read once that the human eye can only see three miles. The curvature of the earth cuts off after that." I shield my eyes with my hand and squint into the distance.

"If we're squinting, I'd say it's right up against the three-mile mark then," he says.

"Yeah. Maybe two and a half. Either way, it's going to be a swim."

"How heavy is the raft?"

I frown. "It said sixty pounds on the carrying case."

Jackson looks down at me, but he doesn't say anything. He doesn't have to. Emmy needs to get in the raft. There's no way around that. But pushing her almost three miles through the current with the added weight of the raft isn't going to be easy. The raft doesn't seem to have any oars. There's definitely no motor.

We only have two sets of tired legs attached to hungry, sleep-deprived bodies.

Emmy mumbles something and Jackson goes to check on her. I grab the first aid kit and my bag, and toss both into the far side of the raft before I join him. I check Emmy's pulse, and it's strong. At the touch of my fingers on her wrist, she turns her head and cracks open one eye.

"Hannah?"

"Hey, Em. I've got you."

She shakes her head, but I get the feeling she's not fully aware she's doing it.

I slip my arm under her shoulders, and she groans.

"You're going to hate me in a second," I tell her. "But you have to get up, okay? As soon as you're in the raft, you can lie down for a long time. It's only a few feet. You can do this."

She makes all kinds of noises, but after four attempts, I get her up. We half fall, half stumble our way across the boat, while Jackson hovers anxiously behind us, shouting warnings about the slippery fiberglass. The *Be-Yacht-Ch* lets out another horrible groan, like it's shouting goodbye, and all I can see in my mind is it sucking us under with it when it sinks. Finally we're close enough that I can pull the raft close and ease her inside.

"You next, Jackson."

He looms over my shoulder. "Aren't you going to need help kicking to shore?"

"Later. Right now I just want to push us away from this cursed boat."

He nods and brushes past me, wedging himself between Emmy and the food bag, leaving as much room for me as possible. I untie the rope from the boat, take a running leap, and launch myself into the raft.

The momentum sends us spinning, and we drift away from Captain Keith's boat. It feels more final than anything else we've done so far. After being trapped on that neglected thing this whole time, it's strange to leave it, even when it's half submerged.

The sun beats against the canopy, turning the inside of the raft an eerie green. Still, it's a relief to have a break from the sun. I peek out the opening in the canopy and watch us drift farther from the *Be-Yacht-Ch*. It lets out another groan. It's sinking for real this time.

It's time to start swimming like hell, but I'm stalling. Jackson notices.

"Take your time," he says. "There's no rush."

"There is though. I just hate the idea of sinking my legs into miles of ocean again."

"We're closer to land. It might only be *a* mile now."

I glare at him.

He laughs and reaches out to take my hand. "I'll be right there with you. One more swim, and we'll be on shore. It's going to suck, but you can do it. You can get this raft to the mainland."

I exhale. *I can get this raft to the mainland.*

I look down at Emmy. For her, I can do this.

Jackson goes in first, sliding his feet out the canopy opening. He holds on to one of the ropes that circles the outside of the raft and waits for me. I slip in beside him, hating every single second, and with a good grip on the raft, we start swimming.

This is a marathon, not a sprint. We'll burn out if we swim too fast, so instead we opt to kick at a slow and steady pace, and surprisingly, the wind seems to help. It catches inside the canopy, and I can feel it taking some of the weight off.

Unfortunately I can also feel when the wind shifts, making it monumentally *harder* to make progress. But I focus on the simple mechanical movement of kicking. My muscles burn, and my heart beats wildly in my chest, but we keep going.

Jackson's a machine. Head down, hands fisted beside mine on the raft supports—he never seems to slow. Still, even with his help, it's harder than I expected.

Every time I have to stop to catch my breath, I feel like I'm wasting progress. Every time the wind changes and it gets harder to kick, it feels like we'll never reach the shore. Every time I peek to see how much farther we have to go, my heart sinks.

"Stop it," Jackson says, glaring at me.

I glower back, but I'm too out of breath to respond.

"I know what you're doing. Stop being so hard on yourself. If you need to take a break, take a break. It doesn't make you weak."

Tears prickle at the backs of my eyes. "Fine."

He grins and bumps me with his shoulder. "You know I'm right."

I do, but I won't admit it.

"Look behind us," he says.

When I do, I see the *Be-Yacht-Ch* off in the distance. It's nothing but a little white blip, and it's a lot farther away than I expected.

"Holy shit."

"See? You're doing great. Catch your breath and keep going."

So I do.

The sun climbs overhead until it's shining directly onto my back. I should have put more sunscreen on before I got back in the water, but there's nothing I can do about that now.

After what's probably hours, I peek around the raft and a smile breaks out across my face.

"We're almost there!"

I can clearly see land now. It stretches out in either direction as far as I can see. We're close enough that the Sierra Madre mountains emerge from the haze, rising into the distance like sentries. If I squint, I can even see the palm trees lining the shore.

"Told you," Jackson says. "You're in the home stretch. Take another break, and then we'll power through."

I climb back into the raft to check on Emmy again. She's been asleep every other time I checked on her, and her eyes are closed now too. I want to shake her awake, tell her that we're almost back to shore, but she needs her rest. She's still far too pale.

I ignore the worry in my chest. The moment we get to land, we have to find a way to keep that fever down.

Once I've caught my breath, I sink back into the water and start kicking again.

Something drifts around my ankle and sends a skittering tingle along my skin. My whole body shudders, and I kick faster. This is not the moment to lose my cool.

When I feel the same tingle farther up my leg, I look down, but I can't see anything. The ocean is far from clear after the storms, and the sun glints off the surface, making it almost impossible to see underneath.

The tingle appears at my elbow and again by my knee. I kick out and feel it on the other side of my leg, stronger this time. Like little electric currents pinpricking the length of my calf. I reach down to brush my hand along my leg, and feel the sting along my forearm, then the underside of my arm.

"Ouch! Fuck! What's in the water?"

Jackson startles at my shouting. He cuts a hand through the water, hand splayed. "I don't feel anything."

The stinging is along nearly every piece of my skin beneath the water. It doesn't *hurt* hurt. It's more annoying than painful, but the salt water makes it worse. Soon everywhere I felt the tingle begins to burn. I kick down, wondering if it's sharp seaweed floating in the surf. Is that a thing? Sharp seaweed?

A new pain sears the underside of my wrist.

When I pull my arm from the water, it's covered in dime sized welts that are rapidly shifting from pink to red. They climb my arms, and undoubtedly both of my legs, like irritated Dalmatian spots, some much larger than others. One welt twists around my wrist in a long thin line.

"Hannah," Jackson breathes, letting go of the raft with one hand to run his fingers down my skin, following the red line to where it stops by my wrist bone. "What the hell is this?"

This time, when I look down, a translucent blob about the size of a half dollar floats beneath the surface beside me. As I watch, the outline of another, smaller blob appears, and then I understand.

I swear under my breath.

"We're trapped in a swarm of jellyfish."

CHAPTER TWENTY

We keep swimming, because what other choice do we have? And soon, as quickly as the stinging began, it disappears again. The welts still burn like a bitch, but the sensation of being jabbed with little razors stops.

We must have made it to the other side of the swarm.

I'd sigh with relief if I had any hope of catching my breath.

A wave crests behind us and nearly face-plants me into the raft. I stay there for a second, face pressed against the fluorescent green material, wishing I could close my eyes. Only for a month or two.

"Keep swimming, Hannah," Jackson says, nudging my shoulder. "You're almost there."

By some miracle, my legs keep moving. Though I don't think I'll be able to stand upright once we reach solid ground.

The waves pick up as we get closer to shore, and they save my ass. Each one grabs the raft and propels us closer to dry land. We're so focused on plowing ahead that I don't realize how close we are until my toes graze rock and sand.

I look up in shock. The beach looms a hundred or so feet ahead of us. *Oh my god, we did it.*

A particularly large wave all but spits us up onto the wet sand. We use the last shred of our energy to give the raft one final push, and it comes to a stop just out of reach of the waves.

I stumble, dizzy and exhausted, onto the sand beside the raft, and my legs give out as predicted. Between the sunburn and jellyfish welts, it feels like rubbing sandpaper along every inch of my furious skin as I lie down. I gasp for air, staring straight up into the pink sky.

The sun is already going down.

It was midday when we started.

My fingers curl into the hot sand, and I hang on like someone's going to come along and drag me back to sea.

"Jackson?"

There's a long pause, then, "Yeah?"

"You okay?"

"I'm okay." He sounds winded for the first time since we set off, his voice barely audible from the other side of the raft. "I knew you could do it."

Despite everything, I smile.

My muscles ache, and I'm certain I've never been this tired in my entire life, but I have to get up. I have to help Emmy. With a groan that comes from my very soul, I roll into a sitting position and crawl toward the raft opening.

Inside, Emmy's still curled into a fetal position, the shoulder of her life vest serving as a pillow. She mumbles under her breath. I lean closer.

"...too hot...in the water...he's in the water..."

"Em?"

She shakes her head. "Can't get him out... It's on fire."

I want to crawl into that raft with her and sleep, but I can't rest until she's okay. I grab my bag and dig around for my metal water bottle. If the seizures were from dehydration, she needs water. Lots more water than we currently have.

"Stay with Emmy," I say, peeking at Jackson around the back of the raft. He's flat on his back, knees bent. When he hears my voice, he turns his head. "I'm going to see if I can find a stream or something."

"Will the water be safe?"

I shrug. "I don't know, but we don't have a lot of choices."

"No, I guess not."

"Keep an eye on her. If she wakes up, see if she'll drink that last bottle of water?"

He nods and sits up on his elbows. "Please be careful?"

I tip the water bottle toward him. "I'll think about it."

His laugh follows me down the beach. "You're a punk, you know that?" he calls after me, and despite the stress residing in every inch of my body, I grin.

For the first time, I really take in where we are.

White sand stretches out on either side of us with absolutely no sign of anything resembling civilization. The trees begin about thirty feet from the water, and they get thicker and thicker until they form a wall of green in front of me. Mountains tower behind them, layered with a dense blanket of jungle foliage, and I suddenly feel very small and vulnerable.

The sand burns the bottom of my bare feet. I pick my way across the beach as fast as I can, but my muscles are Jell-O wrapped around toothpicks. I'm lucky to be walking at all.

Angry red welts cover nearly half my legs, and a mean-looking sting wraps around the back of my knee. Every time I take a step with that leg, the skin pulls, and I wince. I didn't even know Mexico *had* jellyfish. Just my luck I'd swim through a whole family of them.

The edge of the jungle is silent, but deeper in there's a low hum of bugs. I stay close to the tree line—no good can come from venturing too far in—and slowly pick my way through palm trees until the vegetation gets thicker.

I hope more plants mean more water. It's a shot in the dark.

I round a clump of trees as tall as me and almost step on a bunch of yellow blobs on the ground. It takes me a second to realize they're mangoes. I rip a fresh one off the tree so fast it sends the branch springing into the air when the fruit detaches. I bite right through the skin. I don't know if mango skin is edible, but I also don't give a shit. The fruit's nowhere near ripe; it's like chomping into a hard peach. Still, it's the best thing I've ever eaten. The mango juice makes my mouth water, and I rip off a piece of the peel and press it to my cracked lips with a sigh.

I eat two more all the way to the pit before I force myself to resume my water search. I take several with me as I reluctantly stagger away, though. If Emmy wasn't in that raft, I'd probably sit here eating these until I threw up.

More vegetation blocks my path, and I weave around a particularly fat palm tree and run straight into a stream. I gape at the water and have another mirage moment, but sure as shit, clear water runs over dark rocks, slowly headed for the ocean to my right. All the mangoes fall from my arms. I drop to my bruised knees and plunge my hands into the water, acutely aware of the layer of salt covering my body.

The stream is only about two feet deep in the middle, but the water is blissfully cool, and soon I'm submerging my arms and legs as far as I can reach, gently running the water over the jellyfish stings. I dunk my sunburned face. The relief is instant. The stream feels like it's purging the sweat and dirt and salt and heat from every place it touches.

The cold water brings down the temperature of my sunburn, and I sit up with a gasp. This is how I'm going to bring Emmy's fever down. I quickly gulp down a couple handfuls of water, refill the water bottle, and sprint back to the beach.

Emmy's in the same spot.

Jackson is not.

I skid to a stop in the sand and spin in a circle looking for him, but he's nowhere in sight. "Jackson?" My voice carries down the beach, but there's no response.

A spike of fear courses through me, but there are no drag marks in the sand. It's not like he got hauled off by a wild animal. He's probably walking along the beach, scouting for help. I climb into the raft with Emmy. If he's not back in ten minutes, I'll freak out, but right now I need to focus on her.

I unbuckle the straps of her life vest and gently tug it off her. She doesn't react at all. I put my hand behind her head and lift her face toward me. Her eyes move behind her closed lids, but she still doesn't open them. I dump half the contents of my water bottle down her face.

She spits water everywhere and gasps, eyes lazily locking on me.

"Stay awake," I say.

I grab the coral bag and pull Emmy up until she's sitting. She blinks about a dozen times, and her eyes don't really focus on my face, but she stays upright.

"Come on," I say, turning to wrap her good arm around my neck. She barely has a grip, so I clamp one hand on her wrist and the other on her hip, and stand. It takes every last bit of my energy to get up and out of the raft with her on my back, and I stumble to the side. Black dots blink in and out of focus around the edge of my vision, but I don't pass out and I don't fall over.

It takes me three times as long to trudge back to the stream half walking and half staggering with Emmy. At the water's edge my knees finally give up, and at the last second I drop my shoulder and all but dump Emmy into the water.

Her eyes fly open, and she gasps and claws at me like she can't quite tell her ass is resting on the bottom. I hold her head above the surface and seat myself behind her shoulders. I whisper soothing things to her until her spine relaxes. I slowly tilt her head back until her hair is running down her bare shoulders and her scalp is cool to the touch. I dip my hand in the water and press it against her forehead, her cheeks, the underside of her chin, as the sun sets in front of us. Slowly, I feel the temperature of her body drop.

The relief is so intense that I almost burst into tears.

When Jackson appears at my shoulder, I do.

He crouches beside me. "Hey! What's wrong?"

"Where did you go?"

He points toward the beach. "Emmy wouldn't wake up long enough to drink anything, so I walked down the beach to see if I could find help."

"Did you?"

"No, but I didn't want to leave her alone for long, so I didn't go very far before I turned back. Scared the hell out of me when nobody was there, but I saw your footprints in the sand."

I pool more water in my hand and run it down the top of Emmy's scalp. "The stream is keeping her cool. I think I can keep her fever from spiking if I can treat her arm, but I don't know how to do that with knuckle bandages and sunscreen."

Even I can hear the frustration in my voice.

"You don't have to save her all by yourself, Hannah. You just have to keep her alive long enough for someone to find us. She doesn't need you to turn yourself inside out trying to create medication from tree bark. She needs you to get her to an emergency room, high-dose antibiotics, and IVs."

I almost laugh. "So what you're saying is, I have to stop channeling *Grey's Anatomy* and lean more... *Cast Away*?"

Jackson smirks. "Something like that."

The gears start turning. We're on shore. We have more resources at our disposal than we had on the boat. We can start a fire. A *big* fire.

Jackson is right. I don't need to perform medical miracles out here.

I have to make us easy to find.

Slowly Emmy becomes more alert. I get one of the cans of peaches from my bag and make her drink all the syrup, to get some sugar into her system. The more she drinks, the more color comes back to her face. She even manages to chew up most of the peach slices. I convince her to finish our final water bottle. Once that's gone, I switch to the stream water.

We probably sit there for upwards of an hour. Long enough for the sun to sink below the horizon and the sky to dim. I would have stayed all night if it meant she didn't have another seizure.

When her skin is almost the same temperature as the stream, it finally feels safe to pull her out. The running water cleaned a lot of the sludge out of her arm too. I pull a wide leaf from the mango tree and press it against her wound to keep sand and bugs out of it.

She walks almost all the way back to the beach, and seeing her hold her own weight has me grinning from ear to ear. She's still exhausted and not entirely coherent, but it's a huge improvement. The second she's back in the raft, she lies down again, and I don't stop her.

Jackson climbs in beside her and rubs her back while she drifts off. "You should get some rest too," he suggests. "You're dead on your feet."

My body is practically screaming at me to listen to him. The thought of closing my eyes for even an hour sounds incredible, but there's one more thing we need before it's fully dark.

"I'll rest as soon as I get a fire going." I dig the calamine lotion out of the first aid kit and quickly slather it all over my jellyfish stings so I'm not scratching my skin to the bone while gathering firewood. When I'm done, I slather it on my sunburns too, then toss it at Jackson for his.

He sets it on the bottom of the raft with a frown. "Do you have enough time to start a fire?"

I stand and eye the horizon. With the sun gone, the sky is getting darker by the minute. More stars blink into view above my head. "I have Ben's lighter, and the beach is littered with driftwood. It shouldn't take too long to get it going, and we'll be a lot safer this close to the jungle with a fire."

Even now, the shadows grow between the trees. Soon it will be a wall of darkness.

Jackson gets up to help me, but I hold out a hand to stop him. "Stay with your sister. She shouldn't be by herself if we can help it. I've got the fire handled."

"Are you sure?"

"Positive. How hard could it be?"

CHAPTER TWENTY-ONE

I'm a miserable lousy failure.

A collection of football-sized rocks circles the stack of driftwood I collected. The more I stare at my terribly built fire pit in the moonlight, the angrier I get. My hand tightens around the lighter in my palm.

Jackson was right. The lighter came right back to life after it dried, but it turns out, even the best lighter isn't much help to an incompetent fire builder. Time and time again, the flame licked along the withered leaves and small branches I collected from the forest, only to smoke itself out rather than catch on the main pieces of wood. I used every last bit of daylight and still couldn't get it going.

I had all the gumption and absolutely none of the skills.

Jackson and Emmy have been out like a light in the raft for hours, but I can't bring myself to wind down enough to actually fall asleep. It's so much darker here than back home. The moon casts weak light along the beach, but I've been leaning against the outside of the raft half the night, and my eyes are no closer to adjusting to the dark than when the sun first disappeared.

And the jungle won't *shut up*.

Can you overdose on adrenaline? I feel like I might.

The bugs I thought were so loud during the day are screaming now. Every buzz, every rustle of leaves becomes some kind of animal ready to jump out and rip my face off. The adrenaline feels like sludge moving through my veins while I wait for something to jump out at me.

So instead of sleeping, I sit motionlessly and wait for the sun to rise again.

How long can we survive out here by ourselves? I'm already hyperaware of what little food we have left. Just one can of tomato soup, one more can of peaches, and some mangoes from the beach.

Emmy woke up in the middle of my bonfire failure, and I made her to eat half a can of tuna before she passed out again. I had to smash the can between two rocks to get to the fish inside. It was the first protein any of us has seen in days. I tried to split the other half with Jackson, but he argued with me until I caved and ate it. I don't even like tuna, but I inhaled it, and when the fish was gone, I dipped my finger in the bits of oil left in the broken can and spread it on my lips to sooth the cracked sunburned skin. It was the closest to content I've been since we left the resort. I can still taste the fish and the oil on my lips, and I sigh.

If we're here for more than another day, I'm going to have to find us another source of protein, and that means going back in the water to catch some unsuspecting fish. One I'll have no way of cooking because I can't even manage to light *a simple fire*.

I fight the impulse to throw the lighter into the ocean and tuck it into my bathing suit top instead. Tomorrow is a new day. I just have to get through tonight, and then I can figure out where I went wrong with the fire in the morning.

The raft rustles, and Jackson steps out. Without saying a word, he comes to sit beside me, his thigh pressed against mine as he leans back against the raft.

"Why aren't you sleeping?" he whispers.

I shrug. "Someone has to keep watch."

"In that case, it's my turn."

I sigh. "I don't think I can sleep."

Without a word he puts his arm around my shoulders. "If you don't want to sleep, neither will I. The least I can do is keep you company."

Warmth spreads through my chest, and I turn to look at his profile in the dark. "You're doing it again."

"Doing what?"

"Saying the exact thing I want to hear."

He laughs and stretches his legs out in front of him. "I don't think that's entirely true. I'm sure there're are lots of things I should have said to you that I never did."

Well. He has me there.

"Maybe."

He's quiet for so long, I wonder if he fell asleep sitting up. A heaviness settles into the back of my head, and I wonder if him sitting here is all I needed.

Jackson's arm tightens around my bare shoulder. "I'm really hating how everything played out on this vacation, but I have to say, there's nobody I'd rather be stranded with on a deserted island than you."

My laugh seems too loud across the dark beach. "We're not *on* a deserted island."

"Semantics."

I smile and close my eyes. "Yeah, well, you're a pretty good castaway companion yourself."

He's quiet again. It's no less dark, the jungle no less scary, but it feels more manageable when I'm not sitting here by myself.

"I shouldn't have ended things the way I did," he says.

I'm unprepared for the change in subject and sit in shocked silence for a few seconds.

When I say nothing, he must get nervous because he starts talking faster than before. "I just…wanted you to know that. 'The one that got away' should know she's 'the one that got away.'"

The one that got away.

I don't know if I want to cry or roll my eyes. Why does it take us almost dying in the middle of nowhere for him to finally tell me what I've wanted to hear all this time?

He removes his arm from my shoulder, and I wonder if he thinks I'm upset. I take his hand and interlock our fingers in the sand between us. It's still warm from the hot day.

"Do me a favor?"

"Anything," he says, without hesitation.

"Tell me all this again when we're back home."

Translation: tell me I mean something to you when the threat of death is no longer coloring every single thing we do. Even our kiss on the boat was in the midst of a catastrophe.

He shifts beside me. "Whatever you need, Hannah. I'm here."

CHAPTER TWENTY-TWO

The boat gently rocks in the wind. I stand at the helm, watching the white sails billow out above my head against a sky full of stars. It's beautiful, but every once in a while, the star I'm looking at will vanish. I shift my gaze to another, and then that one snuffs out too. Soon it seems like the sky is half as bright as it was.

"You better be careful."

I jump. Captain Keith stands over my shoulder. He's shirtless, and the slowly dimming moonlight barely illuminates the tattoo across his chest. Only now, instead of "NICKELBACK," it says "BETRAYAL."

"You never know what's waiting for you out there."

I frown. "What do you mean? Up in the sky?"

He shakes his head and gestures toward the side of the boat.

I blink again, and the helm is gone. We're on the sand, staring at a wall of jungle. A small light comes from inside a bright green raft beside us, but when I take a step toward it, something inside growls.

I freeze, and Captain Keith laughs. "You shouldn't worry about what's in there. You should be worried about what's out there."

I follow the direction of his shaking finger, toward the jungle.

Except we're no longer looking at it from the shore; we're pressed right up against the trees. They loom above us. I take a step back, but Keith wraps a hand around my upper arm and holds me in place, tsking at me. "Hannah, Hannah, Hannah. Don't you know? What the jungle wants, the jungle gets. And the jungle wants you."

A pair of yellow eyes opens in the darkness right in front of my face. They narrow, and before I can scream, a panther leaps from the shadows, claws extended, and tackles me to the ground with a snarl.

I scramble backward, screaming my head off for a full ten seconds before I realize it's not dark. I'm not standing by the trees. There is no panther. I'm lying in the sand beside the raft, and the sun has long since risen.

I get to my feet and look around, pressing a hand against my heart.

God, it was only a dream.

If I thought I was scared of the jungle before, I'm terrified now and I don't even know if panthers are native to this part of the jungle.

I run my fingers through my crusty, greasy hair—careful to avoid the scalp flap—and let out a sigh while I wait for my body to recognize there's no immediate danger and unlock the rest of my muscles. I shake out my arms and roll my shoulders, moving toward the edge of the water. I look up and down the beach. It's quiet except for the gentle crash of the waves as they roll in and slide over the tops of my feet. The sound of the water eventually calms my heart rate.

The sun is up over the trees at my back. If I had to guess, it's probably somewhere between eight and ten in the morning. I have no idea when I finally fell asleep, but as tired as my body feels, it couldn't have been too long before dawn. I feel like a towel that's been wrung out one too many times.

My stomach clenches painfully, and I wrap my arms around myself. I have to make Emmy eat and check her wound again. She's probably due another trip to the stream before I start on this fire bullshit again too. If I manage to get it started this time, one of us is going to have to bounce between her and the fire all day while the other hikes down either side of the beach to look for help. But with the stream and the fruit alone, we're so much better off than we were on the boat.

All we have to do now is survive long enough to be rescued.

I climb into the raft, and I stop in my tracks.

Something's wrong.

Emmy is fine. She's still warm, but not as feverish as she was on the boat, and her pulse is strong. I peel back the mango leaf, and her wound is disgusting, but it doesn't look any worse. The sunlight glints off a piece of her bone, and I quickly cover it back up.

Jackson, too, is fine. He's sleeping soundly beside his sister. Neither of them seem to be the cause of the alarm bells ringing in my head. My gaze slides around the inside of the raft, and I do a double take.

My bag is gone.

I lunge forward and run my hands along the bottom of the raft, which is ridiculous, because if I can't see the coral-colored mesh in this little space, it's clearly not here. That doesn't stop me though. I climb back out of the raft and run around the outside, checking the sand in case Jackson moved it—though I don't know why he'd do that.

No bag.

It's gone, and with it, all our remaining cans of food, the mangoes we collected, my water bottle, my useless phone, and the first aid kit.

The jungle looms over our little campsite, and I feel eyes on me. I scan the trees, but nothing moves beyond them. I scramble back to the raft and shake Jackson's leg until he sits up, blinking hard. I wave for him to follow me, and he does, blearily rubbing his eyes.

When we're more than a dozen feet from the raft Jackson pulls me to a stop by the water's edge. "What's wrong?"

"Did you move my bag?"

He shakes his head.

There goes my best-case scenario. "The food is gone."

Jackson takes a full four seconds to respond. "What do you mean?"

"Our tiny collection of food? All our hope for survival? Everything we had? It's gone. My bag isn't in the raft anymore."

He runs a frantic hand down his face and turns away, like he means to check the raft himself, then thinks better of it. "Well, where did it go?"

"That's a fantastic fucking question, Jackson. How the hell should I know?"

He glowers at me.

I sink to the sand and drop my face into my hands. "Sorry, sorry. That was rude. I'm just stressed out. I don't understand what happened."

"Maybe an animal smelled the tuna and dragged it off?"

That hits a little too close to my dream for comfort. The idea of some animal emerging from the forest and getting close enough to grab a whole bag of our food without waking us is the stuff of nightmares.

We need to get the hell out of here before whatever animal big enough to cart off a bag full of cans comes looking for more and we're all that's left.

I jump to my feet, grab Jackson's arm, and drag him toward the trees. "Come with me. We need some drier wood. We're getting that fire going even if it kills us."

Jackson winces. "Interesting choice of words."

We pick our way through the edge of the jungle, skirting giant rocks and clusters of trees until the canopy overhead is so thick that the vegetation on the ground is drier than anything we've seen so far. I grab a collection of larger branches and brush, tucking dried leaves on top of the pile. When my arms are full, I run back to the relative safety of the beach.

I make a pyramid shaped pyre with the brush and dried leaves underneath and pull Ben's lighter from my bathing suit. The metal is warm from my body heat. I light several of the leaves, blowing on the tiny flames to get them to spread.

"You got it," Jackson says, carefully watching the fire beside me. "Put more leaves there at the bottom. And another smaller branch too. It needs to fully catch on the little stuff before the larger chunks will burn."

I do what he suggests and watch in amazement as the flame actually builds against the larger wood pieces this time. The drier wood makes a world of difference. I should have known not to trust anything on the beach to be dry all the way through. After a few minutes, the fire is small but growing. Once everything in the circle of stones is engulfed in flame, I rip several fresh branches off nearby bushes and smaller trees and lay them across the top of the fire. Right away the green wood starts smoking up a storm, and I watch in satisfaction as it curls toward the sky.

While I wait for the fire to spread through the green branches, I dig giant letters into the sand beside the fire with my hands.

HELP

"What are you doing now?" Jackson asks. He pokes at one of the logs with a stick and sparks fly up in the air, intermingling with the smoke.

"If there's a search party out there, I want to make it easy to find us. I'm going to make the fire as big as I can, but if the smoke catches anyone's attention from the air, I want them to know right away we're not here by choice."

"How very *Cast Away* of you."

"You know, I've never actually seen that movie," I say, finishing up the *E* and clapping sand off my hands.

"It's pretty sad. The guy has nobody to talk to, so he makes friends with a volleyball."

I heft a rock from the tree line and stop to stare at him. "Wait... really?"

"Really."

I drop the rock in the middle of the *L* and go back for another. "Too bad we're fresh out of volleyballs."

He pokes at the fire again, and another spark shoots off. "You don't need a volleyball. You have Emmy."

We both look toward the silent raft, and I take a step toward it.

Jackson shakes his head. "Finish your letters. I'll check on her."

A few dozen trips later, my message is clear as day, carved deep into the sand and covered in dark rocks from the forest. Each letter is about as big as the raft. If we can get the smoke high enough, someone might spot us. By boat or air, I'm not picky.

The sun is almost directly overhead, and it's humid as hell as I cross the scorching sand to get back to the raft. Jackson's worrying at his lip beside Emmy when I climb in.

The empty space where my bag used to sit taunts me, and I scowl at it while checking Emmy's fever. As if I don't have enough on my plate already, now we're going to have to scrounge up more food and water too. And without a water bottle to hold it, keeping us all hydrated is going to be a hell of a lot harder.

I can't wrap my head around what kind of animal could drag my bag out of here without any of us hearing it. The thing was full of metal. How did it drag all that away without clanging up a storm?

"You look angry," Jackson says. "Should I tell the locals to hide their PlayStations?"

"Hilarious." I scratch at my jellyfish stings with the tips of my fingers, trying not to break the skin.

He nudges my shoulder. "What's on your mind?"

"I have a really bad feeling about our stuff going missing. What kind of animal steals a first aid kit? And mangoes that are readily available on the ground?"

"It might be weird if we *only* lost the first aid kit, but it was all in the same bag. There's probably a pile of bandages in the dirt somewhere, discarded by whatever licked the tuna can clean."

Maybe. It still doesn't sit right with me.

Emmy rolls to her side and winces. I check her wound, and more green pus has started to form around the bone. I need to clean her arm in the stream again and get her a new mango leaf. The open yawn of her skin makes me wince, and I wonder if I can find a palm frond or something to pull the skin together.

"She needs to go to the stream again," I say. "Can you look for more food while I take her?"

"Of course."

We split up in the trees. Jackson squeezes my hand and kisses his sister on the cheek before he disappears on his own mission. Emmy and I stumble to the creek, and I make quick work of her wound in the water. She cools down much faster this time and protests loudly when I tie her gaping wound closed with long strips of palm frond, which I think is a good sign. It means she's alert enough to notice the pain. But she's more lethargic on the way back to the raft, and when she lies down, she's babbling nonsense again intermingled with Jackson's name.

We *have* to get her out of here.

After what feels like a long time, Jackson comes staggering out of the trees...empty-handed. He trudges toward me and frowns. "I couldn't find anything."

Frustration balls my hands into fists so tight, my knuckles scream in protest. "What do you mean you couldn't find anything? There's fruit everywhere."

He holds up his hands, looking significantly more wary than a second ago. "I can go back—"

"No. I've got it," I snap. "Someone needs to hike the beach to look for help anyway; I'll see what I can find on the way back. Stay here and keep an eye on Emmy, if you think you can handle that."

The moment the last part leaves my lips I regret it.

Hurt flashes across his face.

I close my eyes and try to relax my hands. "I'm sorry, I shouldn't have said that. The sleep deprivation is starting to get to me."

"It's okay. Do you want me to hike the beach for you?"

I force a smile and blurt out the first excuse I can think of. "No. Emmy's going to want to see you when she wakes up. You're better off staying here to keep the fire going."

And I'm better off taking a lap before I bite his head off again.

He holds my stare for a long time before he nods.

I hurry down the left side of the beach before he can say anything else. We can't turn on each other now or we'll never make it out of this.

I keep to the hard-packed sand by the water to save my feet from the burning hot sand. The beach curves in a gentle arc that seems to go on forever, long after I lose sight of the raft. The sun climbs through the sky above me until I'm covered in sweat. Eventually the smooth sand transitions to small rocks before abruptly climbing up to some kind of stone outcropping that hangs over the ocean. I can't see over the top—it has to be over twenty feet high—but I've already walked at least two miles, and I can't turn back now without seeing what's on the other side.

My feet slide on the smooth charcoal-colored rocks, and I shear off half my fingernails, but I eventually make it to the flat rock along the top. When I stand, all the wind that had been blocked by the rocks hits me in the face and dries the sweat on my body. The outcropping is surrounded with jagged rocks so sharp they look like teeth sticking out of the ocean.

The beach on the other side curves sharply inward in a long, almost pear-shaped inlet that's *miles* long. The far end veers back in on itself and out of sight.

The whole stretch is nothing but water and jungle.

My shoulders sag, and I curl my bloodied fingers into fists at my side, breathing hard.

Fuck.

I debate continuing to the next bend, but it'll take hours to get there, and I still have to explore the other direction and find us all food before nightfall. Turning back feels a lot like quitting, but it's the smartest choice.

When I get back to camp, the fire is low, and Jackson is gone again.

Swearing under my breath, I throw more dry branches on the fire and stoke it back up. He's still not back by the time I'm done, or after I've checked Emmy's temperature.

I walk to the tree line and call his name, but the only response I get is a group of startled birds fleeing the canopy.

The sun is firmly leaning over the ocean now. If I don't hurry, I'll have to wait until tomorrow if I want to venture farther than Jackson made it yesterday. With one last look at the jungle, I set off down the right side of the beach.

Unlike the other direction, this end of the beach stretches out in a seemingly endless straight line after the first couple bends. I can see miles ahead without having to trek the same distance. I look for smoke, or footprints, or *any* sign of life anywhere in the distance.

There's nothing but beach.

And worse, there's absolutely no indication which way might be closest to civilization. They're both equally wild. So even if we could get Emmy on her feet and try to walk our way to safety, we might end up traveling farther from help if we choose the wrong direction.

Defeated, I follow my sad solitary footprints back the way I came. As much as it sucks, staying in one place and trying to make ourselves as visible as possible is probably the smartest option. We may have to get used to this sweaty little patch of sand; we could be here a while.

Captain Keith's story about getting stranded on the mainland replays over and over in my mind as I walk. I can't believe we ended up in the same position, minus the radio that saved *him*. Not for the first time, I curse Ben's very existence. If him and his paddle board had fucked off, we'd be back home by now.

I'm not sure if I believe in an afterlife or not, and it's probably bad form to wish ill on the dead, but I hope he's somewhere getting his toenails ripped out one by one.

I stop by the stream and gulp down a few mouthfuls of water and splash my face before making a beeline for the mango tree. My tired legs have about reached their limit. All I want to do is gather as much food as possible and lie down before I collapse in the sand.

But when I get to the tree, all the fruit is gone.

I stare at the branches, not understanding what I'm seeing. This tree was full of fruit yesterday. How are all but a few rotting mangoes in the sand gone?

That same nagging sensation eats at me, and I wander in a big circle, searching for something else to bring back. Every fruit tree I find is cleaned out except for a cluster of trees filled with bananas. I consider climbing one of them—even though I fucking hate bananas—but even the shortest one is more than twenty feet tall, and there are no branches on the trunks. Climbing that high, as tired as I am, would be next to impossible. I'd probably break something in the process and then we'd really be screwed.

I loop through the area a dozen more times, and the only thing I find is a guava tree with three lonely little fruits on it.

I owe Jackson one hell of an apology.

Itching with frustration, I take my three small guavas and stomp back to the beach. I'm going to have to find a way to fish, but the sun is already going down, so that'll have to be a mission for tomorrow. At least tonight Emmy has something to eat, even if my own stomach is curling in on itself with hunger.

I can wait.

I push my way through the brush and almost drop the guavas.

The beach is covered in smoke. It billows from the fire pit with a hiss as a wave washes up on shore and kisses the far side of the stones.

The ocean put out my fire.

Fuck.

Fuck.

It's high tide. I built the fire too close to the ocean.

I could cry. I almost do. Haven't we had enough rotten luck for a lifetime? Now, instead of sleep, I have to somehow gather the strength to start all over again and build a second fire. Only this time I also have to lug everything back farther from the water.

A single tear falls down my face, and I scrub it off.

I walk to the raft and place Emmy's three guavas inside where they're safe. I find Jackson sound asleep beside his sister, with his arm slung over her side. The sight of it sends an ache through my chest and makes me want to kick something at the same time. It's not fair, and I know it's not fair, but I'm trying my best to keep us all alive, and they're sleeping. I'm so grateful for the ways Jackson has shown up for me in this nightmare of an experience, but I'm getting really tired of doing everything by myself.

I'm in a foul mood as I drag the stones away from the water. I dig a larger hole this time, about five feet wide, and spend a good hour dragging additional rocks from the forest until I have a base big enough for a real bonfire.

It takes me seven more trips into the jungle to gather enough dry material to make a new fire. A much *bigger* fire. This one will go out over my dead freaking body.

I practically collapse beside the stones. My body is screaming at me to lay down and rest, but I ignore it and get to work.

Armed with plenty of dry materials this time, the fire catches along the leaves and then the smaller branches in record time. Soon it's roaring so hot, it irritates the sunburns on my face. When I'm out of dry branches, I chuck in the driftwood that wouldn't catch before, and the fire is so hot it chars the wood straight away, sending thick black clouds into the air. I add the rest of the green branches. The smoke coming off the fire reminds me of the fire on the boat.

Someone's bound to see this. They have to.

And then we can go home.

The thought feels so foreign to me. Home. I can't even sort out how many days it's been since we left the marina. It feels like it could be five or it could be fifty. I'd agree with either number. Especially here. This beach is the kind of place where hours quickly bleed into days.

The muscles in my arms and legs throb. I finally sink to the sand and let myself rest while I admire the smoke kissing the clouds. The midday sun beats down on me, and sweat rolls down my back but it feels so good to sit.

The raft moves, and a moment later Jackson climbs out. He has dark circles under his eyes, and he's paler than the last time I saw him.

"You're back," he says, sounding as tired as he looks. "And you moved the fire?"

I consider telling him the ocean killed the last one, but he'll just feel bad for falling asleep. He clearly needed the rest, and it's not like he could have stopped the tide even if he'd been awake. "Yeah I wanted it to be more visible. And farther from the water."

He nods, but he looks worried. "You need to check on Emmy."

The way he says it has me sprinting for the raft. Before my hand touches her face, I can feel the heat. Her whole body is shaking with fever again. She's turned in her sleep, and the wound on her arm is pressed against the bottom of the raft. I nudge her onto her back so I can see. She's ripped off the scab. Green goo oozes between scraps of mango leaf and the palm frond ties. I rip off the makeshift bandage, and the skin underneath smells like it's rotting. I turn my head so I don't gag.

I send Jackson off to get more firewood while I drag his sister back to the stream. Emmy protests the entire way, but I plop her into the water anyway. The cold clearly makes her uncomfortable, and she makes all kinds of noises. More than she did the last time. Significantly more, but the longer she soaks, the more she quiets. I wonder if the fever is making her skin sensitive. If it is, there's not much we can do about it. I hate to make her miserable, but this is the only way we can lower her fever at the moment.

I carefully wash the goo and the pus from her wound while she soaks, and before I help her out of the stream, I tie a new mango leaf to her forearm. I walk her back into the raft, and she grabs my hand before I step out to let her rest.

"Hannah."

I fold myself beside her. "I'm right here."

"Ben…"

My stomach sinks, and I gently brush the wet hair from her forehead. "I'm sorry, Em. He's gone."

Her forehead wrinkles, and her hand tightens on mine. "No… he…"

She doesn't finish her sentence before she's out again. She took so long to ask about him, I thought maybe she wasn't going to. Or that she didn't care *what* happened to him. Preferably the second option.

The urge to sleep crawls over me, and with Emmy passed out, the fire raging, and Jackson nearby, there's no reason to fight it. I fold my arms under my head and try to get comfortable.

As soon as I close my eyes, I hear a sound that doesn't belong. I jolt upright. It's like a buzzing, but not a natural one. Not a jungle bug or a bird.

It grows louder, and I climb out of the raft. When I stand, dots dance along the edge of my vision, and I grab the raft canopy for support until they clear.

I turn my head, trying to place the direction of the sound, and finally piece together what I'm hearing.

A *helicopter*.

CHAPTER TWENTY-THREE

I spin in a circle, screaming to get their attention before I can even spot the damn thing. The sound of the blades slicing through the air gets louder by the second, but I don't see it anywhere over the ocean or down either stretch of beach.

I run toward the water, trying to see over the trees and the helicopter parts the canopy and flies straight over me. It continues out toward the sunset and I wave my hands over my head, trying to flag them down. I scream for Jackson at the top of my lungs, and relief has me laughing between breaths.

Oh my god, it's over. They found us. It's really over.

We're going home!

Jackson races from the trees. "Hannah! What's wrong?"

I point at the sky and sob, "They found us!"

But when I turn to show him, the helicopter vanishes into thin air. The answering silence is deafening. I stare at the sky like whatever black hole swallowed our impending rescue will spit it back to us, but it doesn't happen.

The only thing above our heads is a smattering of pink clouds.

"But...it was right there," I say, my voice hoarse from yelling.

"What was?"

I gesture helplessly at the empty sky. "A helicopter..."

I rip my gaze from the clouds, only to find him staring at me like I've grown a third eye. The pity on his face nearly breaks me. The reality of what just happened settles in, and I sink to the sand. Jackson drops with me. We kneel in the surf at the water's edge, and I begin to shake.

"There was no helicopter?" I guess.

"No."

It was a hallucination.

I feel like I've been kicked in the chest. Tears stream down my face.

Jackson wraps his arms around me, and I let my forehead fall against his chest.

"It's okay," he whispers, his voice soothing. "You're exhausted, you're dehydrated, and you've barely eaten. That's bound to catch up with you in unexpected ways."

He's right. We're isolated, sunburnt, overheated, beat-up, and we're drinking from a stream of what could turn out to be contaminated water.

I'm surprised it took this long to start seeing things, but it's no less terrifying.

I replay the helicopter vanishing into thin air again and again on repeat while Jackson rubs circles on my back. I swear I could feel the wind it displaced when it flew over my head. Feel the sand it scattered prickle at my legs. It was so real that if it hadn't vanished, there's nothing he could have told me to convince me it wasn't there.

"It'll be okay," he says, holding me tighter. "You're going to be okay. Someone will see the smoke from your fire. You have to hang on a bit longer."

I nod and let him lead me back to the raft, but I can't help but wonder how I'm supposed to get us home if I can't tell the difference between what's real and what's all in my head.

I don't sleep.

Again.

Jackson watches me closely the rest of the day. Everywhere I go—into the trees for more firewood, searching for another fruit tree, forcing Emmy to eat all three of those guavas, watching the sun set—he's right beside me with a worried little fissure between his eyebrows. When I can't take the scrutiny anymore, I lie down in the sand between the fire and the raft and pretend to sleep.

Eventually I hear him get up, and when I lift my head I find I'm blissfully alone. I peek into the raft, and he's wrapped around his sister like a watchdog. I want to climb in with them, but I know I won't be able to sleep. Instead I sit sentry in front of the fire, making sure it doesn't go out again.

Might as well be somewhat productive while I spiral.

The nonexistent helicopter rattled the hell out of me. Probably more than it should have, if I'm being honest with myself. Hallucinations in survival situations are the brain's reaction to stress, and there's been no lack of stress these last few days, but I can't shake the feeling that I'm missing something important.

It's making me restless, jumpy. Sleep would probably help, but I'm too full of adrenaline and worst-case scenarios. I scrub my grimy hands down my face and close my eyes. I lectured Jackson about keeping his cool in the wake of Emmy's seizure, and here I am, falling apart over an imaginary helicopter.

I *need* to get a grip.

The fire lets out a big crack, and I startle in surprise. I scoot back to keep the embers off the tops of my feet, and something moves in the corner of my vision.

I whip around and wait, but nothing moves within the trees. I pinch the bridge of my nose, frustrated with how jumpy I am. I just told myself I couldn't lose it, and five seconds later my mind starts playing tricks ag—

A branch snaps behind me.

I'm on my feet in a flash and sprint to the other side of the fire. I scan the trees, and this time, hear something moving in the darkness. Back and forth. Back and forth. The same branches move, the same thumps on the forest floor.

"Jackson," I whisper.

There's no response from the raft.

"*Jackson.*"

Silence.

The figure in the trees paces back and forth again, and I narrow my eyes. There's no way that's a jungle predator. A panther doesn't stomp around. They're stealthy. I'd probably be half eaten before I even knew a true predator was out there.

Whatever's in the trees is *watching*.

Or...waiting?

I back around the other side of the raft and creep down the shore until I'm out of the firelight's reach. Then I sprint as quietly as possible up to the trees near the path I've been taking to get to the stream and double back toward the campsite in the shadows. Maybe whatever's in there will creep out when it doesn't see anyone by the fire, and I'll finally solve the riddle of what the hell made off with our canned foods.

Are there jungle rodents? It sounds big. Maybe a monkey? A monkey definitely could have made off with my bag.

I hide behind a palm tree, listening carefully. The pacing stops. It's quiet for so long that I begin to wonder if this is another helicopter situation. Did I also hallucinate something in the trees?

The silence stretches on until I'm ready to abandon my stupid plan and stalk back to the fire when a figure slithers out of the shadows. Their back is to me, but it's definitely not a panther *or* a monkey.

It's a man.

The firelight glints off the bare skin of his torso, but his face is all shadow as he moves closer to Emmy and Jackson in the raft. Before I can scream a warning, there are three quick popping sounds as he jabs something into the raft.

"Hey!" I shout, sprinting from the trees.

The man jumps and hauls ass across the beach, kicking a wall of sand at the fire as he passes. I'm hot on his heels, shouting for him to stop. He dives back into the jungle.

I'm only about *ten feet* behind him, and yet somehow, when I crash into the trees a moment later, everything is silent. I stand in a patch of palm trees, turning in a slow circle. The jungle is almost *scary* silent. Even the bugs don't make a sound. It's like…

He vanished into thin air.

Except this time, I *know* it's not all in my head. He was considerate enough to leave me with ample proof. Part of the fire is dark where the sand extinguished it. There are footprints by the slowly deflating raft full of fresh punctures.

No, this wasn't a hallucination. We're not alone on this beach.

I stand there listening for any sign of him, but the only sound I hear is Jackson fumbling with the deflating raft and frantically shouting my name. I back out of the trees, so he doesn't freak out when he can't find me, but I keep my gaze trained on the jungle.

"You scared the hell out of me!" he says when I reach the light of the fire. "I heard you yell—and what the fuck happened to the raft?"

He's practically shouting across our camp, and I shush him. "There's someone here."

He's at my side in an instant, watching the trees as closely as I am. "Are you sure?"

"I saw him. He stabbed the raft with something and kicked sand at the fire."

Jackson shakes his head. "That doesn't make any sense. Why would someone deflate the raft? That seems so...benign. If someone wanted to hurt one of us, Emmy and I were sleeping right there."

I had the same thought. "I'm telling you what I saw. The moment I was out of sight, he slithered out like a little rat."

"Who was it? Who'd even be out this far? We haven't seen a soul."

"It would have to be a local, right? I don't know why a local would want to steal our food and destroy our shelter though."

Sounds more like Ben, a little voice in the back of my head whispers. But that's impossible. He got washed overboard without a life vest. In the middle of a storm. While we were any number of miles from land. There's no way it could be him.

Jackson frowns, and places a hand on my shoulder. "Don't punch me for saying this, okay?"

"I make no promises. I already don't like whatever you're about to say."

"Is there any chance you dreamed it? Maybe kicked the sand at the fire yourself before you woke up all the way?"

I smack his hand off my shoulder. "Oh for sure. I sleep-stabbed the raft too. Better watch out, you're probably next."

He laughs and crushes me to his chest. "Well, that sucks. It would be really great if you dreamed it."

"*Why?*"

"Because then we wouldn't have another thing to worry about."

Little by little, the noises in the forest pick up again, and my skin begins to crawl. All the hairs on the back of my neck rise, and though I don't hear any more pacing, I can't shake the feeling that whoever that was, is still out there.

Watching.

CHAPTER TWENTY-FOUR

The moment the sun starts to lighten in the sky, I burn anything green I can get my hands on. Piles of fresh leaves. Branches I rip off trees. Whole bushes I uproot from the ground, until a thick stream of cloying smoke rises so high in the air that it seems to merge with the highest clouds overhead. The fire doubles, then triples, until it's pressing against the confines of its stone circle.

Hallucinations be damned.

Creepy assholes in the trees be damned.

Someone's going to find us today if it kills me.

Jackson watches me like I've lost my damn mind, and honestly, I might have. He tries to get me to sit, to drink water, to go find something to eat, but I don't stop. I'll eat once we're rescued.

"Would you please, for the love of god, sit down?" he asks for the fourth time. "It's a thousand degrees, and if you don't stop, you're going to pass out."

I wave him off. "Later. I'm busy."

He steps in my way and knocks the branch I'm about to throw on top of the fire out of my hands. "If you go get a drink of water, I'll give you my car."

I snort. "I have my own car."

"You can have two cars."

The concern on his face crumbles my resolve a bit. For so many years, I would have killed to have him look at me like that. To care about what I do, or where I go, or how I'm taking care of myself. I drag his forehead down to meet mine and smile. "I don't need two cars. I need us to all get home safely. Preferably within the next twelve hours."

He presses his lips to my forehead and sighs. "Lofty goal."

I pull away. "My favorite kind."

He rolls his eyes and backs away, dramatically lifting his hands. "Fine, I surrender. At least let me help with the brush."

"I've got this. But if you can find any more fruit, I'll give you *my* car."

He gives me a mock salute and wanders down the right side of the beach.

I check on Emmy. I had to unearth her from the deflating raft last night, and now she's lying on top of it, using the deflated remains of the canopy as a blanket. Eventually I'll have to find a way to prop it up so she has some kind of protection from the sun, but for now she looks comfortable, so I leave her alone.

Her wounded arm stretches out across the top of the raft, mango leaf still tied to her skin. Every time I pull it back, I brace for maggots, but thankfully that nightmare hasn't happened quite yet.

I stand up and look down the beach. The sky could not be bluer. The water is sparkling. The sand pristine. It's another beautiful day in paradise.

And I never want to see any of it, ever again.

My stomach aches with hunger, so I head into the trees to grab more green branches to distract myself from it. God, I hope Jackson can find something to eat this time. If not, we might have to venture much farther from camp, but there's got to be more fruit trees around here somewhere. And when we find them, I'm hiding food everywhere. Everywhere. Let's see that asshole try and steal from us again when I've filled the beach with little stashes of food like a fucking squirrel.

Ten feet into the trees, the hair on the back of my neck lifts, and I freeze.

The jungle has gone silent again. It's like nature itself is telling me something out here doesn't belong, and I'd be willing to bet Jackson's car that it's the same shirtless asshole who stole our food last night.

A flash of skin moves to my left, bolting through the trees.

Got you!

I shout for him to stop and take off after him. The forest floor bites into the soles of my feet. Branches catch on my bare skin. I trip over rocks and roots and brush, but I don't let up. I'm not letting him slip away this time.

He runs in a zigzag pattern away from camp, around groups of trees and brush, keeping parallel with the beach. Flashes of sunlight, sparkling off the water, shine through gaps in the trees and glint off his back.

He fucked up. He should have waited until nightfall to mess with us again, because now I won't stop until I have answers.

I'm gaining on him.

The trees ahead thin, and he bolts through a swampy area full of sludge. He splashes through the ankle-deep water and shoots out the other side. I crash in after him. Halfway through, something catches my foot, and I almost fall face-first into the disgusting mosquito breeding pool, but I catch myself on a stump and wade out the other side.

When I right myself, he's gone.

I round a cluster of palm trees, expecting to spot him on the other side, and kick something hard across the jungle floor. Pain radiates through my toes, and I swear up at the canopy, jumping on one foot to see what I kicked.

My sticker-covered water bottle is on the ground.

I stare at it in shock. Footsteps thunder through the trees to my left, and I shake off my surprise and tear through the trees after him.

Who the hell is this person? Someone who doesn't want us on their beach? Fine, report us to the authorities. Do us all a favor and get us the hell out of here. I don't understand the point of stealing our things and ruining our shelter.

I run through a wide thicket of branches and skid to a stop.

I'm standing in a small clearing, only about twenty feet across, but someone's clearly living here. A rickety-looking shelter made of branches and palm fronds leans up against a thin tree that bends under the weight. The cans of stolen peaches and tomato soup are smashed open on the ground beside a rock.

My mesh bag hangs from a nearby branch.

I step closer, listening for movement in the trees, and snatch my bag off the branch. The first aid kit is still inside, and so is the waterproof pouch with my phone. The sunscreen is gone.

On the ground beneath it is a huge pile of fruit. Mangoes, bananas, guavas, even a couple avocados. More than any one person could eat before it went rotten. In fact, it looks like all the fruit that went missing from the trees around the campsite.

My heart thunders in my ears.

Someone's going out of their way to make sure we suffer out here.

I need to leave, right now. I don't hear him in the trees, and if he doubles back for the camp, Jackson will be Emmy's only line of defense. If this guy is willing to watch us starve, what else is he capable of? I have to get back and tell Jackson what's happening.

I put the water bottle into my bag and turn to leave, but my gaze catches on the shelter. A piece of dirty fabric is stretched across the ground inside. White fabric with tiny little buttons.

My blood runs cold.

Oh my god. I know that shirt.

Something moves behind me, and I whirl around as a huge branch swings for my head.

CHAPTER TWENTY-FIVE

I throw myself back, and the branch misses me by inches. I land on the ground. Hard. My head slams into the ground, and I groan as pain wraps around my neck.

Bennett Mulholland looms over me, holding his branch like he's stepping up to bat in the major leagues. He's bruised to hell. One of his eyes is shadowed in deep blue. One side of his chest is so swollen and purple, I think he must have broken a rib or two. There's a gash down his calf and a line of what looks like a rope burn around both forearms. Dried blood tangles his blond hair over one ear.

Otherwise, he looks great.

"Surprised to see me?" he spits.

I nod.

"I should probably thank you for that," he says, gesturing to the other side of the clearing. The boat's emergency flotation sits propped against a tree. "If I didn't have that thing wrapped around me when I went over, I'd have probably drowned."

I scramble away from him. I have that feeling again.

Like I'm missing a vital detail.

I try to think of something to say. "I'm glad you made it, Ben. I never wanted anyone to get hurt."

"Could have fooled me."

"I was defending myself. You didn't give me much of a choice."

He leans forward. "That's funny. When you do it, it's because you had no other choice. When I do it, I'm a criminal."

"Because that's what you call someone who's committed a crime. You know, like murder and arson and assault."

"*You didn't give me much of a choice,*" he says, mimicking me.

I scoot back, but he closes the distance.

"Did you have a choice when you started stealing our food? Our water? When you destroyed our only shelter and put out our fire? We could have been working together to signal a rescue, and instead you're out here making sure we—"

It all clicks together a second too late. Ben quirks an eyebrow at me, amusement dancing across his features. As if me putting the pieces together is the most hilarious thing.

I feel the blood drain from my face.

The thefts, the sabotage—it all makes complete sense now. My stomach rolls.

"You were trying to starve us?"

He shrugs. "Starvation, dehydration, exposure...I'm not picky about how you go, just that you do. *Dead men tell no tales* and all that."

I gape at him. "After everything that's happened, after everything we've already survived, you're still trying to cover your tracks?"

That sparks his anger. His face turns red, and he hefts the branch up over his shoulder. "You still don't understand, do you? Washing ashore alone was the first peace I've had since that dickhead went overboard. I might have been stranded here by myself, but there was nobody left to rat me out. I'd find a way home, and everyone would talk about how terrible it was that a greedy, careless captain took advantage of us. A man who had no business bringing four teens out to sea with a storm looming. What a shame only one made it home…"

As he talks, I can see how the media, the survival story enthusiasts, would run with his version. It's front-page gold: the unfortunate teen who wanted to spend the day on the ocean with his new friends, only to watch them all die after they trusted the wrong man to keep them safe at sea.

Nobody would ever know the truth of what happened out there.

What we did to survive.

What *he* did to *us*.

He'd be celebrated as the lucky hero who made it home—instead of the psychotic asshole responsible for the deaths of four people.

Ben raises the branch with a deep sigh. "But no. You had to keep going. Always Miss Dependable: getting to shore, finding food, breaking fevers, building bonfires the size of a fucking car. If you just quit for *once* in your life, you would all be dead. But you're too fucking tenacious, so now I have to take matters into my own hands before someone sees your miles of fucking smoke."

He takes a step closer, and my fingers fist in the sand.

"I'm sorry it has to be this way, Hannah, but unfortunately, it's you or me…and I'll always choose me."

He tenses to hit me with the branch, and I throw the fistful of sand in his face. He rears back and drops the branch to shield his eyes. I scramble to my feet and swing my bag at his head with all my strength. My metal water bottle connects with his jawbone, and his head snaps back. I drop the bag and *run*.

He screams a string of f-bombs behind me as I race out onto the beach.

I have no idea where I'm going. Only that we're less than a mile from camp, and I can't risk leading him to Emmy when I don't know if Jackson's back from his search yet. I just know I have to get the hell away from Ben.

I race down the hot sand toward the rock outcropping.

I hear him crash through the brush behind me, and he snarls my name.

He's on me in a flash. He grabs my hair and yanks. I fall to the sand with a grunt, and Ben straddles my stomach, knocking the wind out of me. He rears back and punches me in the face. Pain rockets through my skull, and blood gushes from my nose.

My hand scrabbles through the too-hot sand.

His sweaty, angry face hovers over me, as he pins one of my arms. "Jesus, you never stop! You've already failed!"

My fingers close around a palm-sized rock. "Not yet."

I smash it into his temple.

His scream carries down the beach, and he lists to one side. I dump him off me and twist to my knees. He grabs an ankle before I can get my foot under me, and I kick back. He lets out another grunt, and my ankle comes free.

"Fuck!" he shouts.

I sprint to the hard-packed sand along the waterline and pick up more speed. I have to hide or find some kind of weapon, but I can't do either with him right on my heels.

My lungs catch fire, but I don't slow until the big outcropping of rocks rises a few hundred feet down the beach. I don't have time to climb it. He'll catch up to me long before I reach the top. I cross the soft sand and plunge back into the jungle.

A tree root catches my foot, and the next thing I know, I'm on the ground. Dirt and sand grit in my teeth, and I taste blood. More blood drips down the side of my face, and when I tap my fingers to my forehead the flap of skin and hair is gone. The fall ripped it off. I try to lift my head, but everything spins. I drag a knee under me and force myself up, but he's too fast.

Ben grabs the hair at the back of my head, his breaths sawing in and out of his mouth. "Gotcha," he gasps.

His grip tightens, and he hurls me out of the trees by my hair. I land face-first at the base of the stone outcropping. The sky is dotted with black smudges I can't seem to blink away. Blood streams from my nose. I can't make myself get up.

He might actually win this.

I think of Jackson and Emmy on the beach. They have no idea that Ben is still alive, much less what he's about to do. Will he leave them to die on their own? How long before he grows impatient with starvation and goes after them too?

Ben comes to stand beside me and folds his arms. Fresh blood coats the side of his face from the rock. "You have to do everything the hard way. I really wanted to keep my hands clean this time and let nature do the dirty work."

I spit blood onto the rock beside my head. "Sorry to disappoint."

"What is that, your life motto?"

He reaches for me, and I slam my elbow down on the top of his foot. He lets out a howl and stumbles back. I scoot away, and the black spots in my vision get bigger. There's nowhere else to go but farther up the rock, toward the water.

Ben hobbles around, cursing me with every breath, and a sick sense of satisfaction courses through me. I might die here, but I'm not going to roll over and let it happen. I'll give him hell. And if he wins, I'm coming back to haunt every moment of his pathetic life.

His gaze locks on me, rage burning in his eyes, and he lunges. I blindly kick in his direction and somehow connect with his knee, so hard I can feel his kneecap move.

He drops, cradling his knee to his chest. "Son of a bitch!"

"You should see what I can do with a PlayStation."

I roll to my knees. A hollow ringing fills both my ears, half drowning out Ben, the sound of the ocean, even my own heartbeat. I need to buy myself some time—long enough for my head to stop spinning, so I don't fall off the side of this rock. It feels like trying to brawl on a merry-go-round at full speed.

"What about Emmy?" I shout, blinking hard to clear the shadows. If I can see him more clearly, I'll have a better chance of hitting my mark when I lunge for his smug face. "I know you're a selfish prick, but I watched you make goo-goo eyes at her all week long. What's the plan? Kill me and watch her starve? You'd really do that to her?"

I stagger to my feet, and the ocean, the rock, the trees, they all spin.

Ben puts all his weight on his other knee and leans down to grab a rock. "Emmy's death will be...regrettable. I really did like her, and if things had gone differently on the boat, I might have spared her. But if there's one thing I hate, it's a liar. She was ready to let me die the moment I put my hands on *you*. Bullshit recognizes bullshit, and your friend is a terrible liar."

Fuck. She really is.

"Besides, there's no point in sparing her now. She's half dead anyway. I'll be putting her out of her misery. Don't worry though, I'll really talk her up when I get home. She'll be famous. You both will. *The girls who fought for their lives and tragically died at sea.* Hell, it'll probably end up a Crimflix special. I'll say nothing but good things when they interview me." He holds up one hand. "Nobody will know you're both manipulative little bitches. Scout's honor."

I can't process what he's saying. It's such a glaring example of how disconnected he is from reality—the idea that the *story* he tells about a person makes up for murdering them. That the best he can offer Emmy is stardom in a documentary because our status as girls who famously died at sea is valuable currency in his mind.

Our lives are expendable. Not *his* future, not *his* reputation, not *his* family name. No, those are untouchable. Us, on the other hand? We are nothing.

"What about Jackson? He's not going to stand by and let you kill his sister."

He frowns and tips his head to the side. "What—"

The ringing in my head gets louder...only now it's more of a buzz. Ben freezes. His eyes widen, and he whips around to stare down the beach, first in the direction of our little camp, then the other way.

I follow his stare, but all I see is the thin line of dwindling dark smoke coming from my fire and the same curved pear-shaped section of beach that was here before—

Something moves across the sky, far off in the distance.

It's not my ears that are buzzing. It's another helicopter.

Only this time, Ben stares at it with dawning horror on his face. This one isn't in my mind. There's *actually* a helicopter in the sky. And it's heading our way.

Ben looks at me, then toward my smoke signal, and I can see the gears turning. He's wondering how he can get rid of me *and* Jackson and Emmy before the helicopter reaches us.

I open my mouth to tell him it's too late, but he seems to disagree, because without hesitation, he hurls the rock in his hand at my face.

I barely move in time. The rock glances off the top of my shoulder and rips through the skin. I gasp in pain, but before I can scramble away, he's got a grip on my hair again, and I feel myself being dragged backward.

I dig my heels into the rock, trying and failing to find purchase. The distance between us and the edge quickly disappears.

He's going to throw me off the fucking cliff.

Frantic now, I claw at his arms, at his legs, at the ground. Flashes of jagged, tooth-shaped rocks sticking out of the water fill my head. I know what's waiting for me over the edge, and it seems Ben does too.

I plead with him to stop, but he only laughs at me.

"I told you, Hannah. You don't know when to quit. I'm stronger than you. This was always how it was going to play out."

I twist and wrap my legs around his until we're tangled like a pretzel. I hang on as tightly as I can, and he frowns, trying to shake me off, like I'm some unruly toddler.

We're two feet from the edge now.

"You'll be charged anyway!" I gasp, desperate to poke a hole in his logic. To make him doubt whatever parts of his plan still seem viable in his mind. "Your story doesn't make any sense!"

He rolls his eyes and tries to step on my calf, but I curl my knees tighter around his ankles. The effort brings back the black dots in my vision, but I ignore them.

"Think about it!" I croak. "How could all three of us die of starvation or dehydration or exposure, but you're totally fine? How are you going to explain how you kept yourself fed and hydrated while the rest of us withered away?"

At that, he pauses.

He looks...confused.

"Never mind that Jackson will never let you within a hundred feet of Emmy," I say. "Killing me will only double your jail time. There's no fucking point. You have to see that!"

Ben looks even more confused. Waves crash against the jagged rocks below. My heart is beating so hard, it feels like it's bruising itself against my rib cage.

He starts laughing. He actually throws his head back and laughs. "What the fuck are you talking about? Do you have brain damage or something?"

I... What?

He shakes his head and crouches down. His expression shifts, his lips pressing together with something that looks a whole lot like pity. "You delusional little thing. Your dream boy isn't here with you. I killed him on the boat."

CHAPTER TWENTY-SIX

I killed him.
 I killed him.
 I killed him.

I stop breathing. My heart might stop too—the entire world along with it.

He...he doesn't know what he's talking about. Of course, Jackson is here. He's been with me for *days*. I found him in the water...

Ben trails a finger down my cheek. "You don't remember?"

When I say nothing—because I can't—he keeps going. "The wave overshot the top of the boat, and we all got slammed into the deck instead of washed off it. The water receded, and the three of us were tangled in the lifelines, but you were out cold.

"Part of the railing by my shoulder snapped off when we hit, and it hooked through the rope around the flotation ring. I couldn't stand to get to the hatch. Your fucking boy toy took *my* knife out of his pocket, and instead of cutting me loose, he sliced through a line on the deck and tied it around *you*."

I think I'm going to be sick.

"I told him he was wasting time, that we had to leave you and get to the hatch, and he looked me dead in the eye and said, *You're not going to make it, but she will.* He was so focused on tying you to the boat that he didn't even notice me pick up the knife."

No no no. I don't want to hear this. I *can't* hear this.

"In hindsight, he probably meant that *none* of us had time to make it to the hatch before the next wave, and he was right. I lodged my knife in his neck, and the wave hit. It felt like the boat got punched by a giant. We rolled, and I blacked out. The force must have knocked me loose of the lifelines. Woke up floating in the pitch-black ocean, and everyone was gone."

"No," I say, my voice sounding hollow. "I found Jackson floating in the water with the emergency ring. It's what kept him alive, I..."

But I also saw the life ring at Ben's camp, leaning against the tree.

There was only one on the boat.

"Sorry, no," he says, not sounding sorry at all. "That's what kept *me* alive. I still don't know how I managed to hang on to it all night, but by the morning, I could see the shoreline. You and Emmy appeared half a day later with your raft."

My hands fall away from him and land limply in my lap.

Oh my god.

I remember Jackson standing on the flipped boat while I dove to get the raft from the cabin, only to vanish when I needed him to help me haul it up. I remember dragging Emmy to the stream over and over to break her fever. Jackson never offered to carry her. I tried to give him food, water, sunscreen. He refused it all. Kicking the raft ashore, the jellyfish only stung *me*, and if I stopped to take a break, so did he.

If you don't want to go down with this ship, you need to make a plan.

You. *You* need to make a plan. Not *we*.

Keep swimming, Hannah. You're almost there.

You don't need a volleyball. You have Emmy.

Someone will see the smoke from your fire. You have to hang on a bit longer.

You. You. You.

I see Jackson floating in the ocean, plain as day. Waving me down as soon as I started to crack under the pressure of keeping Emmy alive all by myself. Wearing the "Game of Holmes" shirt that he never put back on after I used it to sop up the blood from Captain Keith's broken nose.

He never came up with a single plan. He never cooled down in the creek. He never added to our pile of food or firewood. He talked and encouraged me and said all the things I needed to hear, but he didn't actually *do* anything, touch anything, interact with anything on the beach except…me.

He was never here.

Ben looms very close to my face. "It's sort of romantic, if you think about it. He died for you, and now you'll die thinking about him."

He grabs me by the throat, but all I can hear is Jackson telling me to keep trying, to not give up. I straighten my leg between Ben's and press my heel against a cluster of rocks for leverage. I twist and throw my elbow into the back of his injured knee, and he lets out a yelp, windmilling his arms to keep from tripping over the clothesline I've made with my legs.

I grab his ankle and yank.

Ben's upper body tips back, leaning precariously over the edge of the rock face.

And then, he falls.

His scream splits the air and abruptly cuts off. I feel the end of his life in every part of my body. I wobble to my feet and peek over the edge. What's left of Bennett Mulholland is splayed out in the surf and rocks below. He landed in the middle of the sharpest section of rock. His limbs are bent at unnatural angles. As I watch, a wave crashes through the rock teeth and lifts his body. First, he's pushed closer to the base of the cliff, and then it pulls him farther out. He's slowly being dragged out to sea.

His eyes are wide open, staring at the sky.

I turn and puke off the other side of the cliff. Almost nothing comes up, but I retch the bile left in my stomach while that blank look on his face makes a home in the back of my mind.

I know what would have happened if he'd been the one to leave this rock. He would have gone straight for Emmy. The coward that he is, he probably would have killed her in her sleep. What I did was not only for self-defense but to protect her too.

Still, my whole body is numb as I scramble my way back to the sand.

The roar of the helicopter races overhead, just like it did in my imagination, only this time it blows sand everywhere and displaces the seawater. This time it's real.

I stick my hand in the air and wave it down the beach as I stumble back toward the raft.

I have to get to Emmy and—

Emmy and…

Memories of the last few days replay in my mind. Only now, they shift.

Jackson no longer stands on the hull, holding the rope for me while I dive for the raft. The rope is tied to the boat, and I dive for the emergency raft alone.

Jackson's holding onto the raft, swimming beside me until he dissolves, and I swim alone. Whispering assurances to myself the whole way.

I see him asleep next to his sister, and then I blink and she's lying alone.

I replay our time on this godforsaken stretch of beach, except now there's one set of footprints leading to and from the jungle.

Mine.

Because only Emmy and I made it to shore, and she's been asleep for days.

Something cracks open inside me, and a coldness spreads through my body.

I blink, and I'm standing in front of Emmy, with no memory of walking down the rest of the beach. Big gasping sobs rip through my chest as I take in our little camp. The fire is still pouring smoke into the sky. It scatters when the helicopter nears.

Emmy's still asleep on top of the ruined raft. I collapse at her side before my legs can give out, pressing my forehead against hers. The helicopter makes another pass overhead and lands a little distance down the beach.

She stirs. "Hannah?"

"I'm here, Em."

Shouted commands fill the beach as help arrives, and I hug her tightly.

"We're going home."

EPILOGUE

ALMOST A YEAR LATER

For the first time in months, the sun is out. The Linfield grounds are full of students sitting against trees and gathered around picnic tables to catch up on last-minute assignments before spring break. It's warm enough that I shed my sweatshirt as soon as I drop my stuff at an empty table, thrilled to have escaped the library, even if it's only for a few hours.

As I sit, my phone pings with a message, and I fish it from my bag. Emmy.

I click it open right away. It's a photo of her posed in front of an old castle, with weathered stones and moss. She's smiling ear to ear. It makes me smile too. She must still be in Scotland.

I haven't seen her in six months. Not since I dropped her off at the airport with a single bag and a one-way ticket to Spain. She's been to about a dozen countries since then, and I couldn't be prouder after everything she went through to get there.

It took Emmy months to recover from her injuries. The infection in her arm was so bad, she almost lost it. But she was well enough to leave for her world tour in October—much to the delight of the internet. Between her Instagram account and the travel blog she started, Emmy's basking in our post-survival internet fame.

I, on the other hand, made all my accounts private, and that's how they'll remain. Everyone wanted to hear from the girls who survived being trapped at sea with a murderer; meanwhile, all we wanted was to put the whole thing behind us and forget it ever happened.

To this day, neither of us has done a single interview about what happened out there. The public seemed to settle for watching Emmy travel the world in place of getting the answers they wanted. If they couldn't satisfy their curiosity, they could at least watch her "heal" and "move on" and whatever else people say in the hundreds of thousands of performative comments. Emmy's using the publicity to her advantage though. She's got brand deals out the ass, and she actually seems happy. Somehow.

I'm…not exactly happy, but things aren't as dire as they were when we first made it home. I'm at school. I'm settling in and getting through.

But it's hard.

I rarely go home anymore. Everywhere I turn there's a memory of Jackson. My own kitchen. His bedroom window on the second floor of the house next door. The corner where he broke things off with me. His Mazda sitting in the driveway. His devastated, hollow-eyed parents, going about their lives like zombies.

I can't look them in the eye, knowing Jackson's dead because of me.

My dad is trying his best, but he doesn't understand. Before our trip, he wanted me to stay at home and commute to college, and he doubled down after we were rescued. I couldn't do it. I couldn't even bring myself to walk the stage at graduation, because they planned a moment of silence for Jackson as part of the ceremony. If I saw his face on the screen, I would have lost it.

They mailed me my diploma instead.

I almost bailed on Linfield too. It felt like my dreams belonged to another version of me. One who went out on that boat and didn't make it back. But Emmy wouldn't hear of it. She sat me down and asked me to imagine my life ten or fifteen years in the future. Once the grief lost its edge, and I was no longer thought of as "one of those girls who almost died on vacation," where did I see myself? And while I couldn't imagine the grief as anything but all-consuming, I also couldn't imagine doing anything but helping people.

So, at the start of the semester, I was here.

Emmy helped me move into my dorm.

She's the only person who understands.

She's also the only person who knows Bennett Mulholland didn't die when the boat went down.

They never found his body, which feels like some kind of poetic justice. Thanks to him, they'll never find Captain Keith or Jackson either. Ben's parents threatened a wrongful death lawsuit for a minute, but with the owner of the boat dead and Ben himself having booked it, they eventually had to back down. They've done several interviews claiming their son wasn't the violent, unstable person the media made him out to be, but public opinion has landed squarely against them.

Despite their best efforts, Ben Mulholland has gone down as the villain in this story.

A burst of laughter shakes me from the past, and I glance around the campus. A group of girls are clustered around someone's phone, laughing so hard they have tears in their eyes.

I glance at the empty seats around my table and sigh. I should really put more effort into make friends here. My dorm-mate is from Seattle, and she's invited me out with her friends a handful of times, but I keep finding excuses to stay behind. Which is probably for the best—I'm not the best company at the moment.

Next week is the one-year anniversary of our doomed voyage.

I've been trying and failing to find a way to commemorate it. If I treat that week like any other set of days, it'll pass that way. I'd much rather make it matter, so that maybe I can find the closure I need to leave what happened in the past. The worst parts of it, anyway.

I just can't figure out how. Jackson's parents are throwing a memorial at their house, but the thought of attending breaks me out in a cold sweat. And I'm running out of time to find an alternative.

My phone rings in my hand, and a picture of my dad's bald head fills the screen.

I swipe to answer. "Hey Dad."

"Heya, child o' mine. How's your week?"

We chat for a minute about classes and the weather, the same things we cover every single time he calls. Which is often. He's clearly anxious about me living in the dorms, but each time I tell him about my day and it doesn't include some kind of maritime disaster, I think he calms a little more.

"Are you coming home this weekend?" he asks, sounding hopeful. "I can trade shifts with someone at the hospital if you want to stop by."

I smile. "I'm almost out of clean pants, so it's probably time."

He lets out an affronted gasp. "I see how it is, using me for my free laundry facilities."

"Well, that and you feed me."

He laughs. "Where are you? The library again?"

"No, actually. I'm trying to soak up some weak sunlight while it lasts. Why?"

He's quiet for a beat. Then, "No reason. Have you eaten?"

I blink at the phone screen and put it back to my ear. "What? Why?"

Someone sets a bag of takeout on the table, and when I look up, Emmy's standing beside me. I squeal so loud, about fifty heads turn in my direction. I launch myself into her arms, and she laughs.

"Oh my god! What are you doing here?" I practically yell in her ear.

"Visiting you, of course."

I let go of her and spot my phone on the ground. When I pick it up, my dad's already hung up.

"He was in on it," Emmy says, sliding onto the other end of the bench. "He picked me up from the airport. He's right over there, actually."

I follow her pointed finger in time to see his car pulling away from the curb across the lawn, and I can't stop smiling. That's why he was being so shifty. I sit beside her. "I thought you were in Scotland."

Emmy grabs a burger from the bag and uses it to wave me off. "It was raining a lot, and I figured if I was going to get caught in the rain, it might as well be here with you. Besides...next week is the big one. I didn't think either one of us should be alone for that."

Tears burn behind my eyes, and I blink them away.

Emmy has very little memory of what happened once the boat flipped. Everything before the second storm is clear, right up until

Jackson and I shoved her into the cabin, but it gets blurry after that. She knows I took care of her, but she has no specific memories of being trapped in the boat or surviving on shore, and I'm so grateful for that. I remember plenty for the both of us, and Emmy lost her brother, which is trauma enough.

We scarf down our burgers in silence in the weak March sunlight. It glints off the jagged scar on her arm, still pink and several shades lighter than the skin around it, but fully healed.

"How long are you here?" I finally ask when we're done.

"As long as you need me."

I lose my fight with the tears and let my head fall to her shoulder. She wraps her arm around me, and for the first time since I left her at the airport, I don't feel alone.

"How are you really?" she asks.

"I'm...alive?"

She laughs. "I can see that. Please elaborate."

It takes me a bit to find the words. "I'm finding my place here, I guess. I love my classes, and my dorm-mate is really nice. But it's taking me a little longer than I expected to feel normal."

Emmy snorts. "Nobody's normal. Nobody is okay. Everyone's losing it in their own way, Hannah. You're doing fine, all things considered."

I lift my head. "You sound like your brother."

Her eyes shine. "Thank you."

Rain sprinkles the top of the table, and I jump into action, grabbing my books and the study sheets I'd spread out across the wood.

Emmy helps me gather it all and stuff it in my bag. I suggest we move this reunion to my dorm, and she slings an arm around my waist as we cross the campus. "So what's the plan for spring break?"

"No idea. I've been trying to think of something to do for Jackson, but I'm coming up blank. I'll probably stay on campus. We can find something to do around here if you're planning to stay the whole week? Maybe go to the beach or something?"

She flashes me a mischievous smile. "What if you came to Italy with me instead?"

I stop under the awning over the front entrance of my dorm and drag her to the side so we're not blocking the doors. "You're finally going?"

Emmy skipped right over Italy when she started her world tour. She said Ben ruined it for her. In fact, she crossed out the whole country on her chaotic travel wall behind her bed.

Emmy takes a deep breath and shrugs. "I don't want him to have it, you know? He took so much. He almost took you. Why should he still have any power over me or my plans? The memorial my parents are throwing is going to be a whole thing, with people looking somber and skirting around what happened so they don't make my parents more upset than they already are. That's not how I want to remember my brother."

My throat closes up, and I hug her so tightly, she squeaks.

"But," she says, pushing me away with a laugh, "Only if you'll come with me. I don't think it's somewhere I want to go alone anymore. If you'd rather not, that's fine too. We could go somewhere else instead."

I imagine us wandering ancient buildings, eating amazing food as this dreaded anniversary passes right by us, and I can't think of a better way to honor Jackson. Nothing would make him happier.

"Italy sounds perfect. But I have one condition," I say, pulling her into the dorm and out of the rain.

"Name it."

I hold out my wrist, still wrapped in our frayed friendship bracelet, and she presses her matching one against it.

"No boats."

CREDITS

SOURCEBOOKS FIRE

PUBLISHER AND CEO
Dominique Raccah

CHILDREN'S PUBLISHER
Jennifer Gonzalez

EDITORIAL DIRECTOR
Jenne Abramowitz

EDITOR
Annette Pollert-Morgan

EDITORIAL ASSISTANT
Jenny Lopez

COPY EDITOR
Aimee Alker

PROOFREADER
Neha Patel

MARKETING & PUBLICITY
Karen Masnica
Lia Ferrone
Delaney Heisterkamp

CONTENT DELIVERY
Thea Voutiritsas
Jessica Thelander

ART & DESIGN
Sophia Chunn
Erin Fitzsimmons
Stephanie Rocha
Ash Jon

INTERIORS
Laura Boren
Diane Cunningham

EBOOK PRODUCTION
Ashley Holstrom
Holli Roach

SALES
Paula Amendolara
Sean Murray
Tracy Nelson
Jess Elliott
Valerie Pierce
Margaret Coffee
BrocheAroe Fabian

RIGHTS
Kate Boggs
Liz Logback

EMERALD CITY LITERARY

AGENT
Mandy Hubbard

CONTRACTS MANAGER
Kirsten Wolf

FILM AND TELEVISION RIGHTS MANAGER
Linda Epstein

ACKNOWLEDGMENTS

Story time! Several years ago, I went on a girls trip to Puerto Vallarta. We spent our days on boat tours of the bay, snorkeling, riding horses to a waterfall, and eating at beautiful beachfront restaurants. Overall, it was an incredible vacation... But one person in our group made a few questionable decisions regarding her own personal safety that could very well have ended in disaster. Everyone made it home safe and sound, but it planted a seed that eventually grew into the events of *What We Did to Survive*, a story about changing friendships, trusting the wrong people, and fighting to stay alive even when all hope seems to be lost.

First, I'd like to thank Mandy Hubbard. We've been in this together for a long time, and it still never fails to amaze me how well you understand my brain. You're often more excited about my book ideas than I am, and that's saying something. Working with someone who not only shares the same taste in books but also champions all my wild ideas and ambitions makes navigating a complicated industry so much easier. I appreciate the hell out of you.

Annette Pollert-Morgan! This is our third book together, and each one has been an adventure. I love that we can be talking about edits and production timelines one minute and take a left turn to cannibals the next, and you're right there with me. You've been such an incredible champion for my books, and I'm so excited for everything we have planned for the future.

Thank you to everyone at Sourcebooks Fire. Dominique Raccah, you're amazing, and I'm so grateful to have found a home in this incredible author-centered space you've created. Todd Stocke, Karen Masnica, Delaney Heisterkamp, Lia Ferrone, Deanna Maloney, Valerie Pierce, Margaret Coffee, Emily Luedloff, BrocheAroe Fabian, and Jennifer Steinhagen, thank you for everything you do to get my books into the right hands. I'm consistently blown away by this team and the incredible work you all do. And thank you to Sophia Chunn and Erin Fitzsimmons for creating the pink thriller cover of my dreams!

Huge thank you to The Sea Scouts and more specifically, to Sabine. I would like to preface this chunk of appreciation by saying I know as much about sailing as the characters in this book, and when I first drafted this, I hadn't even been on a sailboat. When I reached out to The Sea Scouts to try to find someone to talk to about how these boats work, I didn't expect to find a reader who was more than thrilled to talk to me about boat parts and logistics. Sabine, you were a lifesaver (pun intended), and I'm sure I still got something in these pages wrong, but everything I got right was because of you. Thank you so, so much.

Courtney Gould and Rosiee Thor, this book wouldn't exist without the two of you talking me off the ledge so many times. Thank you for the trips to the beach to meet my deadlines, the hype, the brainstorming help, and being overall amazing people.

Clare Edge, thank you for dropping everything to read this when I'd convinced myself I'd forgotten how to write. Even though survival stories aren't your jam and you were writing three hundred books of your own. Having you in my corner means so much to me.

To L and P, I know your friends have discovered your mom writes books, and at least one of you finds the mere mention of your initial in these back pages to be incredibly embarrassing but...too bad. I'll never not thank you for being the kindest and sweetest little humans on the planet. I love you so much.

And finally, to my readers, I've said it before, and I'll say it again: You're the reason I get to keep doing this job that I love. Thank you for all the ways you show up for these books that make you cry and throw things. There are lots more in the works, and it's all because of you.

ABOUT THE AUTHOR

Megan Lally is *the New York Times* and *USA Today* bestselling author of *That's Not My Name*. When she's not writing dark and twisty young adult novels, you might find her barefoot at the ocean, drinking one too many lavender lattes, or arguing about the validity of glitter as a favorite color. (It's absolutely a color, and it's the best one.) She lives in the Pacific Northwest with her family.

sourcebooks fire

Home of the hottest trends in YA!

Visit us online and
sign up for our newsletter at
FIREreads.com

Follow
@sourcebooksfire
online